Praise
and *Girl in White*

SUE HUBBARD is an award-winning poet, novelist and free-
lance art critic. She has published three acclaimed novels and
numerous collections of poetry, and was commissioned to create
London's largest public art poem at Waterloo. Her fourth novel,
Flatlands, is forthcoming from ONE.

Girl in White

Sue Hubbard

AN IMPRINT OF PUSHKIN PRESS

Pushkin Press
Somerset House, Strand
London WC2R 1LA

First published by Cinnamon Press, Blaenau Ffestiniog, 2012

First published by Pushkin Press in 2022

3 5 7 9 8 6 4 2

ISBN 13: 978-1-78227-912-9

Designed and typeset by Tetragon, London
Printed and bound by Clays Ltd, Elcograf S.p.A.

www.pushkinpress.com

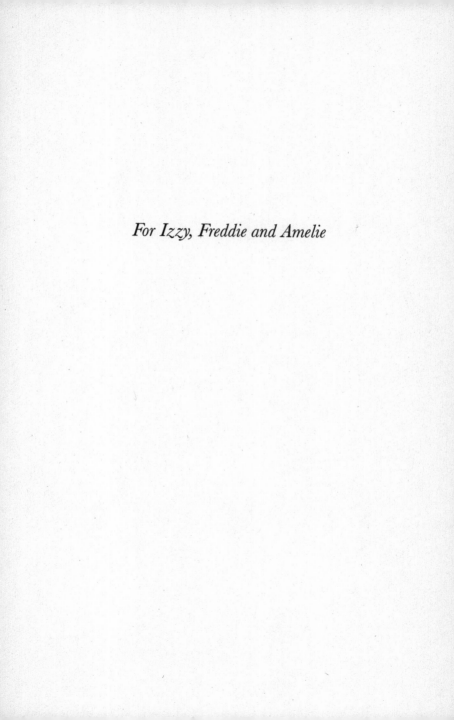

For Izzy, Freddie and Amelie

The work of Paula Modersohn-Becker is not much known in this country. As a painter she was far ahead of her time and deserves a place alongside the likes of Gwen John and Frida Kahlo. I have broadly followed the events of her life and, although some incidents are fictitious, my aim has been to give colour and texture to her singular existence, as well as to place her against the background of her times in Germany where, after her death, her work was denounced as degenerate by the Nazis. Her intense relationship with the poet Rilke, her struggle to find a balance between being a painter, wife and mother, are issues that many women can still relate to today. The role of her daughter, Mathilde, is one of pure imagination. I chose not to know anything of her real life and used her to provide a narrative perspective. I am grateful to her, and hope that she would have approved. But above all my thanks is due to Paula; for her paintings and for her diaries. Without these this book would not exist.

In art one is usually totally alone with oneself.

PAULA MODERSOHN-BECKER,
Paris, 18 November 1906

MATHILDE

AND THEN IT BEGINS TO SNOW. As I step from the bus large white flakes land on the rim of my felt hat, soak my lisle stockings and seep into the leather soles of my new T-bar shoes. It's the first fall of the year and has come too early. I should have dressed more sensibly, but hadn't expected this turn; nothing is normal these days. That's why I had to come now. Soon it might not be possible. I've heard the hectoring tones over the airwaves, seen the crowds gathering in the streets; the banners, the torchbearers and the flags.

I can smell it in the air, another war.

It terrifies me, but I can't think about it now, about what it might mean for the future; mine and this country's. Today's my birthday. November 2nd, 1933.

And what else should I do to celebrate the day of my birth other than come back here to visit my mother? Who else should I turn to with my broken heart? On the bus from Bremen I got out my little diary with the black calf cover to count the weeks again, just to be sure. But there's no mistake.

I thought feeling sick was simply a symptom of grief. It never occurred to me, naïve as it sounds, that there might be some other reason. I'm not even sure when it happened. But this simple fact changes everything. It gives me a reason to go on. After you left there was nothing to live for. I wish more than ever that my mother, that Paula, was around. I'm sure that she'd have understood. Maybe coming here I'll feel a little closer to her, be able to make some sense of everything that has happened.

As I hurry from the bus, turning up the rabbit-fur collar of my coat against the flurries of damp sleet and pulling down my felt hat, I pause by a clump of tall birches, uncertain where to go. I've pictured the village so often that now I'm actually here, I feel disorientated. From where I'm standing I can look out over the open landscape at the paths and canals that criss-cross the dark moors. The sky is the colour of dishwater and low clouds lie in a heavy blanket over the horizon. I make my way along the cobbled pavement past the cottages with their high thatched roofs and whitewashed facades latticed with black crossbeams. A few lights glow in the afternoon dusk and I stop outside the gate of Heinrich Vogeler's Barkenhoff, basically a farmhouse like the others, though it's more isolated in its large garden. I know it, of course, from his painting: the green gate and high windows half hidden by pink rambling roses. I've always known it. My father, Otto, bought the painting when we moved away the year after my mother died. I grew up with it, knew the names of all those sitting on the terrace that summer evening, talking and playing music. On the left is my mother, with my father, Otto, and Clara Westhoff-Rilke. Vogeler's wife, Martha, is standing on the steps in the middle of the picture flanked by two bay trees. She's wearing a green satin dress with a white lace collar and leaning against the balustrade, holding a large wolfhound on a leash. On the other side of the terrace are Heinrich Vogeler and his brother Franz, playing a flute. Someone else is playing the fiddle. A group of young friends in a garden on a summer evening seated among roses and potted pink geraniums, reciting poetry, making music, and dreaming dreams.

But when I reach the actual house it looks nothing like the painting. It's rather run-down and a group of whey-faced boys with cropped hair and chapped knees are planting potatoes in the garden. I make my way in the flurrying snow through the village, up the sandy path to the church with the white wooden clock tower. It was here that my mother Paula and her friend Clara climbed the belfry one balmy August evening and rang the bells out over the sandy mound of the Weyerberg. Thinking there was a fire the frightened villagers ran from the houses clutching their pots, pans and brooms, still dressed in their nightshirts and petticoats. I want to find the little carved cherub and painted orange sunflowers that the pastor demanded from Paula and Clara by way of a penance.

Inside a group of women is decorating the church for a wedding. They look up as I come in, smile, and then turn back to their work. They are tying small bouquets onto the ends of the grey-painted pews; lilies, white roses and ivy. Aluminium buckets and vases half-filled with water stand among the aisles. All the women seem to know each other and chat while they work. The walls are whitewashed, as if the snow has blown in under the door and through the cracks, filling up the little church. The scent of lilies is overpowering. Cut stalks lie scattered on the stone floor in the zinc light. At one end of the knave is a simple carved altar, at the other an organ, its gleaming pipes graded like a set of shining steel teeth.

I wonder what it would be like to be a bride. What it would have been like if things had been different. And for a moment I can't think of anything other than that last kiss on the crowded station, snatched amid the stream of embarking and disembarking passengers, the warmth of your mouth, your smell mingling with mine before you pulled away and walked out of my life forever. A slim figure in a long tweed coat and felt hat, carrying your violin.

I watched as long as I could, as you made your way past the kiosk with its hoarding for Manoli cigarettes, past the elderly businessman waiting on the corner in a black coat with an astrakhan collar, past the young soldiers and porters, watched as you walked towards the train that would take you back to your American wife; out of my arms forever, to safety across the sea. So many leavings and partings. Brothers, husbands, lovers, sons, and then the whistle, the high-pitched wail of the train, like a knife in my heart.

I return to that image over and over, rummaging in my brain like someone searching for an old photograph at the back of a drawer. But I'm afraid of spoiling it with overuse, so that it becomes as faded as an over-washed dress. Memories are all I have now. It was a risk to say goodbye, let alone snatch that last kiss. But how could I have asked you to stay? I imagine you, now, on that ship, halfway across the Atlantic, halfway across the world, dancing with your wife in her ivory chenille dress that shows off her thin white shoulders and slender neck with its string of milky pearls. I can see the band in the ballroom. Their white tuxedos and black bow ties, the trombonist's cheeks puffed out like two balloons: *I can't give you anything but love, baby...*

and I remember that afternoon when I came for a lesson and you put that record on the phonograph, lowered the needle and took me in your arms, humming those words in my ear, as we danced round your study, watched by the plaster busts of Beethoven, Handel and Chopin.

I came here because I need to make sense of the past. My childhood was spent with my father Otto and with Louise who, to all intents and purposes, acted as my mother, and with Elsbeth and my young half-brothers, Ulrich and Christian. Then there were the years of music study in Munich. It was a well-regulated, ordered life. How hurt Father would be if he knew that I'd come to Worpswede. I think he'd feel betrayed, as though he hadn't done enough. Of course he did his best, but what did he know about bringing up a small child? This place belongs to Paula and he never talked of her. That part of his life is a closed chapter. As far as the world's concerned he's Otto Modersohn, the famous artist. No one remembers her. No one remembers Paula Modersohn-Becker.

My parents married in May. It was a simple enough wedding. Paula in a white muslin dress, my father, Otto, ten years older and a widower looking, from the photograph I still have, stern and professorial in his dark suit, with his wire glasses and newly trimmed beard. Paula is much shorter; her hair looped simply at the nape of her neck. I'm told by those who knew her, by my Aunt Milly and my grandmother, that I look a little like her. It feels strange to think of these family events that preceded my birth. I try to imagine them, but I can't. In the wedding picture my half-sister, Elsbeth, is holding a small nosegay. She looks very serious and seems to be embracing her role as handmaiden. She spent seven years with my mother. I only had days.

Was Paula happy on her wedding day? I think she must have loved my father then, or at least believed that she did. But how can I possibly know? Perhaps, in the end, all relationships are a compromise. Who knows why anyone else makes the decisions they make. Why the squat little man with a receding hairline is the focus of one woman's passion, or what the blond boy sees in his older married lover? And I'll never know for sure how much Paula really wanted me; really wanted a child or if, given the choice, she would have stayed on in Paris working in the thick of things and not have come back to Worpswede. In the end, despite me, Father, and even Rilke, painting was the most important thing in her life. I treasure these photographs and carry them everywhere. For me my mother will always be defined by the one taken by the photographer who came from Dresden days after I was born, where she stares dark-eyed directly into the camera from her bed, as I, Mathilde, lie in her arms testing out my week-old lungs.

The snow is falling faster now, scattering over the well-tended graves like a coating of icing sugar. As I walk through the church porch into the cemetery I hear a crunch on the gravel and look up to see an old man clearing the paths. He has a shaven, bullet-shaped head and wears a coarse potato-coloured jacket. He nods as I pass, then looks down again and goes back to sweeping the falling snow.

It's very silent, as though the world is slowly being buried. Spruce and small fir trees line the paths. I'm not sure where my mother is as I search among the moss-covered tomb-stones carved with angels and fat-faced cherubs. Many of the headstones are inscribed in old Gothic script. I brush off the falling flakes with my bare hands, but still can't decipher the inscriptions, and continue making my way up and down the rows, stopping at a pale upright slab and a simple rough-hewn granite stone. Then, as I turn a corner and walk down a path I've not walked before, I see it on the far side of the churchyard by the hedge.

How could I have missed it, the carving of a woman with bare breasts draped in Grecian robes, reclining on a mauso-leum? A small child sits in her lap. I go up closer and see the woman isn't touching the child, but is staring up at the dark sky. It's Paula—my mother—with me, carved in white marble. The mason's made me look older than I was when she actually died. It feels odd to be part of a memorial to the dead whilst I'm still alive. I don't know who paid for it, but I doubt it was my father. I stand staring at the statue thinking about the cells dividing within me, cells half-made up of your DNA, and realise that whoever we are, whatever we've done, we'll all end up in a place like this. Then I unwrap the white roses I brought from Bremen, and lay them in my stone mother's arms. Soon the fragile petals are covered in snow.

Is that why I came? To fill the space left by you, Daniel, with the memory of her? I want to go back to that yellow house with the red roof where I spent my first weeks. For me it'll always be more than just a house with a sloped attic, flowered wallpaper and a vase of freshly picked sweet peas on the sill. For me, it'll always be home.

17

It's getting very cold now. I try to retrace my footsteps to the gate, but they've disappeared beneath the falling snow. I have to find somewhere to stay before it gets really dark. Tonight, while I sleep in some strange bed, I'll dream, as I always do, of you.

And tomorrow? Well, tomorrow, I shall begin my search for Paula.

PAULA

THE ELBE WAS CLOGGED with ice and flood water streamed off the mountains. Torrents of rain alternated with flurries of snow, piling in drifts along the roads, hedgerows and railway lines. Though a conscientious man, Woldemar Becker couldn't worry about his wife. He'd have to leave that to the midwife. The new railroad embankments along the river were giving way. Not only were millions of Deutschmarks at stake, but his reputation as an engineer. Men were battling up to their knees in the icy slush, shoring up the banks with wooden stakes and iron girders, trying to prevent collapse.

After the old nurse had cleared away the afterbirth, wrapped up the bloodied sheets, swaddled the baby and placed her in her mother's arms she changed her stained apron, heated some coffee and overfilled the paraffin stove so the flames shot up in an inferno towards the velvet curtains. Screaming, she ran to the young mother's bedside, where, despite her recent long labour, the young woman had the presence of mind to extinguish the blaze. What with the commotion, bad weather and the worry that her husband would be buried beneath an avalanche of snow and mud, Mathilde Becker developed an infected breast, which had to be wrapped in hot poultices and then lanced. Yet even though it took her six months to recover from her confinement, she didn't love her third child less than any of her others.

Inside the freezing church the pastor held the lace bundle in the crook of his arm, dipped a big beetroot hand into the stone font and marked the child's forehead, just beneath her frilled silk bonnet, with the sign of the cross. The icy water made her scream, but Woldemar Becker looked on indulgently, for he'd never been one of those men who only wanted sons.

'Look, my dear,' he said, turning to his wife, 'at her snub nose. And those lungs! Our little daughter has quite an opinion already. See how she grips my finger and reaches for her old Papi's beard.'

As Paula knelt on the Turkish rug among the swirls of dark acanthus leaves she could feel the scratchy wool even through her thick winter stockings. She had rushed through her sums and music practice and was laying out her pencils and sticks of charcoal next to a large sheet of paper on the floor. On the far side of the room was her mother's bureau with the little drawers stuffed with letters tied in red ribbon, and the Venetian glass paperweight with green florets that went on and on forever when she held it up to the light. And by the door there was the mahogany cabinet of Dresden china that had belonged to her grandmother. The silver samovar her father had brought from Odessa, which sat next to the tawny owl in a glass case, that stared down at her with its beady yellow-glass eyes from its high shelf. Above the fireplace was the portrait of Mutti in a dove-grey dress, her long hair tied with a blue bow, painted before she married Papi. She must have been about eighteen. Only seven years older than Paula was now.

The coals in the grate glimmered making shadows in the room's cold corners and, despite the heavy velvet curtains, there was still a draught. As Paula pulled the stick of charcoal over the paper, the carriage clock on the mantel ticked into the silence. *Chiaroscuro*; recently she'd learnt that this was the word for the effects of contrasted light and shade. The great artist, Leonardo, Papi had told her, when'd he got down the big leather book in his study to show her the engraved plates, had been the pioneer. Other artists such as Caravaggio and Rembrandt had also experimented with it. It was one of the great discoveries of the Renaissance and, if she wanted to be serious about her art, then she'd need to master this difference between light and dark.

Chia-ro-scuro: she rolled the Italian word round her mouth like a lump of barley sugar. Then, sitting back to admire her handiwork, wiped her fingers on her pinafore leaving black smears on the clean white cotton. Why weren't the marks on the paper she made more like the thing she actually saw? She tried to make the charcoal lines look like the cat, but they remained flat and inert. With the ball of her thumb she smudged the edges to soften the contours but as she did so the cat got up, stretched and walked off with its tail in the air.

She laid her left hand on the paper and traced round the square nails and ragged cuticles that Mutti was always scolding her for biting. So what if the cat left? She didn't care. She would be her own model. She got up and went to the mirror by the door and examined the tawny eyes and slightly bulbous lips reflected back at her. She wished that she had Mutti's mouth. But that was just vanity. She had nice chestnut hair and rosy cheeks and should be satisfied with what God had given her. She may not be as pretty as her big sister Milly, but it wasn't a bad face, at least one she could draw whenever she wanted.

Outside in the snow-filled streets she could hear the muffled shouts of the errand boys dropping off pumpernickel and pickled herrings to Frau Linderman, and the clatter of the iron rings on the beer kegs as they rolled over the cobbles into the cellars. It was even too cold for the dogs to bark. They'd slunk back into the warmth of their kennels.

Earlier that morning Paula had gone with Kurt and Milly to the park. The sky had been the colour of slate and the ground iron with frost. They had slid across the frozen lake, laughing and falling in heaps, bumping their knees and blowing on their raw hands. One or two of the other children had real skates with steel blades, but the Becker children just slid around in their button boots. Across the ice they could smell the chestnut-seller's brazier. He'd been there every winter they could remember in his hat with ear flaps, his fingerless mittens and dirty charcoaled hands. Paula wondered where he came from with his strange accent and where he went in the summer. Some of the other children said he was from Silesia and that if you weren't careful he'd steal you away like the Pied Piper and you'd never be seen again. Others swore he lived in a hut on the edge of a forest and was married to a witch. One day, as he was setting up his brazier, some boys threw stones at him and ran off shouting that he was a dirty Jew. Yet he always smiled at them showing his broken black teeth, and added an extra chestnut to their brown-paper twist.

On Sundays there was usually a puppet show in the park. There was also a zoological garden where, on warm days, the whole family would go to watch the Siberian tigers padding backwards and forwards behind the thick iron bars, and the monkeys with rude behinds rattling their cages, demanding peanuts. Further up the hill there was a museum and a castle filled with antiquities. It was there that Papi had shown her Raphael's *Madonna di San Sisto* in its room with crimson fabric walls, and the *Madonna* by the younger Holbein, as well as Carreggio's *La Notte.* But her favourite painting was of the English King, Charles I, with his Queen and their children, by Van Dyck. She wondered what it would have been like to meet them, these boys and girls dressed in their fine silks, who would have been the same age as her, and her brothers and sisters. She could have practised her English: *the weather is a little inclement for the time of year; I live in the beautiful town of Dresden.*

But her favourite spot was where the park was left to grow wild. On fine summer days they would take their skipping ropes and sketchbooks, their apples and flasks of milk and spend the afternoon lying amid the poppies and long grass, listening to the thrush in the willows. Across the lake she'd watch the families taking the air, the nannies in starched uniforms pushing their charges in big black perambulators.

Dresden was the only place that Paula had ever lived during her twelve years on earth. She knew nowhere other than this city with its cupolas and towers, spires and copper roofs, where the *Altstadt*, with its rococo churches, was separated by the slow running Elbe from the *Neustadt*, and connected by five bridges. How lucky she was, Papi insisted, to live in the German Florence. What better place to grow up for someone who wanted to be a painter.

Perhaps she should have guessed that something was up when, flushed from skating, Mutti had hurried them to wash their hands and get to the lunch table quickly. Their father had something to tell them. Papi didn't usually join them for the midday meal. Normally he dined with the engineer and the accountant in the hotel next to the town hall where they ate sausage and sauerkraut, drank beer and sat in the dark smoking room with their cigars, talking of stocks and shares and the newly built sections of railway for which he was responsible. Rivets, sleepers and bolts, that's what made a good railway. A line was only ever as good as the engineer who designed it and the builder who built it, he insisted, wreathed in clouds of smoke.

But today Papi was to eat lunch at home with his wife and children. First they said grace—though Paula knew he only bowed his head in deference to Mutti—before slicing the black bread and ladling out the pork and cabbage from the steaming tureen. Kurt was served first, then Milly and her. After that came Günther and the twins, Herma and Henner, for this was a household where the girls were given their rightful places in front of their younger brothers. As they ate her father spread his napkin on his lap and cleared his throat. Change, he announced, built character, and they were all about to experience a major

24

change. They'd soon be moving to Bremen for he had recently been appointed Inspector for the Construction and Maintenance of the Berlin–Dresden Railway.

With his salt and pepper beard, mop of greying hair, and his navy blue jacket with the brass buttons, her Papi looked well-suited to this important new job, which was perfect for a man passionate about technology and the latest scientific developments. He followed, with a keen interest, the developments in electro technology and engineering being used to improve new factories along the Elbe, turning the old crafts of paper and soap-making into modern industries. He devoured the writings of Nietzsche and followed the debates of the Englishman Darwin, with his progressive ideas on the origin of the species. Darwin, much to Mutti's sadness, was Papi's hero; and, like Darwin, he had lost his faith in God. Sometimes her Papi could seem rather fierce. But Paula knew that was because he was often troubled. She was never sure why the world seemed to sit so heavily on his shoulders. Why a man who read so much, a kind man, should have such dark moods. She wished he was a believer and, every night before she went to bed, knelt and prayed that he would be returned to his faith. But, young as she was, she understood that he had a different map of the world.

She tried to be good and make him happy. She loved it when he crept up behind her when she was drawing, so she didn't know that he was there until she felt his whiskers on her cheek and smelt the familiar tang of pomade and cigar smoke.

'That's very good, Paula. Well done. But look, the cat's front leg's too long. Can't you see? You need to measure more carefully if you're going to be a proper artist.'

Her Papi was a creature of habit. Most evenings he read in his study until well past midnight. Long after she should have been asleep she'd see the sliver of light from his desk lamp escaping under his shut door. In the morning he'd rise early before the rest of the house and weigh himself on a pair of scales in his dressing gown and socks, then mark the result on a little chart that he kept pinned to the wall. He always took breakfast alone in his room, except on Sundays: stewed apple, pumpernickel with cheese, and a glass of hot water with a slice of lemon. While he ate he read books on philosophy or the genetics of plant propagation, which he propped up against the honey jar. He never left his room unless properly dressed; his socks neatly held up with garters, and the correct dimple pressed into his cravat. The last thing he did was fold a clean handkerchief into four squares and tuck it into the pocket of his double-breasted jacket.

At a quarter to eight on the dot, after selecting his overcoat according to the weather, he left the house. He'd slip his arm into the right sleeve, then shake the chosen coat up onto his shoulder and insert the other arm, adjusting the hang of the cloth in front of the long hall mirror. When dressed to his liking he'd pick up his letters and newspaper; kiss any of his children that he happened to pass in the hall on the top of their heads, before taking a brisk walk to the office of the Inspectorate of the Dresden division of the Prussian railroads.

*

Woldemar Becker discussed everything with his wife, and this move to Bremen was no exception. Later that night, when the children were asleep, he listened for the rustle of her skirts as she made her way down the tessellated tile hall in the dim gas light to his study. He knew she'd take the change in her stride; that she had a rare gift which he did not, with his melancholy nature, of attracting people into her orbit. He'd been lucky in his choice of bride. Not only had she been beautiful—and still was in a solid mature sort of way with that lovely mouth of hers, even after seven children and the death of little Hans—but she exuded warmth.

And she had been a great comfort to him; for somehow he'd never quite got over the loss of the boy. He'd often wondered what it had been that had made him so special among his children. He always suspected it was because he'd been conceived on their wedding anniversary, when the apple tree was in bloom.

Hans had shared his interest in the natural world and loved to go down to the pond at the bottom of the garden to collect newts and frogs' spawn. He'd take the boy by one hand, in the other carrying a net and jar, and sit for hours watching him fish in the green water. Then they would carry back the murky container and set up the brass microscope on the mahogany table, and he would explain how tadpoles grew legs and shed their tails to become frogs. Woldemar Becker believed in encouraging his children's interests. Drawing in Paula, natural history in Hans, to whom he read about each stage of the amphibian life-cycle from the large encyclopedia. But these were things that he never spoke of now and kept shut away in his heart.

He knew that he'd not been much help to his wife in the days after the boy had been taken by scarlet fever. He had no words for the loss of the small son he had watched fading in the narrow bed, set up in quarantine in the little attic room away from the other children. Alone in his study, late at night, he could still see the child's eyes shining in his flushed face. Yet despite the poultices, the hot flannels soaked in mustard, the enemas and bed baths, nothing had cooled the child's fever. If Becker had ever doubted there was a God, he knew it for certain now. That was something he shared with the great Darwin; for he, too, had lost his beloved daughter and, with her death, his faith.

After the funeral, when his other children had stood in a forlorn huddle underneath the damp yews in coats stitched with black armbands, watching as the little white coffin was lowered into its grave, Woldemar Becker shut himself away in his study with his books and a hole in his heart.

It had been Mathilde who'd held the family together, despite her own grief; who had helped his children through their tears. In the dark, cold hours of morning, she'd held his head to her breast as he'd sobbed like a baby and reached for the comfort of her beneath her flannel nightgown. And it would be Mathilde who would ease their transition from Dresden to Bremen. It would only be a matter of time before she was calling on the neighbours, inviting them to evening soirées where she'd serve spiced wine and poppy-seed cake. His warm-hearted, congenial wife would soon have exchanged visiting cards with half the neighbourhood. And with this new job as administrator of the Prussian railroads for the city-state of Bremen came an official residence—a spacious house with a big garden that would provide plenty of room for the children to play.

No, it wasn't altogether a bad thing this move to Bremen.

And Paula; what did she remember of Hans' funeral? Above all she remembered the rain. How it had soaked into her coat with the velvet collar and run down her neck. That Hans was dead she knew. That her little brother was never coming back she understood, but standing there in the cemetery as the autumn leaves drifted among the graves, she couldn't make any sense of it. How could he just not exist any more? Suddenly everything seemed so fragile and uncertain. All the things that had defined her childhood were changing. Her brother was gone and they were moving to another city.

After the funeral she went to her father's study and lifted down the large atlas to look at the map of Bremen. Papi had explained it was one of the Hanseatic cities that occupied the sandy plain on the banks of the Weser and had one of the finest buildings in northern Germany. The fifteenth-century Rathaus—with its Renaissance facade studded with windows made up of hundreds of tiny leaded panes—dominated the market square. She wanted to see the famous statue of Roland—who was said to be very handsome—and explore the winding cobbled streets flanked by massive gabled houses. But Hans' death had affected her badly. Bremen might be beautiful but it wasn't her home. And she couldn't bear the thought of leaving little Hans here, alone, in his newly dug grave with no one to visit him or lay flowers on his headstone.

*

She was to have the large room at the top of the house with the slanted gables and a window seat that looked out over the walnut tree. Her elder sister Milly had been given the bed furthest from the door, whilst she was to have the one in the alcove. This was a grown-up room, not a nursery. The walls were moss green and the curtains sprigged with Alpine flowers. In the corner was a washstand, a basin and a jug. The first thing Paula did was unpack her paintbrushes and crayons, which she lined up in old coffee tins on her desk beside her sketchbooks. When she'd organised everything to her liking she curled up on the window seat and sat staring out into the wet garden.

'Milly, come here,' she said, drawing her knees up under her pinafore and beckoning over her sister, who was arranging her undergarments in the chest of drawers. 'Look, at the end of the garden, do you see, there's a swing? Oh Milly, we're going to have such fun. Come and sit by me. Tell me what you plan to be when you're grown-up and your little sister is a famous painter?'

Maybe now that they'd left Dresden Paula would leave the nightmares behind. She couldn't bear it any more. The dead-white face that appeared in the middle of the night, leaving her sweating with fear. She had loved her cousin, more than her own sisters, more even than little Hans. Only eighteen months older than Paula, they had been like twins. Cora had grown up in Indonesia and had only recently returned to Germany. With raven hair and a serious demeanour she had quickly become her younger cousin's confidante and friend.

'Oh, do tell me about your visit to the Buddhist temple, Cora. It sounds so exotic. Will you read me *The Little Mermaid* again while I draw you? Do you think you could ever do that, divide your tail into legs, even though it felt as if you were walking on a thousand knives? Can love really make you do such things? I'm not sure I could, even for a Prince. I want to be a painter.'

It had been a long hot summer afternoon. Six children had been playing in the park, flying kites and sailing wooden boats on the pond, pushing them out onto the sparkling water with sticks to catch the wind. In the heat they had taken off their shoes and stockings to build a castle in the sandpit near the linden trees, but the boys had become bored and started to scratch at the sand on all fours like dogs, sending it flying in all directions.

'Look, we're digging to the other side of the world. Come on Cora, come on Paula, get in. Now pat it down. Oh my God, quick, somebody, quick…'

She could still feel the weight of the sand pressing against her ribs, feel the grit in her nostrils and mouth, hear her brother's frightened voice calling and calling in the distance, as the faint whimpering slowly faded to silence. Then they led her away from the crumpled heap splayed on the sand like a rag doll. She was told not to look back, yet deep inside she knew what had happened.

It had been no one's fault, they told her. She shouldn't blame herself. But why had her cousin been taken and not her? Why had she survived? Surely some day God would punish her. She lay on her bed for days, not eating and staring at the ceiling, as a fly buzzed inside the frosted-glass shade. Gradually it dawned on her that life was not what you deserved, but what was dished out to you and she was afraid. Afraid of the future, afraid that she'd never be able to make anything of herself and justify her survival, afraid that there wouldn't be enough time to learn all she needed to know, that she didn't have the talent or the grit to become an artist. Night after night Cora appeared to her, her dark hair floating about her white face, like someone drowning.

'Oh please God, not tonight. If I'm good and not stubborn or egotistical please, please tell Cora that, though I love her very much, I'd be grateful if she stayed in Dresden.'

Nothing fancy. Some gingerbread, coffee and a little sweet wine. He'd have no vulgar display, no pretence that his family was anything that they weren't, Papi insisted, as Mutti announced she would be giving a small house-warming party.

Paula and Milly were stirring flour through the big sieve, adding brown sugar, cinnamon and ginger into the white mixing basin as they discussed what they'd play for their guests. Mutti wanted Paula to play the Brahms but Milly preferred Schumann.

'We could do both,' Milly suggested, squashing the butter into the cake mix with the back of a wooden spoon. 'But there's not much time to practise, Paula, if you're also going to paint the backdrop. The twins can play a duet. That always goes down well. Even when they make mistakes everyone thinks they're sweet sitting side by side in their sailor suits.'

'And Günther can do his card trick, and Kurt recite a poem,' Paula added, pouring the mix into the floured tin. 'Then Mutti can sing some *Lieder*. You know how much everyone enjoys that,' she added, licking the last of the mixture off the spoon. 'No one will notice if I don't play.'

They weren't rich, she knew, but Mutti loved beauty. The house was always filled with vases of flowers arranged in the Japanese style and small dishes of gourds and quince that her mother gathered from the garden. Mutti had even hung all the paintings in the house herself, going from room to room with her little hammer and picture pins. And everywhere there were books: new editions of the German classics, works by modern English and French writers. This evening's gathering was to include Paula's governess, Fräulein Lindesmann, and their neighbours the Schlegels and the Schäfers, as well as the local doctor. The day they'd arrived from Dresden he had knocked on the door and, with a low bow that had made Mutti blush, presented her with a bunch of violets. And today Paula was going to meet her new drawing tutor. She had begged Papi to let her have private lessons and finally he had relented, agreeing that if she was going to be an artist then she'd better take her studies seriously. He had made enquiries. A local painter by the name of Wiegandt seemed suitable. He had studied in Berlin and spent a month touring Italy, drawing the churches in Venice and Rome, and now made a fair living as a society portrait and landscape painter. What's more, he was newly married and came from a respectable family.

'Should I put clips in my hair, the little tortoise ones I got for Christmas, or tie it back with my brown ribbon? What do you think, Milly?'

But there was no time to fuss. She still had to lay the table with the best Swiss lace cloth and put out the silver coffee pot, the creamer and sugar bowl with the little tongs. Everything had to be perfect. At last she was going to study art, not just sit at the table in the morning room on rainy afternoons drawing the cat or Kurt slumped in his chair.

After Milly played the Schumann, Paula handed round the refreshments. Despite Papi's insistence on simplicity, they had baked a large cheesecake, which her mother was slicing onto the best Dresden plates. She took a piece over to Fräulein Lindesmann seated on the ottoman. When she grew up she wanted to be like her teacher and have a plaid dress with a silver brooch at the throat. She loved the way Fräulein Lindesmann wound her blonde hair around her head in a thick halo of plaits. She was far too lovely, the beautiful, the divine Fräulein Lindesmann, to be a governess for long. Surely some handsome man would come along and whisk her away and marry her. But Paula had to pluck up courage to offer a plate of cake to Frau Schlegel with her bosom like a shelf in brown bombazine, and grains of face powder that quivered in the dark hairs on her upper lip.

The Golden Section, Herr Wiegandt explained the following afternoon, was a portion in which a straight line or a rectangle was divided into two equal parts so that the ratio of the smaller to the greater was the same as that of the greater to the whole. Perhaps, he asked, adjusting the buttons on his velvet waistcoat with his long white fingers that reminded her of early asparagus, she'd come across the value of pi in her study of geometry?

Paula shook her head. She'd no idea that learning to draw would be so complicated.

Luca Pacioli, Herr Wiegandt continued, as she studied his pale face, was the most famous mathematician of his day and a close friend of Leonardo da Vinci. He'd written his master-work, the *Divina Proportione*, in 1498. Maybe, eventually, she'd study Italian and read it for herself in the original. He always carried a copy on his excursions around Florence.

Next he set her to draw in pencil, demonstrating how to hold it at arm's length and close one eye in order to take measurements, which she then had to mark on the paper. The cat's head fitted into its body twice. The door was one and a half times the height of the fireplace. Perspective was the method used to represent depth on a flat surface, using the convergence of parallel lines.

'And who developed the fixed central viewpoint, Paula?'

'Oh, I know, Herr Wiegandt. I learnt it last night. Wait a minute, please, I'll remember in a second. Oh, it's… Brunelleschi!'

'Well done young lady. Now to the still life.'

For this he'd arranged a pile of apples in Mutti's blue-and-white Bavarian bowl, beside Papi's meerschaum pipe and a glass decanter of port. The Dutch masters were particularly keen on this sort of arrangement. She had to consider, before she started to draw, the negative space between the objects. These were as important as the objects themselves. It was what gave them volume and weight. She should also note the direction of the light, and the way the shadows fell. If he'd set her this exercise before luncheon they would have been different. Look how the light caught the lip of the decanter, how the cut-glass facets reflected the window and the apples changed the colour of the glass and seemed to have no edge because they were round. How was she going to convey that roundedness? He wanted to see apples; to know that they were apples and not pears.

'And don't forget to measure, Paula; draw nothing in isolation. Everything relates to everything else.'

In between lessons she practised in the new sketchbook Mutti had given her.

She drew the women in the street washing their front steps and cleaning windows with paper dipped in vinegar. She drew the maids on their knees polishing the knockers and brass letter boxes, and the street boys playing with a mangy dog. She sketched the man who sold blocks of peat for fuel from a horse-drawn cart, and the street hawkers and fishmonger, as well as the fashionable ladies out for a morning stroll in the market square. She made drawings of everything that caught her eye; from a cat on the wall to the baker's boy carrying a loaf of bread. As she became more confident she ventured down the cobbled alleys of the Schnoor, the area built by fishermen on the low hills by the river, crammed with fetid workshops where cobblers, watchmakers and carpenters jostled in the dark alleys between the peeling gables. She would stay out for so long her mother would scold her, but once she started to draw she forgot the time. At home she spent hours in the garden. She drew the mauve aquilegias and forget-me-knots, and the snails, which she searched out by their trails of silver slime. The world was so full of shapes, textures and colours. How could anyone not want to be a painter?

When she wasn't drawing she made lists of artists and philosophers, and the Kings and Queens of England. She liked to test her memory. She wrote down the names of different countries with their capital cities and the rivers that ran through them, compiling a chart of primary colours. She even made a note of the small eruptions of her body; a scratch here, a bruise there, observing how they turned from red to black then yellow.

'Turn round, slowly. Oh do stop fidgeting,' Mutti complained through a mouthful of pins. 'Milly, that hem is all crooked.'

Paula was standing on the high stool in her stockinged feet as Milly held up the edge of her white lawn dress for her mother to shorten the hem. Was this what it felt like to be a bride, all this fuss about tucks and cuffs? It was the eve of her confirmation. After which she'd be leaving for England to stay with her Aunt Marie, her father's half-sister who was married to an Englishman and lived on an estate near London. She was to learn English, as well as how to run a household, clot cream, and make polish from beeswax and turpentine for the heavy oak furniture, arrange flowers, cook and make English tea.

'Milk first and then the tea; remember, Paula, you have to let it brew. They like it strong, so the spoon stands up,' Mutti joked, 'not like the lemon tea we drink in the little glasses Papi brought from Odessa.'

Her aunt would expect her to work hard, but Mutti had promised to write and ask if there was a chance that she might continue with her studies in drawing.

'And guess what, Paula? Today I've received a reply. But you'll have to keep still and let me pin this if you want me to tell you what your uncle said,' she teased. 'Now how's this? He's agreed to pay for classes at an art school in London?'

The sky was overcast and the air thick with salt. As she stood on deck, waving goodbye to Papi on the quayside, gulls swooped and mewed overhead. She was on her way from the Hook of Holland to Harwich. Papi had brought her to the Hook by train and she was going to be met by her uncle in Harwich. There'd been talk of a chaperone, but Papi believed she could manage the crossing alone. Up on deck she watched the white horses ride the waves as queasy passengers clung to the rails. Wrapping her shawl tight around her shoulders she turned her face into the wind, feeling the slap and tug of her bonnet ribbons against her cheeks. Along the deck a young father was holding his small son in his arms, pointing out the wheelhouse, the lifebuoys and the sailors in blue mopping the deck. As the boat tossed up and down in the swell, the small boy squealed with delight. How the twins would've loved this. All around her she could hear the babble of German, Dutch and English; it was like the Tower of Babel. She would write to her family as soon as she arrived.

Harwich was a scribble of tall masts and rigging. Ships from all over the world were moored on the busy quayside. Merchant seaman jostled and shouted, their voices carrying away in the wind, as they unloaded timber, sugar, jute and huge bales of wool. Carts and wagons clattered across the wet cobbles as people ran to and fro. It was raining cats and dogs. That was the expression in her English textbook. At the entrance to the disembarkation lounge her Uncle Charles was waiting for her under a big black umbrella, wearing a pair of rubber galoshes.

Paula had never been away from home, never had to rely on her own resources. The next morning she woke to the sound of rain. Outside her window everything was green; the lawns, the trees and fields. Later her aunt took her up to the dairy where she was shown how to make butter. At first she was nervous of the cows, but by the end of the morning she was milking them without any help, sitting on her three-legged stool, leaning her cheek against their dusty flanks.

It was much harder than she'd expected and it took a while to get into the rhythm. During her first attempt Cowslip kicked over the pail with her back leg, sending the contents running in a white river across the yard. Later she learnt how to scald the milk and place it in the heavy churn, then add just the right amount of salt, before slapping it into shape with a pair of wooden paddles. Fridays were butter days. She had to wear a white apron and cap; for the dairy had to be spotless or the milk would curdle. She was shown how to wash the tiles and mop the marble surfaces with hot water. There were also three Dutch girls staying in the house and they'd all made butter before. Her aunt's regime was strict and she was anxious that she wouldn't be able to keep up.

She wrote to her parents telling them what she'd been doing and tried to imagine the Sunday morning letter-opening cere- mony when Mutti came downstairs in her brown dressing gown to pour the coffee and sort the letters. It was her job to slit them open with her little silver knife. Everything had to be done in the correct sequence, so Kurt's letter from the barracks would be read before hers. Mutti could barely hide her disappointment if the mail was opened by anyone else.

The following week Paula received a letter from Papi. Surely four pages describing the entire process of butter-making were excessive? There must be other things to write home about.

How was her aunt, and how were her studies in drawing coming along?

They'd come up to London by train. Crowds spilt from the pavements in the filthy, smog-filled streets. Hansom cabs clattered against the cobbles as gentlemen with furled umbrellas and top hats stepped gingerly between the steaming horse droppings. On every corner there was a flower seller, a costermonger, or a newspaper boy barking out the evening headlines. She couldn't understand a word as they made their way past a milliner, a haberdasher and a crowded pie and mash shop, where the rich meaty smell wafted out across the pavement.

Their uncle was taking them to the theatre to see Mr Volodin from Leningrad who was billed as a 'Mind Reader, Mesmerist and Magician'. She'd seen a picture of him in a black opera cloak on a hoarding in Holborn. Not only could he read minds but he was an expert phrenologist. Just as she was about to step out into Drury Lane her aunt grabbed her sleeve to prevent her stepping in front of an oncoming cab.

Paula had never been to a theatre before and was delighted, as they sat in the fifth row of the stalls, by the cream and gold boxes and ladies with feathers in their hair peering at the stage through opera glasses. As the gas mantles were turned down there was a roll of drums and Mr Volodin appeared in his black cape from behind a pair of heavy red curtains. With a flick of his silk handkerchief, three doves flew across the stage out of nowhere and were greeted with a round of applause. After that he invited a lady in a spangled costume to lie in a box while he sawed her in half. Paula could hardly watch. But when she opened her eyes the young woman was standing on the stage, in one piece, smiling.

When they visited the Natural History Museum, the marble halls reminded her of St Peter's where she'd been confirmed. She couldn't believe the dinosaurs. Had such things really walked the earth? She stood beside a skeleton and felt like a midget. She'd hardly grown more than half an inch in a whole year. Wherever she went she drew. Everything was different in England; the shape of the houses, the gardens, even peoples' clothes. On their final evening they went to see Sir Henry Irving in *King Lear*. Ellen Terry was playing Cordelia. Paula could hardly bear to watch the mad old man raving and muttering on the heath, unable to recognise his own daughter.

Back in the country it did nothing but rain so they couldn't get into the garden to play lawn tennis, which had become a favourite with her and the Dutch girls. On fine days they organised tennis parties with the boys from the neighbouring estate, home from Harrow for the summer. They would arrive in white trousers and plimsolls, their blue jerseys knotted round their necks, carrying armfuls of rackets. Paula had become rather good at the game, hitching up her long skirts and tucking them into her belt. She was hitting more balls than she missed, though she couldn't quite manage the backhands. But now the gardener had rolled up the net and the chalk lines were being washed away into the wet grass.

She hated not being able to go outside. There was nothing to do but sit in the morning room and watch the incessant downpour through the French windows, as it smashed the tall blue delphiniums in the herbaceous border, and poured off the roof into the rain butt. She drew and tried to read Sir Walter Scott's *Rob Roy*, but there were so many difficult words. Every day before luncheon, from twelve to one, she had to practice her English pronunciation by reading to her aunt in the drawing room. She'd begun with simple stories, but had moved on to biographies, starting with Thackeray. Her aunt was very exacting.

'You don't like being corrected, do you Paula? You need to be a little less opinionated, young lady. We all have to learn by our mistakes and you make more than are strictly necessary.'

She was taken aback. Maybe her aunt was right. Perhaps she was opinionated. She wasn't used to being told off so directly and felt something inside her shrivel. Only that morning she'd been scolded for remarking on the arrangement of fans in the drawing room. Yet when Mutti put a vase of flowers on the window ledge, she always commented on how pretty they looked. But, according to her aunt, her remarks were uncalled for. It wasn't for her to comment on other people's affairs.

The next morning she got up early. She'd been woken for the last few days by headaches. She sat at the table in the bay window trying to finish the watercolour of the rose garden, with its spokes of gravel paths that led to the lichen-covered stone fountain where a chubby cupid with a pot on his shoulder poured water into a pool of speckled goldfish. Everything in England was so green and lush. As she sat staring into the wet garden, her eyes filled with tears. She knew she was being foolish. She was sixteen; not a baby, but she missed her home and her family. She wiped her face with the back of her hand

and forced herself to finish her sketch. She would send it to Mutti in the next post.

At breakfast the following morning she unfolded her napkin hoping to find a letter. The previous day her uncle had hidden Günther's inside the starched linen, but today there was nothing and she had to fight back her disappointment. She knew she had to disguise this gnawing homesickness, that it would be rude to show her aunt and uncle how unhappy she was, how badly she slept, and how very much she missed her brothers and sisters. She was finding her aunt's regime difficult. She was never sure whether or not she'd offended her, or if her curtness was simply the English way. The time between letters from home seemed interminable. But she knew she was lucky to be in England and have the chance to learn so much. If only she wasn't so tired all the time, if her head didn't ache and she could manage the unfamiliar food.

Alone in her room she cried a good deal. Of course, it was only in private. For how ungrateful her relatives would think her if they knew; how lacking in character. And it would reflect badly on her parents. The next day there was a letter from Kurt. Cholera was taking hold in Germany. She was frightened; worried that her family weren't eating enough fruit or boiling the water.

St John's Wood Art School: 'The Wood', as it was known locally, was run by Mr Ward; RA. Paula was to start on Monday. Lessons were from ten o'clock to four o'clock. The first exercises were simple. Students drew from two-dimensional models, then moved onto Greek casts, reliefs and jointed dolls, and finally to still life. Much later they were allowed to draw from a model.

She wasn't sure what to take, so sorted some recent sketches in her portfolio to show the teacher. She sharpened her pencils, placing them neatly in the new wooden pencil box that the twins had given her before she'd left for England. When she arrived there were about sixty ladies and gentlemen in the studio and she was by far the youngest. Mr Ward, a middle-aged man with wispy hair and a velvet jacket, worn with a loose cravat in the French style, showed her around. He spoke so fast she worried that she wouldn't understand a thing. Another student, Millicent Webber from Hampstead, offered—what was her strange phrase?—to show her the ropes. What ropes these were, Paula had no idea. But she was grateful for her kindness as they shared an apple in the break and Millicent went through everything Mr Ward had taught them in case Paula hadn't understood. While enjoying a glass of milk, Paula remarked on Millicent's brooch with its pink, white and green enamel, which she always wore at the throat of her lawn blouse.

'Do you know what these colours stand for, Paula? Have you ever heard of Women's Suffrage?'

Paula admitted that she hadn't.

'You've never heard of the Women's Franchise League? Sylvia Pankhurst is my heroine. She's a close friend of Mama's. They visit the workhouses in the East End. You can't believe it, Paula, the conditions in which those women are forced to live. Dirt, deprivation, no self respect, separated from their husbands and children. You wouldn't keep a dog in such a state.'

Paula didn't know what to say. She had no idea that people had to endure such hardship.

*

The women in the class far outnumbered the men. They were all ages and sat at their easels, in baggy smocks, looking very serious. Being so much younger Paula was afraid she wouldn't come up to scratch. At first she was only allowed to use pencil to practise arabesques and shading. Then, as she progressed, she was permitted to move on to charcoal and copy the plaster casts. After three weeks she was ushered into the life room. There were only women present. The men had been sent off to another studio where they were to draw the figure nude. Here, the model was wearing bathing drawers, with a swatch of material wound over the top and passed between her legs, secured with a leather strap.

As the older women set up their easels Paula kept her eyes on the floor. She'd never been in a room with a half-naked woman before, except her sister. She felt embarrassed, but as she started to draw she became lost in the curve of the shoulder jutting from beneath the white skin, and the soft fall of the model's heavy breasts set free of the constraint of her corset.

It was a real pea souper. That was the English phrase. She couldn't see a thing in the smog except the fuzzy sulphurous glow from the lamps of the oncoming trams. Her aunt was surprised at her determination but, when Paula insisted that she had to attend her class, she made her wrap up in a thick woollen muffler and tam-o'-shanter.

'You need to cover your chest in this weather, Paula. We don't want you coming down with bronchitis now, do we? What would your Mutti say?'

45

Paula made her way to the life room where the other students were already at work. The model on the dais was dressed as a monk. She tacked a fresh sheet of paper onto her board and settled herself in a corner. Deep lines, like a map, etched the model's face. She wondered if she would ever be able to convey such emotion. That's what was lacking in her work. She was too preoccupied with form and the outward appearance of things rather than their essence. In the hushed concentration of the room a wave of nausea washed over her. What an earth was she doing here? Who did she think she was? What did she know either about art or life? She was just a silly girl from Bremen.

The next morning there was a letter from Papi:

'My dear girl,
    I just received your first watercolours in the post. I know you expect my derision, but I'm very proud of you. The bits of fruit you sent are beautifully executed. I almost wanted to take a bite out of them, but are they lemons or oranges? I wasn't quite sure. Form, Paula. It all comes down to form. That's what you have to remember. But the main reason for this letter, my dear, is to remind you that it's the duty of every well-educated young woman to strive for independence. Art is your chosen path, but you should never forget the sudden changes that we're all subjected to in this modern age. None of us should take the good life for granted. Hopefully there'll always be a call for well-trained teachers.

I know, too, that you'll be pleased to hear that Kurt's rheumatism is a little better. Now he only has pain in his left arm. But he's fed up with being in hospital and the Doctor has insisted on another two weeks, so please send him a postcard with one of your little sketches to cheer him up. The other piece of news is that Günther's left for boarding school. It's hard to think of him being so grown-up. Finally, though you may not be aware of this, your aunt recently wrote to me suggesting two options. The first is that you enrol in an English boarding school, and the second is that you cut short your visit and come home. The offer of a school is very generous, but your aunt expressed some concern about your health, Paula, though you've not mentioned it in any of your letters. I understand that your headaches are more frequent and that you've been having fainting fits. My own feeling is that you should come home and be with your family so that your symptoms can be monitored. Of course, it might be nothing more than growing pains, but Mutti believes it is homesickness. And Mutti is usually right about such things. Anyway, you know what a fusspot she is and she would prefer to have you where she can keep an eye on you. Let me know which course of action you'd prefer to take and I'll make the necessary arrangements.

Your loving, Papi.'

The cherry trees were in bloom and everywhere there was the heady, urgent smell of spring. It was good to be home. Back in her own bed under the eaves, talking far into the night with

Milly. Paula knew that going away had opened her eyes to the world, which was essential if she was going to be an artist, but she'd been very homesick. Yesterday she'd restarted her lessons with Herr Wiegandt and he had paid her the compliment of saying how much her drawing had matured in England.

Now, whenever possible, she drew from a live model. Her preference was for charcoal. She set up a studio in the old stable block at the bottom of the garden and bribed Herma and Henner to sit for her. Sugared almonds usually did the trick but they got easily bored and never stayed for long. It was hard to find anyone willing to pose for the hours she needed to finish a drawing. Mutti was always trying to enlist volunteers. Recently, taking tea with the Doctor, she'd suggested that he might pose for her. The trouble was he wasn't at all impressed by the way she had emphasised his jug-like ears.

When she wasn't drawing she played lawn tennis with Milly, a habit she'd brought back from England. They set up a temporary court at the far end of the garden, down by the laburnum where not much grew, laying down boundary ribbons to mark out the court and putting up a net between two sticks. Sundays were their tennis days when they invited the boys from two houses away. They took the game very seriously and didn't like losing to a pair of girls.

'They're not—what's the English phrase, Milly?—*good sports.*'

After the match they would sit in the shade of the laburnum drinking lemon barley water. But though she enjoyed socialising, more and more she felt after her time away, the need for solitude. When she wasn't playing tennis or helping her mother, she'd sit on her bed drawing and reading from the leather-bound

Browning her aunt had given her as a leaving present. *The Dramatic Lyrics* were her favourite, though she still struggled with some of the long words. Despite her aunt's strictness, she had learnt a good deal in England.

Worpsweders. That's what they called the artists showing at the Kunsthalle because they lived in a colony in the village of Worpswede out on the moors, some thirteen miles from Bremen. It took half a day to get there, down wooded lanes and bumpy cart tracks, to the handful of low cottages hunched among the bogs and windmills. This was Paula's first *vernissage*. She and Milly were both wearing their new winter coats. It seemed as if all of Bremen was in attendance. Women in feathered hats and furs gathered on the stairs tut-tutting at the ugly modern paintings. Why should anyone want to paint bogs and filthy peasants instead of charming views of Paris or scenes from ancient Rome, they asked sourly.

But Paula was entranced. She'd never seen anything like Mackensen's *Sermon on the Heath* before. He'd painted it from a glass-covered wagon built especially so that he could be out in all weathers. In a clearing of silver birch a congregation of peasants sat listening to a pastor's sermon: the women dressed in their white Sunday bonnets and shawls. It was as if she could simply reach out and touch those peat-blackened hands lying in the shallows of their starched aprons.

After her stay in England life, at home, was beginning to feel suffocating. She loved her brothers and sisters, and her parents, but none of them really cared about the things that mattered to her. Even Papi's views on painting were quite different to her own. Technical ability was what mattered to him, not sentiment or expression. Of course, she still had a good deal to learn, but she wanted to convey what was real, even if it that was mean and ugly.

There were times she felt very lonely, when she'd go for solitary walks around the city and spend as much time thinking as drawing. She tried to imagine what it would be like to have someone to share her innermost thoughts. Yet happiness wasn't something she could quite envisage for herself. She thought of her parents, of how much love there was in their marriage. But that was because Mutti always put Papi and the family first. But she knew she wasn't so selfless, that what she wanted, above all, was to paint. Did that mean, then, that she'd never find love? And even if she did, what then? Maybe like a glint of light on water, it would be there one minute and then gone the next, so that in contrast everything would just seem darker.

These Worpswede painters were pushing back the boundaries of what it meant to be an artist, rejecting conventional academicism for something more authentic. She was particularly struck by the gritty realism of Otto Modersohn. The sepia and russet tones with which he suggested the low-lying fields and dykes around Worpswede. The sense of desolation moved her. She could smell the damp peat, hear the cries of the circling rooks, and feel the leaden clouds gathering over the moors. Yet his paintings were more than mere copies of nature. They were attempts to translate what it felt like to be part of the landscape. Beside Herr Modersohn's paintings those of the young Heinrich Vogeler, with their fairies and medieval knights, appeared stylised and contrived. They reminded her of the English Pre-Raphaelites, the Holman Hunts and works by Dante Gabriel Rossetti that she'd seen in London. Vogeler's paintings were charming, but they had little to do with the harsh realities of modern life that she had seen in parts of London, or the poorer parts of Bremen. And that's what she wanted to paint. The world in all its dirty poignancy.

It was April, and she couldn't go out without an umbrella for fear of getting caught in a shower. What a cosmopolitan city Berlin was compared to Bremen. How lucky she was to be here and it was all thanks to Mutti. For although she'd been accepted by the Drawing and Painting School of the Association of Berlin Women Artists, Paula had no idea how she was going to pay the fees. It had been impossible to bring up the subject with Papi for fear of sending him into one of his bleak depressions when he'd disappear into his study for days, asking for his meals to be sent in on a tray, refusing to draw back the curtains, as if the morning sun would further illuminate his shortcomings.

For in his eyes—and nothing his wife or children could say would change his view—he was a failure. The Office for the Management of the Bremen Railways had recently decided that the Bremen line was unprofitable and had shut it down. As a result, Papi had lost his post. Despite his qualifications, his learning, and endless letter writing, he couldn't find another suitable job.

'They say I'm too old. Too independent, the idiots, the fools. What do they know about engineering?'

They'd even taken away his uniform. Paula couldn't bear to see him hanging about the house in his old black jacket with the patched elbows, all too aware that his family now had to manage on his meagre pension. But Mutti had heard of a young American who wished to lodge with a German family in order to improve her language skills. Without a moment's hesitation she had suggested that the young woman should join them as a paying guest and take conversation classes with her every morning from ten to twelve o'clock.

'She'll have two rooms and I'll get three hundred marks a month for room and board. But don't say anything for the moment to Papi, Paula. You know how he's always accusing me of encouraging you in what he considers to be reckless plans, and he does worry so about money. But now my dear, you'll be able to go to Berlin.'

She had to change trains in Hamburg and was anxious about finding the right platform as she struggled across the station concourse with her heavy leather suitcase, drawing stool and box full of brushes and paint. Despite the spring weather, Mutti had insisted she should bring her winter coat and she was boiling. Exhilarated, but a little nervous to be travelling alone, she clambered up the steps, hauling her bags after her into an empty compartment where a large Jewess was sitting, eating a sandwich. Paula could feel herself getting hotter and hotter as she struggled to lift her luggage into the overhead rack before collapsing, exhausted, just as the train pulled out. Despite her florid complexion and big lobster hands covered in rings, her travelling companion turned out to be very pleasant.

In fact she didn't stop talking. Paula learnt that she worked as the Kaiser's hairdresser and was a specialist in beard trimming. Oh, the beards she'd tended! The dukes and counts, the lawyers and lechers who'd passed through her hands! She did like a neat perfumed beard. You could tell a gentleman by the way he kept his beard. If only Paula had seen the one belonging to her late husband, a diamond dealer, and a most elegant man, she prattled on, stopping only to offer her a salt beef sandwich.

When the train finally drew into Berlin-Friedrichstrasse the thudding pistons and screaming sirens of the great trains beneath the soot-covered glass roof amazed her. Suddenly the whole world seemed to be on the move. A grandmother was waiting for her grandson. A soldier for his young wife who emerged from a cloud of steam and smoke, carrying a basket of pears. Lives coming together and pulled apart by the railways. As she climbed from her carriage, Kurt was waiting at the barrier to take her to her aunt and uncle's where she'd be lodging.

This time she was determined not to feel homesick, not to experience the loneliness that had laid her so low with headaches and fainting fits when she'd stayed in England. She wondered if she would always feel this pull between the need to venture out into the world and the desire to stay at home. How much easier it would be if she simply wanted to make a good marriage rather than be a painter. But she was older now and needed to learn to be more independent. Papi expected it. She knew that in his heart he didn't have much faith in her ability to be an artist. A teacher, maybe, but an artist? She was aware, too, of the sacrifices that her mother was making on her behalf. In his last letter Papi had criticised her for her prim disdain towards others. She'd been taken aback. Was that really how he saw her? But perhaps he was right. Maybe she did judge too quickly. She didn't mean to. It was just that she wanted so much from life.

Yet for all his gruffness she sensed that her father had an inkling of what she was trying to do and loved him for it. She imagined him in his study full of pipe smoke, sitting at his heavy mahogany desk with its little wooden letter rack, matching pen-holder and paper knife, writing her a letter. Art, he insisted, was more than the subject, more even than craftsmanship.

'A painting, Paula, has to make you care.'

Her first drawing lesson was far more formal than anything she had experienced in London. She missed the casual ease of the classes at The Wood, her apple breaks with Millicent, and their chats about her mother's work for women's suffrage. There she'd been protected by the older women who'd clucked round her, making sure that their 'little German friend' understood what was going on. And, unlike the balding Mr Ward, Herr Alberts was terrifying.

'That's rubbish Fräulein Becker, complete rubbish,' he'd stammer, spittle flying from the corners of his mouth as he stood beside her easel. Then, when she didn't acquiesce quickly enough, he would throw down his charcoal in a rage and rush off to the next student.

'No talent at all,' he'd screech at some hapless girl on the verge of tears. 'Or maybe you're just too stupid to look. Not that it matters either way because it's worthless,' he'd spit, taking a piece of bread from his pocket and smearing the inert charcoal with his meaty hand, so the whole drab drawing sprang to life.

Herr Alberts might be frightening but he made her see with new eyes. Slowly she began to understand that drawing was a process of discovery. It forced her to look at the world in a different way. To dissect, weigh and analyse the object in front of her. A line or a tone was important, not because it recorded what she saw, but because it charted her thoughts. She had to judge the distance between a model's ears and eyes, the triangle between the nipples and navel in relationship to the hips. Notice how the weight-bearing leg remained tense, while the other became soft and relaxed.

Hurrying home along the Potsdamerstrasse to her little room with the yellow curtains, she imagined drawing the woman in the bakery with a goitre, or the school porter with his warty cheeks. These human oddities intrigued her. On the tram she studied the way a prominent nose cast a shadow, or a cheek-bone pressed against an unshaven cheek. She knew she was still drawing shadows too distinctly, as if they were separate from the object. Until she could master these subtleties then nothing she drew would have any depth. That's why Herr Alberts was good for her. He knew each student's ability and demanded that they live up to it.

'It's a sin if you don't pursue your art with devotion, a sin,' he spluttered as white flecks of spit landed on the paper.

But charcoal was difficult. Herr Alberts didn't have to tell her that her drawings were rubbish. She knew. On Mondays and Tuesdays she had a class with Stöving, the little Swede with bad breath and legs like a stick insect. He didn't reprimand her

as severely but she learnt far less from him. She needed someone to goad her on. Stöving had no vision. He could only see
individual lines, never the intention behind them. Back in her
room she began a self-portrait. Sitting staring at her reflection
for hours was very intense. Her features seemed to dissolve and
regroup: the pile of coppery hair, the tawny skin and brown
eyes. If she could only describe in paint what it really felt like to
be her. But the gap between her emotions and their execution
seemed almost unsurpassable.

Saturday mornings were free of classes so she got up early
and made a simple breakfast of cheese, black bread and coffee.
Afterwards, she would go downstairs to bring up a jug of hot
water from the kitchen two floors below to perform her toilette
at the washstand in the corner. Then, if it was fine, she'd stroll in
the park or visit a museum with her new friend Freda. Freda was
only a year above her, but had already sold two paintings. Paula
was educating herself in the German masters. Rembrandt was,
to her mind, the greatest of the northern painters, combining
the everyday and the sublime. Over and over again she found
herself drawn back to *The Vision of Daniel*. You didn't have to
be pious to experience the ecstasy conveyed in Rembrandt's
intense, dark tones.

Fräulein Bauck was in her fifties, stout, with a heavy, mascu-
line jaw. Like many female teachers at the art school she was
unkempt and shabby. In the past she'd probably taken better
care of herself, but poverty and neglect had taken their toll,
and now her hair was piled on top of her head like a mound of
old feathers. In class she always wore the same blue-chequered

blouse without the aid of a corset to hold her in place, so her large breasts lolled in opposite directions as she moved. But her strong views, her outspoken opinions and yellow nicotine-stained fingers, all entranced Paula. She wasn't like any woman she'd ever met before. Sometimes they went to the theatre together when Fräulein Bauck's idea of dressing up was to wrap an old Egyptian shawl over her brown dress.

'Just because you're a woman, Paula, doesn't mean that you're intrinsically inferior to a man, let alone a male painter. You have to hold to your vision and work hard. There's no place for sloppy sentiment if you want to be serious. You don't mind if I smoke, do you?'

They saw the new play by Hauptmann, and Ibsen's *The Doll's House*. For days Paula couldn't get the image of the downtrodden Nora out of her head. Next morning she received a letter from Papi. He warned that it might not be possible for her to continue with her studies. His money worries were mounting. He realised she'd only begun to scratch the surface of her subject so didn't expect any significant success yet. But whatever the future held, even if he could find the means to support her, she would have to prepare to become independent.

Why did he always give with one hand and take away with the other? If she had it in her to become a first-rate painter then he made it clear it would already have become evident. A teacher, that's what he saw her as. He talked of her achieving better-than-average results if she applied herself, but she knew that he didn't consider her an original talent. He thought Mutti indulged her, that Milly had more mettle; and that she was an unworldly, moody girl who may have learnt how to arrange flowers in England, but didn't have the grit to make her own way in the world.

She felt defeated. Didn't he understand that she had dreams? She tacked up the drawing she'd done that morning in class on her bedroom wall and suddenly saw that, maybe, she was on the right track after all, that nothing could hold her back.

The next day she tried to draw everything in two dimensions, but she hated the results. She longed for Herr Alberts to stop at her easel and praise her, but he simply hurried past without a second look. She missed Milly and the twins and longed to be at home helping around the house or sitting with Herma down by the hutch, drawing the old black rabbit.

Just as she was feeling particularly low Fräulein Bauck invited her for the weekend to stay with her sister in Hamburg. On the train Fräulein Bauck chain-smoked and talked of her heroine, Artemisia Gentileschi.

'She was precociously gifted, Paula. One of the greatest painters of the Caravaggio school and a formidable personality, though if it hadn't been for her famous father she'd have been nobody. Can you imagine how hard it was for a woman in the Renaissance to lead an independent life? Rape and torture, that's what she had to put up with. I think they felt insulted by her talent. At least all we have to contend with is the narrow-minded indifference of a few stuffy old academics. Would you like an apple?'

In Hamburg they walked along the shore, holding on to their hats in the breeze, as they watched the black cargo ships disappear over the horizon and talked of art and what a woman might expect from life. Whether it was possible to be a serious painter and married. Then, on Saturday afternoon, they joined the crowds in the old town where Bismarck was paying a visit. Suddenly a huge cheer went up and, as the crowd surged forward, Paula found herself right beside the Chancellor's open landau and handed him a rose. But he turned away without taking it, irritated by the cheering hordes.

At last she was going to be allowed to paint in oils. Herr Dettmann had made a point of telling her how impressed he was with her drawing of corncobs and had invited her to join his Monday class. Now she'd be able to work in colour. And only this morning her mother had sent her the money to buy a length of material to make a copy of her aunt's light-blue cheviot-wool dress. Mutti insisted she should choose something of good quality as it had to put up with hard wear. But a new dress! She'd only brought her brown serge skirt to Berlin and three serviceable blouses. But what pleased her most was that Mutti reported Papi had taken the drawings she'd sent for his birthday into his study, only to emerge half an hour later and announce how good they were.

Every Friday she had to submit a red chalk study for the inspection of the whole class. Some of the other students didn't like the fact that she'd been singled out. It didn't make her popular, but she was making real progress under Alberts, though he never let her get above herself, praising her one day, then finding fault the next. She was also learning more about women's suffrage. It was the subject on everyone's lips. Last Friday she'd dragged Kurt to a lecture on *Goethe and Women's Emancipation*, though he'd protested that he would rather have a beer with his medical student friends. All through the lecture he'd poked her in the ribs and whispered that the lecturer, in her heavy tweed jacket and short cropped hair, looked like a man. As they were leaving a young woman approached to ask if Paula would sign a petition, but Kurt grabbed hold of her sleeve and dragged her off: 'Paula, you're such a ninny. You don't have to do things just because other people do.'

She knew that she should have stood up to him, but perhaps she didn't have it in her to take on the world.

This time, when she changed trains in Hamburg, she 'knew the ropes'. She read and drew a little and mostly had the carriage to herself. She had enjoyed Berlin but missed her family and was pleased to be on her way home. Twenty-five years! Could her parents really have been married that long? She had made them a present: a little book of watercolours that she'd bound herself. By way of a celebration they were all taking a trip to the country. She was longing to see Milly and the twins. They would play dominoes and go for long walks along the canals. She couldn't wait.

MATHILDE

Is this right? How do I know if it's right? I know so little about my mother's life, just the few facts gleaned from my grandmother and Aunt Milly. All I have are her paintings and a clutch of fading photographs. As I walk round Worpswede I try to imagine the tenor of her daily life as she stopped to chat with the farm children or made her way to the Poor House to draw the old woman she befriended there. And I try to guess what she would have done if she'd found herself in my position. She was spirited and brave, and that's what I must be.

I've taken a room in a small guesthouse. The landlady has ruddy cheeks, solid ample hips and a country air. It's people like her and her husband, farmers and war veterans, who support the political changes that are overtaking us. Wedded to this soil and these peat wetlands, for them, these silver birch and buckwheat fields are Germany. They stand between them, ruin and starvation. As yet they're largely untouched by the chaos in the cities. The daily prohibitions, the random acts of violence, and the never-ending propaganda that streams from the wireless.

I'm worried about my little cat, Hölderlin. I hope the girl downstairs has remembered to feed him. She said she'd keep an eye. He's a stray I rescued and rather nervous. He sleeps in my bed and I don't want him to disappear while I'm not there. I don't want to lose him too.

The landlady is obviously curious about me. She probably wonders what I'm doing here, a young woman on my own with one small bag. But she said nothing as she led me up the steep wooden stairs to this little sloping room at the end of the landing. I was pleased to get out of my wet clothes. At the cemetery it was snowing heavily and I got soaked, though the snow didn't settle and now has turned to slush. Outside the sky is steel-grey as if more is on the way. Lying in bed under the heavy feather quilt listening to a branch tapping against the window, I remember another tree and another window, that first time I woke in your little room where you taught, next door to the Café Grössenwahn. There was an upright piano, and on the lid, marble busts of Handel, Beethoven and Chopin, and piles of sheet music everywhere.

Your wife was expecting you home, but you telephoned to say that you were rehearsing late and for her not to expect you for dinner. You'd just made love to me on the red velvet chaise longue. Afterwards we lay in the dark, my back pressed against your chest, your arms wrapped round me, as you cupped my breasts gently inside my chemise. We'd already known each other for six months and I'd loved you from the first. But I never imagined that you had noticed me, a junior member of the orchestra. Through the thin curtains the street lamp cast shadows into the dark corners of the room and I remember willing it not to get light, not to be morning, knowing that to love this much, this unguardedly, could only be dangerous.

But that was a different world, one filled with music. Now I can't listen to music at all, let alone play. How could I get through Mendelssohn's Violin Concerto? It's what you played, what you taught me. German music. Jewish music.

How could Paula have understood, living out there on those moors, where all this talk of land and soil would lead, how their vision would become corrupted? I need to understand what these windswept wetlands meant to her. Of course, it's there in her paintings. The wide skies, the deep green dykes and red-roofed barns set against yellow haystacks. She had such a feeling for the ordinary people. For the rickety children and the toothless old peasants languishing in the Poor House. She painted them with such love. Surely she'd have been shocked at the state of the country now. That so much hope should have ended in all this hate. Perhaps history isn't so much what actually happens, but what we least expect. But it's her self-portraits that speak to me most directly. It's then that I feel closest to her. In her heavy lidded eyes and Slavic cheeks I see something of my own face.

Slipping a woollen shawl over my nightdress I sit staring out at the wet trees, the picket fence and gravel path. I stay like this for ages not wanting to do anything or go anywhere. I like the sensation of not feeling or thinking, it relieves me of the responsibility of choice. My entire morning is framed by a window and a patch of snow-laden sky. Everything is shrouded in silence and a veil of grey cloud. I feel like a nun. An old man walks past carrying a bundle of sticks, and then a girl in a beret cycles past; people getting on with their lives the best they can. For them the horrors of the city are still only a rumour. I get up and make tea on the little stove in the corner of the room, then take the pink china cup bordered with roses back to the table in the window. The sleet outside has turned to freezing rain and drops are chasing down the windowpanes. I sit with my tea watching to see which one will finish first, as if such things are suddenly important.

The day passes. I lie in bed, read a little, dream a little and think of you. Then I try not to think of you. I walk from one side of the room to the other and reorganise my few belongings before staring out of the window again, trying to picture a future. To imagine what I'll do, where I'll go, and how I—no, we—will live. I like this watery half-world, it's soothing. It helps me to forget what I've seen in the city. For the moment this is all there is, this room with its high bed, its table and chair and this cluster of cells dividing inside me oblivious of the disruptions of history. Above the chest of drawers is a painting of an Alpine sunset. The mountains are snow-capped and tinged a celestial pink.

I've no idea what time it is, whether it's two in the afternoon or seven in the evening. The lights in the little house opposite come on, one by one. A woman in a black coat, carrying a basket of vegetables, hurries up the path to the front door, shutting it against the growing dark. I'm still not dressed. What would be the point in getting dressed? And I'm not hungry, so there's no need to go out.

I go to the mirror and brush my hair. All I have to choose is whether to sit or lie down, read or look out of the window. It's such a relief after Berlin; the fear, the anxious queues and sense of mounting panic. Days after the Reichstag burnt down

I saw an old man I've known for years, standing outside the Jewish bakery he owns on the corner, crying. A young soldier had walked in and helped himself to a loaf. When the old man protested the soldier had hit him in the face with his gloved fist. The old man had just stood there, his glasses smashed, blood streaming from his broken nose; as the young man nonchalantly tore chunks out of his stolen loaf and chatted with his friends while stroking the butt of his pistol. No one dared do anything. I felt sick and wanted to protest. But what could I do? Fear makes us all impotent. I tried to call you, to warn you what was going on. But when I picked up the phone there was no reply and I was frightened that Lola would answer. I was frantic that something had happened to you. I knew your old friend, the librarian in the music department at the university, had lost his job, along with many other Jewish academics. But I suppose I couldn't believe that anyone would treat you like that. After all, you're a famous musician.

Before I got on the bus in Bremen I bought a small calfskin notebook. I want to keep a diary while I'm here and try to make sense of all this anguish. When you left, I couldn't eat. I existed on tea and cold toast and my bed was full of crumbs. I didn't wash and my hair became greasy. I spoke to no one except Hölderlin. Lying in bed I'd pretend that his muscles rippling beneath my hand were yours. I knew what was happening outside, the controls being exerted on the press and on the radio, but my world had become reduced to my room.

Everything was unravelling, but all I could think of was your touch. I waited endlessly for the telephone to ring, or for a scribbled note to let me know that it was all a mistake; that you'd decided, after all, to stay in Berlin. I think I was losing my mind.

Now you're on your way to America to take up your place as guest violinist in the Chicago Symphony Orchestra. A position secured by Lola. That was the deal: the marriage for your future. She had connections, or her father, Howard Ritchie, editor of the *Chicago Tribune*, a friend of the mayor's, had connections. Lola called him from Berlin to ask for his help. She was frightened, she told him, that her husband's citizenship was about to be revoked. He may be a world-famous musician, but as far as the authorities were concerned he was an undesirable alien.

What could he do? Howard Ritchie had never met this violinist husband of hers, this Jew. But the fellow seemed to be what his daughter wanted and he appeared to be famous, so he did what she asked, booked tickets, made phone calls, twisted arms.

'What choice do I have, Tille?' you asked, your face buried in my hair, mine wet with tears. What choice is there for any of us now? You know I love you—but it's too dangerous. There are times when love isn't enough, when it can't protect us. But, my darling, you've made me so happy. No one could have asked for more.'

And now, I am carrying your child.

As I try to picture your face there's a knock on my door. I panic. It's the woman who owns the guesthouse. She wants to know if I'm all right. She hasn't seen me all day. Why do I feel so guilty? I know she's looking for clues as to why I'm here. She asks if I'm ill, but I assure her that I'm fine, just tired after my journey, and that now I am on my way out. I know she's being kind as well as nosey, but I don't need this sort of interest. Still it forces me to get dressed. To do what I came to do: go and look for Paula.

PAULA

I T TOOK THE SMALL anniversary party three hours to get to Worpswede along the bumpy country road. Paula's parents had invited her to bring along a friend to keep her company and she'd asked Freda, with her dark fringe and thick black eyebrows like a pair of crow's wings. Located amid soggy marshland on Lüneburg Heath, Worpswede, with its purple heather, weeping willows and peat ponds seemed to belong to another age. An enormous sky hung over the distant chain of hills and fields, where whitewashed cottages squatted among the dykes, and peat smoke curled from the chimneys. There was something Russian about these flatlands with their limitless horizons, silver birch and red stalks of freshly cut buckwheat shivering in the wind.

Papi was very keen to meet Mackensen who had discovered the village in the early 1880s and lived there ever since, attracting artists disenchanted with urban life. Some came for weeks, others for months, even years, to breathe the clean country air and live as cheaply as possible among the peat cutters, the basket weavers and clog makers whose lives had remained unchanged for centuries. Paula knew these artists believed that creeping industrialisation and mechanisation threatened their creativity. That the new factories producing steel and electricity, and the growing railway system, were turning them into unwilling cogs in the fast-moving wheels of modernity. As the party drove into the village with its timbered cottages, surrounded by meadows and dykes, she felt a surge of happiness at the wild beauty of the place. No wonder it attracted painters.

But Mackensen sent a curt note to say that he was busy working on a large triptych and couldn't spare the time for social engagements. Papi was most put out. Though they did meet Otto Modersohn, and some of the other painters including Carl Vinnen and the handsome young Heinrich Vogeler. Mutti made a point of inviting them for coffee and cake. Papi was surprised by the gangly, bearded Modersohn. From the name he'd expected someone more Semitic. Modersohn, like Mackensen, had lived in the village for some time and seemed older than the others.

With a peat stove burning in the corner of the rustic living room, Mutti poured coffee and cream and passed round the spiced apple cake. Outside the twins played in the garden. Papi was in his element seated by the fire chatting, though he found it hard to hide his irritation when Vinnen claimed that he hated books and, if possible, never read them.

'I ask you,' Papi grumbled after they'd left and Mutti was clearing the plates, 'what else is there to do here in the evenings? All that nonsense about keeping his ideas pure and not being influenced by others. How can the man learn anything with such a closed mind? It's just a form of affectation. It's hardly surprising the rest of the world thinks these Worpsweders are a load of dilettantes. It's odd how people who're so extreme in their art can be so conservative in their politics. But that

Modersohn fellow has something about him, I thought. Though he doesn't have much small talk, does he? Presumably that's why he brought along his wife and little girl, to help him out.'

Paula had fallen in love. This was what she'd been looking for, only she hadn't known it until now: these dykes and wide skies, the copse of spindly silver birch. A week wasn't nearly enough. She never wanted to leave. She had to persuade her parents to let her stay on. If Freda was allowed then, maybe, they would agree too. She begged them to write to Freda's father, who wrote back by return giving his permission. So it was settled. They would remain for another three weeks and lodge with a widow in the village.

Whenever they could they went walking. Paula couldn't get enough of the brown moors with their willow-fringed canals and asphalt reflections. The River Hamme where the dark sails of the wooden peat barges seemed to cut across the flat fields, as they carried their cargoes upstream to Bremen. At first the villagers ignored her, but after a while they got used to seeing her sitting on a wall sketching the goose girl, or the old man whittling willow outside his cottage. They would stop and stand behind her, holding a pail of warm milk or a peat shovel, and watch with bemused curiosity as she drew, before wandering off without a word.

But over the last couple of days they'd begun to pass the time. She learnt that many of them had never left the village, that they believed this was the Devil's Moor, and that the souls of unchristened children and lost travellers wandered here. One toothless old woman, dressed in a filthy red-spotted headscarf, spoke of a giant who'd trudged down from the mountains with a sack of sand that had been ripped open by the wind, to create the sandy plain of the Weyerberg. They talked of monasteries and castles sunk beneath the bog, and of spirits dressed in clothes woven from the white cotton grass.

Dawn was Paula's favourite time, when the mist rose over the moors. Or late afternoon, just before dusk, when the trees stood etched against the navy sky and the cries of the crows circling above the ploughed fields punctured the silence. There was something primitive about the drained light and eerie desolation that touched her. It was as if a part of her had always known this place; the name of every flower, berry and bird.

She and Freda had a couple of small rooms in the widow's cottage; a bedroom and a sitting room where they painted. They collected ferns and stones, picked wild flowers which they arranged in jars on the window ledge. Every morning they brewed coffee on the small iron stove and sat down to a breakfast of black bread, honey and fresh eggs, before strapping on their rucksacks and tramping to the edge of the village to set up their easels. In the afternoons she took lessons with Mackensen.

The loneliness of these vast skies and bleak moors moved her profoundly. She saw it in Mackensen's work more than in the other painters, this connection that the peasants had with the soil. He'd managed to catch something both of their steadfast endurance and their vulnerability. And yet, as she became more familiar with his work, she felt he was too eager to organise things into a harmonious arrangement. Mackensen was a kind man, and she relished his encouragement, but he lacked that visceral power she imagined she had seen all those months ago in his *Sermon on the Heath*. Now that she'd got to know Worpswede better she saw that his work was too tame, too concerned with artistry. Where was the rushing wind, the wild storms that battered her windows at night, and the celestial light that suddenly broke through the leaden clouds after rain? In her lessons he spoke of simplicity. But that wasn't enough. She wanted—no, needed—to strip things bare. To go to their heart.

She got up early while Freda slept. Leaving her brushes at home, she set off with her lunch and a copy of Goethe's poems in her rucksack, to climb the steep track past the lonely farmstead; and through the spinney of pines, to the green meadow that ran along the river and opened out onto the heath of purple heather. In the clearing she lay down on a springy bank and watched the racing clouds, remembering how she'd once lain in the park in Dresden listening to the song thrush in the willows. She spent the morning walking and drawing in her notebook. Then, when rain threatened, she packed up her things and wandered back along the banks of the Hamme.

Slowly she was getting to know the artists who made up the community. Heinrich Vogeler was her favourite. Not only was he handsome, he was younger and more eccentric than Mackensen, and much more sociable. A bit of a dreamer, he always carried a volume of verse in his pocket, which he read out loud as he ambled through the woods and fields. When Paula and Freda visited the derelict old farmhouse that he was restoring he would get out his battered guitar and play, urging them to sing along, even when they didn't know the words or the tune. Occasionally, his fiancée, Martha, would be there. It was good to forget about the demands of painting for a while, to laugh and drink tea, and while away the afternoon.

On one occasion there were a couple of other visitors, among them a painter from Berlin, a man with delicate hands, dressed in a brown velvet suit. It struck Paula that there must be some sort of intimate liaison between him and his companion, an old friend of Heinrich Vogeler's, with whom he'd studied in Paris. Heinrich had often spoken of her beauty and unconventional behaviour. After all he'd said Paula wasn't surprised when she arrived at the lunch table dressed in trousers and spent the entire meal with her hand resting on her friend's arm; as if touching a man in public was the most natural thing in the world.

That evening they were all invited to Hans am Ende's. Paula had only met him once before. A turf fire was burning in the hearth and the low-beamed cottage was bathed in candlelight. She couldn't help but notice the way Hans talked to his new wife, how tenderly he kept using her name and reaching out to touch her as he spoke. As the evening wore on the men lit their pipes, more wine was poured, and Carl Vinnen asked: 'Have you read Julius Langbehn yet, Paula? You should read his *Rembrandt as Teacher* if you want to become a real Worpsweder. Ask Heinrich. Langbehn was a big influence on his painting of the girl in a white dress, the one standing among the silver birch. She's the embodiment of German youth, isn't that right H? You see, Paula, for Langbehn, Rembrandt stands against everything that's decadent in Germany. He writes of a renaissance of German culture, and believes that after the domination by the Catholic South, the Protestant North will finally rally with this new art. We have to rid ourselves of all extraneous foreign influence. Did you know that German museums are bulging with French art? We are being swamped by outside forces. We have to return to our roots, to our forests and fairy tales, to the soil worked by the peasants living out here. Isn't that why we came,' he continued, looking round for approval, 'to live the simple life and be proud of what it means to be a true German? Now tell me, Paula, are you enjoying our little community?'

How could she have imagined, only a few months ago, that she'd be living among real artists, discussing the future of art. Yet there was something in Vinnen's words that filled her with disquiet.

And then there was Modersohn. Tall and slightly stooped, with his big fox-coloured beard and brown tweed suit. Paula had only seen him once since the visit he'd paid her parents. He had been out walking with his wife Hélène and their little daughter, and had stopped to lift his hat in greeting and pass the time of day. She couldn't help but notice the dark rings under Hélène's eyes. She seemed so slight and frail as she clung to her husband's arm. But Modersohn's landscapes, with their autumn suns and sulphurous skies, had a strange, brooding quality that deeply attracted her and echoed something of her own sentiments about this wild and lonely region. She would like to talk to him about painting. She'd like to get to know him better, this Otto Modersohn.

She took her easel down to the canal; to a spot that she'd not visited before, where the water was a dark peaty green. That evening she and Freda packed a basket with bread and cheese and a couple of flasks of beer and joined the three Vogeler boys punting on the Hamme. As the brothers took it in turns to punt downstream, Paula lay in the bottom of the boat watching the stars come out.

'You look like Ophelia,' Heinrich joked, as they moored to an overhanging willow branch and spread their picnic out on a chequered cloth. As they ate in silence, listening to the sounds of the river, a pale moon floated up over the horizon and the black sails of a wooden barge glided past with a motionless man at the tiller.

When she could, Paula painted outside her cottage till it got dark. She was constantly moved by the thin pencil lines of the birches silhouetted against the blood-red sky at sunset. One Sunday she took a trip to a spot where the peasants held their church service in the open. She was entranced by the weathered faces of the peat cutters and clog makers, by their stoicism and pious forbearance. The next day she painted her first portrait in the open air of the small blonde girl with pigtails and rough chapped cheeks who lived in the cottage opposite. For nearly two hours the child stood, one scuffed boot resting on the other, her hands in her apron pocket, patiently waiting for Paula to finish.

Little Annie Brotmann came from a big family. There were two girls of twelve and nine—Annie was the younger—a little boy of four and a baby. They seemed to survive on little more than a daily loaf, eaten huddled round a meagre fire, and were hardly better off than the children of the farm labourers who lived in the settlement of huts to the east of the river, who were out with their parents whatever the weather, trimming turnips and digging potatoes in the muddy fields.

Paula couldn't paint these people without doing something in return. She thought of Millicent and her mother working with the destitute in the East End of London and wrote to Mutti asking her to send any clothes that the twins had out-grown. A winter coat or some old boots would make all the difference. Next day she visited the Poor House to ask if any of the inmates would sit for her. A scrawny old man in a rough weave jacket posed in a freezing room. He neither spoke nor moved, sitting stiff as a board until she had finished. A fetid smell of poverty and urine clung to all inhabitants. But Paula was touched by the old man's quiet dignity. People—that's what she'd paint from now on. Not landscapes, but people who smelt of peat and dung and had earth under their fingernails.

Walking through the village one evening with the Vogeler boys they heard music coming from a barn. Poking their heads round the door they found a wedding party in full swing. Sitting on the hay bales was an accordion player, a fiddler and a fellow with a flute. At the far end the cows stood with their heads stuck over the stall partitions, watching. Despite the reek of animals and straw, a long trestle table decorated with jars of flowers and a spread of bread and cheese, had been laid down the middle of the barn. The bride had fallen asleep, and the yawning groom's friends were plying him with ever more tankards of beer so that he, too, was nearly out cold. As the friends stood watching in the doorway, the band struck up and the bride's father, a man with a ruddy, carbuncled face, beckoned them in. Before she knew it, he had grabbed Paula by the waist and was twirling her round the hay bales before depositing her, breathless, back among the sniggering group in the doorway.

'Paula, don't you realise these people are all a bit touched, that they're from the Poor House?'

'So what? I love dancing and, anyway, they dance better than any of you.'

Mein liebes Kind. Frau Brotmann repeated over and over again as she stroked Paula's hair. But Paula was embarrassed. She didn't want to be thanked for the parcel of clothes Mutti had sent. She'd only done what she thought was fair and right. For the rest of the day she painted Becka with her loose yellow hair, standing in front of a vase of deep orange dahlias and then, in the afternoon, she painted Annie holding a bunch of red lilies. It was the best thing she'd done. The next day she would show it to Mackensen.

And then it would be time to go back to her studies in Berlin.

The streets were grey and full of rain and the summer in Worpswede felt like a dream. Every morning she got up early, wrapped her old woollen shawl around her shoulders, lit the stove in her cramped room, and started to paint. She wished, now, that she'd managed to have a proper talk with Otto Modersohn, for something about his work had stayed with her. But then, yesterday, she'd been thrown into a state of despair. Papi had written that by Easter he would be completely dependent on his pension and was worried how he was going to pay for even a partial education for the twins. As a result, there would be no alternative, once her course was finished, but for her to find a job.

But what did he expect her to do? Become a governess to a family of rich dull children? No, she wouldn't, she couldn't, she still had too much to learn. Tears smarted behind her eyes and a tight pain gripped her chest. She felt both guilty and frustrated. Yet when she reread the letter over her breakfast coffee she knew she was being petulant and selfish, and that her father had no real option. But this was the only thing she had ever wanted. For the first time in her life, she had begun to believe that if she worked, if she dedicated herself fiercely and with determination, that she might achieve something.

Of all her classes those with Fräulein Bauck were the ones she looked forward to the most. It was hard to believe that she was in her fifties. Paula hoped that she'd be as energetic and youthful at the same age. Jeanna Bauck was far more inspiring than any of her male tutors. There was passion in her approach. When she'd been young her own tutor had ordered her to paint in the nude, so that 'her skin could breathe'. Now she wanted her class to adopt the same practice and was, Paula realised, quite serious. They went to the theatre and lectures. But Paula hated what was happening at the school. The director was a harridan. Surely it was men who were supposed to start wars? But there'd been some sort of falling out between her and Jeanna. Paula suspected that it was because Jeanna was both a better painter and the more popular teacher. But, whatever the reason, her friend was being forced to leave the school under duress and would now have to try, with only very meagre resources, to set up her own studio. And that, for a woman painter without any backing was, Paula knew, a near impossibility. It was so unfair. The school had become a hothouse of

78

eavesdroppers and informers. If things like this happened in an art school, what hope was there for the rest of the world? When Jeanna's departure was announced Paula hid behind the painting smocks, and wept.

She was sitting by the stove, among the smell of chalk and linseed oil as the weary janitor tidied up the classrooms, writing to her parents. It was the end of term and most of the other girls had already gone home. Beside her was the letter from Papi. She'd read it three times. At first she'd been unable to take in the news that he'd been summoned by the court bailiff and felt sick with anxiety. Had he forgotten to pay a bill, or was there some legal action pending or a creditor after money? Yet, when she'd looked again, she saw that he'd been requested to attend the reading of his great-aunt's last will and testament.

'And guess what, Paula? My old Auntie has left us both a legacy. Six hundred marks for you and fifteen hundred for me. Just like that, completely out of the blue. Perhaps I shouldn't be such an old heathen, after all, and believe in guardian angels. Now, if you want, you can devote another year to your studies and I'll be able to support Kurt through medical school.'

He'd transfer the money on the fourth of June. She could dispose of it however she wished. He'd suggest a deposit in a savings bank. But maybe she wanted to speculate? Sugar was steady, but growth weak; coffee was slack and tea, by all accounts, slow.

Outside her window damp birds were singing in the soft morning rain. She was twenty-two. As she stood bent over her washstand in the small room with its yellow curtains, rinsing her newly washed hair in vinegar to get the soap out, there was a knock at her door. Jeanna and Freda were standing on the step with a bouquet of pussy willow and a cake with twenty-two candles. As she wound her wet hair in a towel they arranged three teacups on the table, put the chocolate cake on her best white plate, and the pussy willow in a pot on the mantelpiece beside the cards from her family. After cutting them each a slice, Freda poured the tea. So this was living: to sit with her new friends eating chocolate cake for breakfast, an unfinished painting on the easel in the corner, the sun making prisms of the raindrops on the attic window. And there, on the mantel, Papi's letter, which meant that she could continue her studies with Mackensen. What better birthday present could anyone want?

It was her first evening back in Worpswede. The cloudless sky was spangled with stars. As she stood on the step listening to the wind in the pines, breathing in the damp evening air and the smell of cut hay, she knew she was really home. A nightingale was singing down in the willows and, on the other side of the river, a new moon hung like a paper lantern in the clearing. How she loved this flat landscape with its tarry waterways and endless sky that covered the moors like a great blue tarpaulin.

The next morning she and Kurt walked out through the misty meadows along the canal towards the yellow mustard fields shimmering beneath the orange autumn sun, and watched the peat barges glide silently past. After a picnic eaten among the birches they meandered back along the towpath, past an old man whittling clogs outside his front door. As he worked, wood chips flew in all directions covering his lap with sawdust. All the peasants wore clogs. Broad ones in the fields, so as not to sink into the boggy peat, lighter, more pointed ones, in the yard. As they walked on, she noticed a group of women on the high ridge bent beneath broad-brimmed hats, ploughing. As they dragged the heavy wooden rakes behind them the men followed, holding lengths of rope to guide the furrows, while, overhead, scavenging starlings circled in a black cloud.

She found a place to lodge. A small bedroom with a bright sitting room attached. After Kurt left for Bremen she wrote to Mutti asking for her bedside clock and the small table from the sewing room. Now that she had a little money of her own she could even contemplate going to Paris. Not that she had any intention of telling anyone her plans. She knew her family would never approve, that they'd consider it a step too far. Yet she'd been dreaming of the chance to see great paintings and meet other painters, of being in the thick of things. If she was serious about being an artist then she had to challenge herself and not languish in a backwater. And now, well, now it might not be so impossible after all. How could she have guessed, only six months ago, that she'd be back here in Worpswede, growing into herself, becoming a painter?

Every afternoon she visited old Mother Schröder, who hobbled around on stunted bandy legs with the help of a willow stick, in the Poor House. At first Paula recoiled from the smell of unwashed bodies, the grime and peeling paint, but slowly she grew accustomed to the place. During the day the men and younger women were out in the fields, so only the old and small children were left for her to paint. Mother Schröder sat on a three-legged stool in the cold stone-flagged room, her gnarled hands in her lap, as if in a prayer meeting. Working quickly in shades of russet, brown and grey, Paula tried to capture the old woman's lined skin, her bristled chin and sunken cheeks that had collapsed over her lost teeth and spoke of the hardship she'd endured.

As the old woman became used to her, she offered up snippets about her life in thick patois. Tales of the grinding poverty that had driven her and her husband into the Poor House, of the four babies that had been stillborn then wrapped in sacking and thrown into a pauper's grave; of the winters of famine when they'd had nothing to eat but watery buckwheat gruel. It had driven her husband to lose his wits and at night he wandered over the moors in his nightclothes, howling at the moon.

'You coming t'morrow, then?' the old woman asked, as Paula was packing up her paints.

'I'd like to if that's all right?'

'All the same to me,' she shrugged, hobbling off down the dank corridor without a backwards glance.

And then there was the little blonde goose girl, whose mother beat her practically senseless. The geese were the only creatures she ever spoke to. She held long conversations with her flock, poking them with her willow stick to keep them in order, and ignored Paula whenever she stopped to draw her. There was such a deep vacancy behind her eyes that it was impossible to tell what was going on in her small head. Paula tried to imagine such a brutalised childhood and realised how lucky she had been to have a loving family.

She also started a portrait of old von Bredow. He sat for hours in the cold male quarters, complaining that his backside hurt. There were rumours that he'd once been a university student, but that something had unhinged his mind and he had ended up as a gravedigger in Hamburg during the cholera epidemic, before joining the merchant navy and sailing to Tahiti and New Zealand. Now he was half mad and spent all day with the cow. Once, the women inmates told her, his brother had come to try and take him home.

'But he was having none of it, Fräulein. He wouldn't leave the cow. He loves her too much,' they cackled lewdly, behind calloused hands. 'But he's rich you know. He has hundreds of marks.'

She got into a routine, getting up early and going for a walk on the moor to get some air into her lungs before returning for a modest breakfast and to work. She tried to draw every day and kept several paintings on the go at once, breaking off only for a little soup and bread at midday. She was permanently cold. The peat in her stove simply smouldered and never gave out much heat. She caught cold and had to take a mustard bath, wrap brown paper round her throat under her scarf, and gargle with honey and vinegar. Her nose was red and permanently dripping. But still she painted, cutting the fingers off a pair of old gloves to save on fuel. She may have become a woman of independent means but those means were slender and she had other plans.

Now she was no longer officially a student she only had her own motivation to rely on, though every few days Mackensen came to give her a tutorial. She looked forward to the sound of his feet on the gravel, his black-coated figure coming up the path to her studio. He may not be as radical as she'd once believed, but he had art in his blood and could teach her about technique. After her lesson she made tea and they would sit either side of the big iron stove eating black bread with the cherry jam her mother had sent from Bremen.

She was invited again to the am Endes. She enjoyed the informality of their cottage, the warmth of their small sitting room, the earthy scent of burning peat, the laughter and music that broke out when anyone picked up a fiddle or guitar. Again it struck her how tender Hans was to his now heavily pregnant wife, caressing her rounded stomach as she passed his chair and how, in turn, she would brush his unruly hair behind his ears as she made her way to their little kitchen. The walls of their modest parlour were hung with reproductions of his favourite paintings that he'd mounted in dark frames. A stone vase of anemones stood on the mantel and a crochet blanket hung over the arm of the chair by the fire. Everything was simple, yet arranged with love and care.

Later that night, as she lay in bed listening to a branch tapping against her window, she tried to imagine what it would be like to have a husband and a child, to love a man completely and have another life growing inside her. Would that, could that, be enough, she wondered, as she ran her hands over her breasts and her nipples hardened against the cotton weave of her nightgown. She pictured Hans and his wife in the attic bedroom of their little cottage, her bodice unlaced, her long hair flowing about her naked shoulders as he kissed her white throat. But Hans' wife was not a painter. She demonstrated her creativity by the way she placed a bowl of tulips or fixed her thick hazel hair and seemed happy just being his wife.

But Paula had to paint. It was no more a choice than breathing. Did that mean she would never experience love? Her heart and body ached for intimacy. Yet this morning, as she'd sketched one of the village women outside her smoky hut breastfeeding her baby, she'd noticed how her grubby toddler had stood wailing and snatching at her free breast as if her only role in life was to nourish others. The following day Paula painted her again. This time in the open air with her brown hair set against the warmth of the red-brick wall. Then she painted her in front of her white clay hut so that the earthy tones of her clothes stood out against the pale backdrop.

Every evening little Meta from the Poor House, with her pinched face and mouth like a crack in a cup, came to visit. She'd stay for a couple of hours and Paula would draw until her eyes ached, breaking off only to give the child some milk. The last time she'd come she had asked her to take off her clothes, but Meta protested, saying that she 'weren't doing nothing like that'. Paula had coaxed so that the girl had grudgingly got half undressed and stood, defiant and grumpy, in the middle of the room until bribed with a new mark coin to remove her grimy bodice and torn stockings. And what a lousy, crooked-legged little thing she was. Paula felt ashamed. She knew that she'd behaved little better than a pimp.

But she was struggling. The gap between what she saw, felt and put down on canvas was so great. She wanted to capture the essence of these people, to show they weren't just types, but individuals in their own right with authentic feelings and lives. It was this failure to grasp the intrinsic humanity of others, no matter what their station in life that led to prejudice and intolerance. It was too easy to turn inwards and only paint what she knew. If she could describe these people honestly, so those who lived in warm houses with drawing rooms decorated with wallpaper and velvet curtains, who slept at night in beds with clean linen, might see them as flesh and blood, not just as objects of derision, then she'd have achieved something. She had such respect for these agricultural labourers, for their grit and good humour, despite the terrible conditions that most of them had to endure. Their way of life, whatever its hardships, had something that was being lost in the filth and clamour of the fast-growing cities. She wanted her paintings to connect with the earth the way the ploughing women connected to the soil. Would she be able to find a painterly language that, like these people, was sober and astringent? Be able to describe their relationship to the changing weather and reveal the truth about their hard lives, even if that truth smelt of sweat and pig shit?

She was aware that for those who lived here there was a daily battle for survival and that these peasants would think her mad for considering that there was anything romantic about their way of life. And yet she needed to believe that their modest ways offered a contradiction to the confusion and disordered uncertainty she'd witnessed when she had been studying in Berlin: the beggars and prostitutes, the abandoned street children selling matches in the filthy, soot-blackened streets. Berlin was a great city full of fine buildings, theatres and horse-drawn carriages, but she'd never felt, outside the art school, that she belonged. She yearned for a place she could call home and Worpswede promised her that.

Mackensen had just returned from the Rembrandt exhibition in Amsterdam. 'He's a giant, Paula; quite simply a giant! There's no one as great. No one has his emotional range or depth. That's what you need to strive towards if you have the patience.'

She'd been anxious all day about his visit. Would he like her new work? Sometimes he could be very harsh. But then he'd make a comment on the way she'd placed a birch in the foreground so that it tied a painting together, or had caught the curve of an arm, and was elated.

'To make art we must depend entirely on ourselves. Yet dressed in these wretched petticoats we're trapped. Marriage, we're told, is the appropriate career for women. But it's a form of suffocation, a slow death. Men have hundreds of opportunities; while we have only one.'

She was reading the diary of a young Russian painter who had died destitute, a few years earlier, in Paris. The young woman's words resonated deeply. Would she ever have the strength to make art the sole focus of her life? Or did a part of her yearn for a husband, a child and a home of her own? Was she prepared for the struggles that lay ahead: the isolation, the loneliness and the sense of failure? Could she, if she worked and put everything else aside, become something, and at what cost? She knew if she pursued this path to its logical conclusion she would move further and further away from her family, that they would understand her less and less. At present she had no right to consider herself a painter when she had achieved so little. She always wanted too much, was too greedy for life. Her old headaches had returned, clutching her temples in their vice-like grip, and she wasn't sleeping. That afternoon Mackensen was critical of everything.

'Paula, you're not looking, and if you *are* then you're not seeing. You're wasting both my time and yours.'

She felt like weeping. After he left she worked until the light began to fade and her hands and face were smeared with paint. But it made no difference. The result was worse than useless. Grabbing her coat and pinning up her paint-splattered hair, she went for a walk to try and lift her spirits, but the gloomy late afternoon only echoed her leaden mood. Wandering among the slender silver birch, their branches streaked across the sky like lines on an etching plate against the darkening sky, she could hear the swollen river pounding in the distance.

She forced herself to draw whether she felt like it or not, tearing up as much as she kept. Her head and body ached as if she had flu or a giant hangover. Life seemed to exist just out of reach in some, not quite, obtainable future. She sat for hours in front of her mirror trying to capture the wide cheekbones, the thin bluish skin that stretched over her face like a mask. And in the face that stared back at her from its halo of auburn hair she could see both the young self she'd once been, and the older self she would become.

*

It was impossible, now, to imagine living anywhere other than among these people. Even if she left these moors she was sure that she would always come back. She had become fond of her little knock-kneed model, and worried about old Renken's rheumatism. He lived alone up beyond the pine trees and made brooms for a living. When out walking she stopped to say hello and found him rocking his small grandson in his lap, singing in a dialect she didn't understand. How easy her life was in comparison. These people had nothing except their affection and loyalty for one another, and the ties of hardship that bound them. During the long winter evenings the women would go from house to house to sit round the peat fires gossiping and telling stories, carding and spinning coarse wool on their wooden spindles. Even the men knitted socks and stockings as they smoked their foul-smelling pipes. She continued to draw the inhabitants of the Poor House, but hated it when the women fought over the chance to pose and earn her modest fee. And still she wasn't satisfied with what she was producing. It was as if she was always running to catch up with herself. At this rate she'd never be able to call herself a real artist.

While sweeping her kitchen floor there was a knock on the door. It was Lise, the voluptuous blonde who'd been in prison for mistreating her illegitimate child. Did Paula want a model? She'd heard that she paid a few marks for sitters. Paula knew she should disapprove of Lise, but as she stood on the step, with yet another baby on her hip, Paula was seduced by the curve of her pale throat and her freckled breasts bursting from her red blouse. Gathering up her paints and brushes she stepped outside and settled Lise on a stool, and painted her as she suckled the baby, her marble skin white against her fiery blouse. Then, without a word, Lise got up, put down her child, lifted her skirts, and squatted to relieve herself just where she stood, before returning to the stool. When Paula had finished she sidled up behind her, looked at the painting, then shrugged and held out a blackened hand for payment, before tucking the coins under her skirt and gathering up the baby.

But Mackensen took her to task. 'Paula, when will you realise that Nature is a more serious subject than people? Why are you wasting your time on these endless self-portraits and studies of peasants? Is it simply pig-headedness or do you think you know better than those of us who've studied art all our lives? And if you must paint people then you should place them in the landscape and show them as an element of it, not just let them float around against a ground of flat colour. There are, Paula, certain things you need to take on board if you're going to make a career as commercial painter.'

'But I don't feel the same way about nature as I do about people. I don't *care* about a tree or a view in the way that I care about Meta or old Renken.'

'Listen, Paula, you have to learn,' Mackensen continued tersely, 'to transcribe the natural world. And you'll only be able to do that if you don't allow your own personality to dominate so much. You need to acquire a little modesty. Your intransigence is not becoming in a young woman.'

He didn't understand. She didn't paint herself because she thought she was special, but because she was the subject she knew best. By exploring herself she hoped to achieve a better understanding of others. She was battling, now, with all her strength to produce something worthwhile. When she'd first come to Worpswede it had been like a dream. But now she had woken up and life was flooding in and she was beginning to achieve something more robust. That night she couldn't sleep and flung open the shutters to find the moon casting hieroglyphs on the fresh snow. It was as if nature was sending her a message, and in the silent dark, she tried to decipher what it was saying.

The curtains were drawn against the January gloom and a fir branch crackled in the stove filling the room with a scent of resin. She'd just received an invitation from Heinrich inviting her to the Barkenhoff. His brothers were staying and were keen to see her. He wouldn't take no for an answer and would expect her at seven.

When she arrived Heinrich was accompanying his brothers on the guitar in the white parlour. They were teaching him a spiritual they'd picked up on their trip to America.

'Paula, come in, come in. Here,' Heinrich said, handing her a sheet of music, 'you'll soon get the hang of it… *Way down upon the Swan-ee Riv-er, far, far from home…*'

There was candlelight and wine. Martha was there too, and some people that Paula had never met, including a painter called Maria Bock and Fräulein Westhoff, a sculptor, who was staying in a cottage just outside the village. Tall and angular, with an intense face, Clara Westhoff was the daughter of a Bremen merchant and this wasn't her first visit to Worpswede.

'I was here last summer with Maria on a bicycle tour. We had a wonderful time. Worked, swam and had a party on a boat. It was so hot I blistered my feet dancing barefoot on the deck.'

There was something wild about this Clara Westhoff that Paula liked immediately.

If it wasn't raining she spent part of everyday out on the moors. She was still discovering the changeable moods of this landscape with its blustery flurries of snow and battering, insistent wind. Walking through a birch copse, as the low clouds raced across the mackerel sky, she stumbled on an isolated hamlet of stone farmhouses covered with moss and lichen, protected only by a windbreak of scattered pines. Climbing to the top of the hill, she stood with her arms outstretched. As the wind uncoiled her hair and lifted her skirts like washing on a line, she felt a tremendous surge of freedom. On her way home she dropped in on the ironmonger to collect the copper kettle she'd taken for repair, and noticed the lights burning in Clara Westhoff's studio.

When she opened the door, Clara's face was streaked with red clay. She was just putting the finishing touches to the bust of an old woman, but, insisted, hooking up her dark hair behind her ear, that Paula must come in. Paula settled herself on a high stool and watched as Clara scraped around the clay nose with a scalpel before, finally, wiping her hands on her smock and announcing: 'There, that's it. Finished.'

Although she was rather aloof, Paula wanted to have Clara as a friend. And Clara was delighted by the little painter who sat perched on her stool without a hat, still in her paint-spattered smock, the warm glow of the copper kettle on her lap reflecting her amber hair.

As Paula lifted her dripping face from the porcelain bowl, she wiped away the cloud of mist from the mirror above the marble washstand, then tied back her hair and patted dry her wet cheeks. It was only when alone that everything superfluous fell away and she was completely herself. She was seeing things with a greater clarity, becoming more independent and focused. She worked hard, but rarely got tired. Even after a full day her head was still clear and she was able to absorb and learn. She was proud of what she was doing, though realistic about her accomplishments. She knew she lacked a critical audience in Worpswede and that if she was going to achieve anything she had to push herself and take risks.

An iron will. That, Mackensen believed, was the essential component of success. Willpower and discipline were important, but they weren't key. What she wanted to express was much harder and lay like an ache beneath her ribs.

That night the storm demanded her attention like a spoilt child. She felt vulnerable and insignificant in the face of the high winds and tremendous rain. Climbing out of bed she stood at her window watching the sheet lightning flash across the sky and felt like a young eagle about to take its first flight in the cold night air.

When the rain stopped she put her coat over her nightgown and went out into the flooded meadows spread like a black lake under the new moon. The inky sky was embroidered with

93

stars. They had never seemed so bright and she felt—what other word could she use?—blessed. Stopping on the towpath among the ghostly willows, she gathered her coat tight against the damp chill and listened to a barn owl hooting somewhere on the other side of the canal. It was a gift, wasn't it, to feel all this; to experience things so intensely? It was this raw austerity that she wanted to reflect in her work and, with luck and hard work, God would grant her wish.

Had she said God? No, not God, but the spirit of this storm-ridden place.

A week in Berlin and it did nothing but rain. She had come to collect the things she'd left behind at her old lodgings. On her way back home in the train she settled down to read Goethe. His ideas on marriage, his insistence that we each follow our own path, struck a deep chord. When she got back to Worpswede the weather had changed. The sky was kingfisher blue and a lark was singing in the hazel bush, which was covered in catkins, just outside her studio. At last it was spring.

But despite the good weather everyone was going down with flu. On the Thursday evening there was a bowling match in the barn in her honour, though neither Modersohn nor Clara was there. They'd both taken to their beds. Paula was touched by the welcome, yet knew that during her week away something had changed. Being in the city had given her a different perspective. She saw how this rural isolation encouraged petty jealousies, how inward and self-satisfied their little group had become. She knew that it would only be a matter of time before she left.

*

She made a point of visiting the Overbecks and the Modersohns but the Overbecks' insularity was stultifying. The Modersohns were more approachable. Despite Papi's comment that Otto Modersohn had no small talk, she found him very amenable, with his pipe and shaggy red beard. He relished the chance to talk about painting. Yet there was something unworldly about him, she thought, as they sat drinking jasmine tea in the conservatory with its wicker chairs, Japanese prints and pots of lemon balm. He had been experimenting working out of doors, painting wet on wet, *alla prima*. This forced him to finish a canvas in one sitting, to capture the immediacy of the landscape without too much reworking.

'You see, what I'm after, Paula, is the feel of the changing weather and shifting light that's often lost back in the studio. I'd be very honoured to have your opinion on what I've been doing.'

Honoured? Why should he care what she thought?

As they sat talking, Hélène got up and excused herself. She hoped that they would forgive her, but she tired easily in company and needed to rest. Anyway, she was sure they had plenty to discuss.

'Otto loves it when anyone will listen to him talk about his work, don't you dear? Do pour Paula some more tea, hers has gone quite cold,' she admonished gently, gathering her woollen shawl around her thin shoulders. There was such a waxy pallor to her skin that Paula wondered if she was seriously ill.

Carl Vinnen had been away much of the spring and was holding a small party in Modersohn's studio. At ten o'clock, as the bats flitted between the barns, Clara came riding over the fields on her rickety bicycle to collect Paula. Balanced on the saddle behind her, Paula clung onto Clara's waist as she peddled back, between the rows of swaying red rye, in the growing dusk.

Two trestle tables decorated with wild flowers and laid with beer, bread and cheese, had been set up in the middle of the studio. Paula was delighted to see Heinrich, though surprised that Mackensen had come, for he rarely attended these gatherings. Modersohn's canvases of silver birch shimmered beneath a string of Japanese paper lanterns. When they had eaten, the tables were pushed to one side to make room for dancing. Weaving in and out of a series of rounds and reels, several people complimented her on her new green velvet dress. She felt very happy. How could she ever have contemplated leaving?

Over the next few days there was a bonfire, a boat ride, and she and Clara went punting on the Hamme, where they picked yellow irises and swam in the cool green water in their petticoats. The rest of the time she spent on life drawings. Her grasp of anatomy was still weak, so she'd ordered a skeleton from a medical school supplier, which now stood in the corner of the studio wearing her winter scarf.

It was late summer and a number of lady painters were arriving in the village. Dressed in straw sun hats and very clean painting smocks, they set up their easels in the most picturesque spots. Many of the usual inhabitants were away, so Paula kept to herself and saw almost no one. She wanted nothing to do with these amateurs. Painting was a hobby for them, a way of filling time between visits to the dressmaker and the haberdashers. She knew if she dedicated herself, if she battled, then she might produce something good enough to enter for the Bremen Kunsthalle in December. The weather was fine and she sketched outside whenever she could. Recently she'd reintroduced colour, which was a pleasure, but also a challenge. Art was a hard taskmaster. She'd have to dig deep if she wanted to produce something that stood out from the decorative watercolours produced by these ladies in their flowered summer dresses. After a week here they'd return home to their husbands and children, and to their household chores. Some people dedicated themselves to their families and marriage, but this was her home, and art her life.

Her goals were becoming more remote from those of her family and, despite her parents' liberal views, they approved less and less. But what choice did she have? She had to be true, to find her own path. Whatever they thought, she was still their Paula, still their daughter. Often she felt lonely and wondered if she was going mad. Surely normal people didn't feel like this, elated one minute and in deep despair the next? She was sleeping badly, waking in the first grey light, imagining that she was back in the old family house, in her little bedroom under the eaves with the sprigged wallpaper that she'd shared with Milly.

Outside it was raining heavily and a blanket of low cloud lay over the moors. There was a knock at the door. She was not expecting anyone in this weather. She put down her brush and, wiping her hands on her smock, found a very wet Otto Modersohn. He had been out walking and got caught in the downpour and wondered whether she might take pity on a damp old fox and invite him in out of the rain. He'd been caught without his umbrella and was soaking. She ushered him in, took his wet hat and coat and hung them to dry by the stove, then fetched a towel for his hair, and made a pot of tea.

'I'd very much like, if I may, Paula, to see what you've been doing,' he said, folding the towel and placing it on the back of the chair.

She poured the tea and turned over the portraits of Annie and the little goose girl, of old Bredow and Mother Schröder, which had been facing the wall. For a long time he sat in silence, then said: 'Paula, these are quite wonderful. You know that, don't you? You haven't flinched from the truth, from being yourself. I'd no idea this was what you were up to.'

As the embers tumbled in the stove, they sipped their tea and waited for the thunderclouds to roll east across the moors. Then, getting up, he slipped on his coat and hat.

'Thank you, Paula, for the shelter, for drying my coat, and for the tea, but most of all for the privilege of allowing me to see your work. Now I must get going or Hélène will think that I've fallen into a canal. Maybe, some day, I can come again?'

Was it really *her* work that he'd just spoken about with such warmth? Were her paintings really strong and courageous? After he left she sat mulling over what Modersohn had said. He was a renowned painter and his good opinion was more than she could ever have hoped for. But she mustn't get carried away. She still had to work hard, but at least, she knew she was on the right track. The important thing was to be patient. To wait and see where her efforts led.

And tomorrow the twins were coming for Easter.

It was the first time that Mutti had let them visit alone. She wouldn't work at all. They'd hard-boil eggs in onion skins to turn them yellow, then decorate them, just as she'd done, each Easter as a child. They'd bake gingerbread, and sleep head to toe in her narrow bed, while she slept on the sofa.

As Otto walked home along the dripping lanes, he couldn't get the paintings he'd seen or the girl in the white dress with the mass of chestnut hair who'd painted them, out of his head.

Who did he think he was this Arthur Fitger? He was just a journalist from the local rag. What did he know of art, let alone the world she was trying to paint? 'We find it regrettable,' he'd written for all the world to see, 'that such unqualified work as that by Fräulein Becker and Fräulein Bock should be allowed to find its way into the exhibition rooms of the Kunsthalle among our more accomplished German painters.'

'*We!*' The pomposity of his 'we'. Was he blind, or simply unable to see anything beyond the drawing room or the academy? Did he have no heart, no soul? Couldn't he see the harsh realities of the lives of those she was trying to paint? The peasants, who in his myopic opinion, were not a suitable subject for art? Well, if she'd been a man with letters after his name, he might have thought differently. But she'd been dismissed as an amateur, a mere foolish girl; a Worpswede *lady*.

And Papi? Well, that was the worst of it. For after all her years of study this Fitger business simply confirmed to him that she had no original talent, that she should set her sights on becoming a teacher and that her time in Worpswede had been a self-indulgent mistake. Thank goodness for her aunt's legacy. Now she would *definitely* go to Paris. Clara had been there for some months and already had a place to live. Paula would join her. But before she left there was one thing she needed to do. To write to Otto Modersohn and thank him for his encouragement and the lecture notes he had sent her.

Fitger indeed! She'd show him!

'Dear Herr Modersohn,

I'm returning your lecture notes with thanks. It's half-past one on New Year's Eve and I'm off on a big adventure. Right now I'm in chaos, packing and saying goodbye to my family. But I just wanted to send New Year's greetings to you and your wife. I hope it's a very happy year for you both. And in the new century, when I'm in that wicked city, Paris, I'll think of your peaceful little house, and of the talks we've had there, and the encouragement that you gave me.

Yours,

Paula Becker.'

MATHILDE

I JUST STOOD on the platform and watched as you walked away into the safety of a future without me—what choice did I have?—watched as you disappeared into the crowds in your familiar felt hat and long coat, carrying your violin. Dan, Daniel, Daniel Zuckerman, celebrated violinist, my mentor, my love.

I can't give you anything but love bay-bee... That's the only thing I've plenty of, bay-bee. Dream awhile, scheme awhile.

Trains jolted and clanked in the siding, as steam hissed from the vents of the black engine and I followed the coil of smoke as it disappeared into the distance with a ghostly whistle. I stood there until there was nothing left to see, then turned back into the crowd not knowing where to go and sat on a bench, watching bits of litter—cigarette packets, an old sheet of newspaper, a feather—scud across the platform, too numb to do anything else. An elderly woman in a beaver coat hurried past dragging a pair of pugs behind her on a double leash, which she scooped into her arms like a pair of drooling babies, before climbing on board the waiting train. I sat on a bench opposite the café and watched the leave-takings and arrivals, the tears, the hugs, the joy of reunions and the sorrow of partings. Finally, I got up and left the station and wandered through the dark Berlin streets without any real purpose, past the street girls freezing on the corner and an old man pressed into the shadows collecting cigarette butts from the gutter.

The truth is that I have no real memory of my mother. No physical memory, only a sense of absence; a void, a mother-shaped hole in the centre of my life where she should have been. As a little girl it made me distrustful even of my own body and my responses to the world. I remember my half-brothers climbing into the branches of the cherry tree at the bottom of the garden, teasing me because I was nervous of heights. Perhaps I knew that there was no one to catch me. No one ever talked of my mother. I used to whisper her name out loud: *Paula, Pau-la, Paul-a,* as if repeating it enough times might conjure her out of the ether. Dream her into existence. I'd imagine her smell—lily-of-the-valley talcum powder, or so I supposed—and her voice soothing me when I fell over on the way to school and got gravel in my knee, or when one of my half-brothers stole my blue hair ribbons.

My father was usually shut in his studio busy with a new painting, preparing for some exhibition. He was already quite famous when I was growing up. He left the care of the house and the boys to Louise. In the evenings he'd disappear into his 'smoking room', in a cloud of rich Turkish tobacco. It's there that he entertained artists from Hamburg, Düsseldorf or Paris. I was left largely to my own devices.

Sometimes I'd play with Elsbeth, when she had nothing better to do, but there wasn't much love lost between us. I think she considered me a bit of a cuckoo. She'd loved my mother, having already lost her own, and saw it as my fault that Paula had been taken from her. Anyway, she was seven years older than me, and when I wanted to play dominoes or cards, she was already dreaming of boys.

I longed for Papa to come and listen to my arpeggios, but if I knocked on his door he'd call out: 'Go back and make sure they're perfect. I'll come later.' But he hardly ever did. And when I played for him he would just nod, and absent-mindedly scrumple my hair as if he was thinking of something else. I don't think he ever really forgave me for killing his beloved Paula.

That's why I retreated into music. I loved listening to my Aunt Milly sing. Dear Milly, who came to get me when I was only a few days old, who did what she could in those early years to love me. When she sat at the piano I'd watch her face and pretend it was my mother's. Sometimes she talked of Paula; of how close they'd been when they were children sharing a bedroom in Bremen; and of my grandfather who'd been the Director of Railways. She used to tell me how they would sit in the window overlooking the garden, telling each other stories. How they dreamt about what they wanted to be when they grew up.

'She was always going to be someone, Tille, your mother; she was always going to be special.'

Now all I have are her paintings. They fill my room in Berlin. Paula with her hair coiled into a chignon, wearing white beads and a brown dress with red spots. Paula with her hair severely parted in the middle, wearing the amber beads that match her eyes, holding a camellia. In that painting she's used warm shades of brown, similar to the tones she used to paint the moors and is standing against a blue sky. My mother has only ever existed for me in paint. Sometimes I try to imagine her stepping out of the canvas, becoming flesh and blood and speaking to me. But I can't remember her voice.

When I do dream of her I'm a baby lying in her arms and the sun's pouring through the window in the yellow house with the red roof, into the bedroom with the flowered wallpaper and onto the high brass bed where I was born. It's ridiculous, of course; I know I'm simply inventing the past, making it into a shape that suits me, but maybe we all do that. Anyway, I was too young to remember anything and now I don't know whether these are things that I've imagined or heard others talk about. Sometimes I think I can remember her hands. Perhaps touch is the last thing we forget. When I'm tuning my fiddle, I imagine that I can see them in the spread of my own.

I must have been nearly eight when Milly took me to see Clara. It was 1915. She wanted me to model for her, to do a bust of my head. I'd only met her twice. She was very tall and dressed in black, and there was something tragic about her. I was a shy child and a little afraid. Her own daughter, Ruth, was not there. I remember the visit clearly; the smell of wet clay and subdued sadness. On the far wall was a photograph of her with my mother in Paris in front of Notre-Dame, both of them in big hats, laughing; two young women with their lives ahead. And on a plinth in the corner was the bust of Rilke.

I sat on a high stool as Clara measured my face with callipers. I knew her primarily from my mother's portrait; the tilted head, the watchful eyes and long swan neck. She is wearing a white dress and holding a rose. I was a very earnest little girl and asked lots of questions. She told me about the time she and Paula got into trouble for ringing the church bells; how cross the villagers had been because they thought there was a fire.

'Tille, I miss her so much. When Paula entered a room it was as though someone had just lit a candle. She was the person I loved most in the world. Your mouth, your hands… they remind me of hers.'

Hurriedly they've all begun to leave Berlin; Paul Hindemith, Arnold Schoenberg, Bruno Walter. There are rumours that Kurt Weill's got out too. Everyone can feel the shadow descending over the city. I realised in May that there was no turning back. We'd been to the cinema, to the Capitol to see *Grand Hotel*, and were sitting in the back row as coils of cigarette smoke twisted in the beam of the projector's light. You'd bought me a box of Turkish Delight and held my hand through the film. Greta Garbo was wonderful as the melancholy dancer, but Dr Otternschlag's words about the hotel that: '*People come. People go… nothing changes*,' sent a shiver down my spine. It made me want to cry. Everything is changing; nothing will stay the same for much longer. The world feels as though it is on the brink of catastrophe.

I knew the moment I arrived that you'd been crying. You tried to hide it, but I guessed that something had happened. I'd just heard that the Goldbergs were moving to Buenos Aires. You know that little Lottie Goldberg; the young flautist with curly hair. They said they couldn't take any more, and were leaving while they still could.

You'd just been to pick up the press photographs for your next tour from Max Hirsch's studio, along with the new photo identity card you needed marked with a J, and had found the shop closed. Barely a hundred yards from Alexanderplatz and the U-Bahn and the S-Bahn on the corner of the Hirtenstrasse, with its grimy restaurants, its grocery store where they pull herrings out of the barrels of brine by their tails, and the old woman sells bootlaces, they'd smashed the windows and daubed the shopfront with crude black swastikas, scrawled *Juden* across the shop window in yellow paint. It was still full of photographs of smiling newly-weds and little girls in veils at their first communion, but Max Hirsch and his family were nowhere. The moment you saw what had happened you lowered the brim of your hat, turned and walked off into the crowd that had gathered on the pavement, then hurried to your room and double-bolted the door. When I found you, you were shaking.

'Tille, I've known old Max Hirsch for years. He's a sweet, kind man. He grows orchids. What have they done to him for God's sake? What's happened to his wife and the daughter who helped him in the darkroom? Where have they taken him?'

I put my finger on your lips, there was no answer, and took you in my arms, cradling your dear head, trying the best I could to shut out the world.

'Tille, I've something to tell you.' I knew it was serious by your hushed tone and pale face. 'I've been trying to avoid this for nearly two weeks, but Lola telephoned her father in Chicago.

He's got two tickets for us. She says he had to pull strings; that it's getting harder and harder, that I have a choice: either I leave with her as Mrs Daniel Zuckerman, or she goes without me and lets me stew here. Even if she and I still had a shred of a marriage left, how can it survive this blackmail? But what can I do, Tille? I can't face life without you, but I can't face it without music either, and if I stay here, well who knows where all this is going to end… And you'd be in danger…

We didn't undress, didn't go to bed or make love. Just sat on the floor by the fire in the dark, wrapped in a woollen blanket like lost children in a wood, as it grew dark outside and we smoked cigarette after cigarette.

But at least we had those two weeks in the mountains. Perhaps some sixth sense told us we needed to take that trip, bottle 'one last memory'. You telephoned Lola to say you had two sudden unscheduled concerts in Munich and would be away for a week.

She probably didn't believe you, but you didn't care. As long as you kept up the show in public that she was the supportive wife, the beautiful blonde American, the backbone of your musical career, she wasn't bothered. She was never very interested in touch; her taut limbs were more comfortable wrapped in haute couture dresses than under your expressive fingers. It was humiliation she feared more than infidelity. What would she be, after all, without you? Just another rich American girl with no entrées into the artistic world she so craved to be a part of. As your wife she had status. Access to those who counted: duchesses, archdukes, professors. Her role as organiser of charity events and galas gave her the opportunity to sweep into concert halls and drawing rooms in her new Schiaparelli, leaving a mist of Elizabeth Arden in her wake. You were her passport. She could find another rich man, but not another role.

For a while you believed it was you she was interested in; you and your music. But slowly, painfully, you had to acknowledge you were wrong. There were scenes, fights and tantrums every time you went on tour.

Looking back, I suppose it was a risk. But we didn't think about it. We wandered in the April sun around Ludwig II's castle—perched over the Hohenschwangau valley—with its twisted turrets like something out of the Sleeping Beauty, its ballroom painted with scenes from *Parsifal*. Took a river trip and sat on the deck drinking beer, watching the barges chug up and down, then walked in the mountains around Tegernesee, where we hiked along shady tree-lined tracks, and lay in the grass by a stream to eat our bread and cheese. There was white edelweiss, I remember, and in the distance, the snow-capped peaks glistened against a duck-egg sky.

We stayed in a little guesthouse, sleeping in a high wooden bed like something out of *Heidi*, caressing and making love all night, as if touch could hold back time. We didn't sleep; just lay in each other's arms until the thin morning light filtered through the gap in the curtains. You wore your old shirt because it was unseasonably cold, holding me to keep me warm, as I held your limp penis cupped in my hand. And I knew then that no one would ever hold me like that again—not so tightly or so safely—and that I had to cherish each second so that I could remember it for the rest of my life.

PAULA

TIME RUSHED ON, despite setting her watch back an hour at the Belgium border. It was the first day of the first month of the new century. What better symbol could Paula have of a new beginning? As she sat with her face pressed against the carriage window in the Ladies' Compartment, towns, villages and snow-covered fields sped past. She thought of all those for whom these places were home, and of her father in his wool muffler and her mother in her fur wrap, waving her off as the train pulled out of the station; and the glow of the candles on the Christmas tree and the songs they'd sung while Milly played the piano and the church bells had rung in the New Year across the Weser, and wondered why such happiness wasn't enough; why she couldn't settle for that.

At Cologne she stopped for a few hours to visit the cathedral with its gargoyles and soaring Gothic facades, which was recommended in her Baedeker guide. When she got back on board a young woman in her previously empty compartment was chatting to a young man loitering on the threshold.

'*Ma petite choux, qu'est-ce que tu pense de mon nouveau blague? Tu l'adore, oui? Dites-moi!*'

Eavesdropping on their conversation, which was peppered with innuendo, it turned out they were variety artistes. After a while the young man, who wasn't allowed into their carriage, got fed up and made his way back to his own compartment. The young woman began to sing softly in a nasal voice, swaying to and fro and making strange dancing motions within her little button boots, as if rehearsing a routine. Paris would, no doubt, be full of such characters. Belgium seemed to go on forever but, at last, Paris was approaching.

She had to pinch herself as she sat in the clattering horse-drawn carriage. She couldn't believe she had, finally, made it. The coachman drove on and on until they reached 203, Boulevard Raspail, where she was welcomed by a concierge in a black dress, with a nose like a mistake. Following her up five flights of narrow stairs, she was shown into a room not much longer than the narrow bed and little wider. Stained wallpaper covered every available surface and the rugs were worn to a thread. In the corner was the tiniest of grates.

But at least it didn't smell.

She woke in the lumpy bed, with its hard bolster, to a view of chimney pots, slanting rooftops and the sound of cooing pigeons. Paris! She was so excited. She dressed quickly, put on her hat and coat and went downstairs to take a cup of bitter coffee in the crowded café over the road. There she made a charcoal sketch of three dray horses attached to a coal wagon in the narrow cobbled street outside, then bought a baguette from the local boulangerie and a pat of unsalted butter to take back to her room. But how filthy everything was. Around every corner there were stinking drains, cabbage leaves and fish heads rotting in the gutters.

Exhausted from her long train journey she posted her first letter home, and then went to bed. It wouldn't be easy living here, she wrote to her parents. She'd have to be strong. The French couldn't be more different to the Germans. Slovenly and dirty, there was a brutality about these Parisian streets that she'd never encountered before. Nevertheless, everywhere she looked there was something colourful and new. The crowded window of a candle merchant's, a shop selling lace collars, or a carcass of meat hanging from a hook above the blood-spattered sawdust in a butcher's. It was as if she'd travelled back in time fifty years.

Just as she was drifting off to sleep there was a noise outside her room. Reaching for her wrap she crept nervously over the creaking boards and opened the door onto the dark stairwell.

'Clara! Oh, Clara. My goodness, you did give me a fright. What on earth are you doing here? But how wonderful! Come in, oh, do come in!'

'Well, my little Worpsweder, I thought I'd give you a surprise and welcome you to this big bad city,' her friend said, standing on the step in a severe black hat, holding out a tiny bouquet of damp violets.

'But heavens, Paula, you're all ready for bed. It's not even midnight. Perhaps I'd better come back tomorrow.'

'Don't you dare! I'm wide-awake now. Come in, Clara. I can't tell you how wonderful it is to see you,' she said, dragging her friend towards the only chair by the little metal stove. 'I'll make some hot chocolate. Take off your hat. It's so damp out. Oh, it's so lovely to see you.'

Clara was, she told her as she took off her coat, already established in her new studio. Paula had to come and see it.

She couldn't wait to show her what she was working on. And they had to go to the Louvre. They'd go tomorrow.

'Paula you've no idea the delights awaiting you. Géricault, Delacroix, Poussin. But what I really want to know is all the gossip. How's everyone at home? Tell me about Heinrich and Otto and Hélène Modersohn? Is she well? I'm longing to hear all the news,' she said, sipping her bowl of steaming chocolate as they chatted far into the night.

The city was bathed in golden mist as they crossed the Seine, making their way past the rows of second-hand bookstalls. They'd only managed a few hours sleep, Clara tucked up under the crochet rug in the little wicker chair, before washing their faces, pinning up their hair, grabbing some coffee and heading for the museum.

Paula couldn't believe she was standing in the Louvre among all the Botticellis and Titians. She hadn't realised what a master Titian was. And Fra Angelico, well this was the first time she had seen his work. Then there were the portraits by Holbein, and the sculpture galleries with early Renaissance statues by della Robbia and Donatello. When they couldn't look any more they strolled though the squares filled with crowded cafés, down narrow cobbled streets with foul-smelling drains, towards the Gothic Musée de Cluny on the boulevard St Michel, and the ruins of a Roman bath. On each corner something caught her eye: an acrobat walking on his hands, a blind violinist, a pair of moth-eaten horses pulling a cart. And everywhere there was the stench of absinthe and men with faces like wrinkled onions, and huddled filthy women.

At noon, footsore and cold, they bundled into a dark restaurant in Les Halles, crowded with market workers in blue overalls. The place was a stench of cigarette smoke and unwashed bodies, the portions very small and much more expensive than cooking for themselves.

'Goodness Clara, how are two strapping German girls supposed to survive on this? No wonder all the French women are so tiny.'

They visited the Jardin du Luxembourg and wandered down the maze of gravel paths where uniformed nannies pushed their charges and fashionable ladies promenaded their little dogs. Then, seated on a wrought-iron bench, well wrapped against the cold, they got out their sketchbooks and drew until their fingers turned blue. After a supper of coarse bread and sausage, taken with some sour red wine back in Paula's room, they set out again arm in arm. What a pair they made! Clara tall, dark and severe, Paula short and vivacious with a mass of auburn hair. They explored the gas-lit alleys of Montmartre that were full of drunks and women plying their trade up against the grimy walls of the narrow streets, going to places they would never have dared to go alone.

'Welcome Fräulein Becker.' Cola Rossi, an extravagant Italian with unnaturally black hair, gathered up her fee. It was Monday and she was enrolling in the life-drawing class at his Académie. The room was very crowded and smelt of linseed and chalk but it was the best she could afford. All the models had a repertoire of half-a-dozen set poses, which they adopted with listless professionalism. Rossi's critiques turned out to be severe, but objective. Paula wasn't yet working life-size, but in the same three-quarter format that she'd used in Berlin. But here she was in Paris, the centre of the art world. She was sure to learn a great deal. And what an opportunity to be able to take free anatomy courses at the École des Beaux-Arts, to have the mysteries of the knee joint explained. Where else could a girl get instruction like that?

Sundays were spent with Clara. They went to the Bois de Boulogne, the Tuileries and the little village of Joinville, out near Vincennes, where they visited friends of Clara's family, the Uhlemanns. The mother, a widow, was completely deaf and had to lip-read their conversations as she clucked round her only son, Alexander. Tall and willowy, with a cluster of features that were too small for his white face, he spoke eight languages, wrote obtuse poems and worked for a newspaper in Paris, where, although only twenty-three, he was having—and no one seemed to care that it was public knowledge—a liaison with a forty-year-old woman. It was all, Paula thought, very 'French'.

That afternoon, as they strolled along by the yellow waters of the Marne, which meandered through the damp meadows, her mood changed. It was raining and everything was shrouded in a dank mist. What was it about Paris? There was something intrinsically melancholy about the place that she couldn't put her finger on, something suffocating and dirty that made her long for the high winds and clean air of her beloved moors. The previous week she'd written to her father telling him about her classes and her growing friendship with Clara. He'd replied by return to say that although it was excellent that she'd found a sympathetic and suitable companion, his advice was that she should attempt to free herself from this liaison. The whole point of being in Paris was to shake off Worpswede's influence and find a new direction. In this friendship with Fräulein Westhoff—though he was sure she'd disagree, but nevertheless this was his impression—she was allowing herself to be influenced by another, stronger personality. 'And I simply don't think that's in keeping with the plan or purpose of your stay in Paris, Paula.'

The problem with Worpswede was that it was a closed community, subject only to reciprocal criticism. That, in his opinion, had been fatal to her development. It may have felt invigorating, but for a mortal such as himself, such self-indulgence was hard to swallow. Given that, Fitger's criticism had hardly been a surprise. Everyone in their circle had grown so used to mutual flattery that they'd become complacent; any outside opinion simply knocked them for six. It had been a tough lesson, but one she needed to learn. The more she could shake off Worpswede and the less store she set by that overwrought word 'Modern', the more progress she would make.

Also all work and no play would simply make her dull. She might do worse than use this time to do a bit of soul searching and stop looking at things through her own myopic lens. Life was drab for those who insisted that the world only accommodate their view. She needed to be receptive to everything and develop her own feeling for form. That's what the French were so good at compared to the stolid Germans.

'You'll soon lose interest, Paula, in your little models with their bloated bellies when you've got used to the more attractive ones available to you at the academy. Then you'll realise that it's much harder to draw those than the unnaturally exaggerated features you've wasted so much time on in Worpswede. Also, I'm concerned to hear that you've moved from your hotel. Are you sure that's sensible? And please take a word of advice from your old Papi; don't walk around the boulevards at night…'

At last, a room of her own. What bliss to be rid of the house-keeper who never tidied up until noon; now she'd be able to look after herself. Come and go as she pleased, even if she didn't have any furniture and the floorboards were crooked. She had looked for bits and pieces in several *bric-à-brac* shops but the prices were prohibitive. So, following the example of her thrifty mother, she made furniture out of old packing cases, dragging those thrown out by the market traders back up the three flights of narrow stairs to her room, then covering them with cheap offcuts of cretonne.

She wanted to show off her new decorations to Clara but hadn't seen her for days. She was also keen to hear what she thought of the young men at the Académie for there wasn't one who struck her as having any real talent. All they were interested in was having fun. But Paris was a tough place. It wasn't that she didn't value her time alone reading in the Tuileries or drawing the horses snorting below her window, but she was struggling to hold her nerve. Whatever Papi said, she needed a friend, someone to whom she could open her heart.

Whenever she felt helpless she let her thoughts wander back to Worpswede, like a ship seeking safe harbour in a storm. She wrote to Otto and Hélène Modersohn about the Millet she'd seen in the Louvre and described her walk across the Pont

Neuf in the early morning as the sun rose over the Seine. She wanted to tell them about the silvery shadows in the Jardin du Luxembourg at twilight and the guitarist who sang *chansons* in the small crowded bistro full of thick smoke where she took her evening meals. She wished she could show them her little room with its table and chair, and its chest of drawers that she'd made herself. But, in truth, there were so many painters here, all jostling to be noticed, that at times she felt quite despondent. Many of them never appeared to do any work and what they did do was often indifferent. They seemed content just to dress the part with their long hair and floppy bow ties. Even sensible bourgeois people wore flowing capes, which they pulled over their heads when it rained, and it rained a good deal. And the French girls were very chic. They knew how to do clever things with their clothes and hair, which made her feel very frumpy and Teutonic. Also, they might be interested to know that Clara Westhoff was living in the same house as her and working on a large sculpture. They'd become firm friends and she sent her regards. But her fire was dying and she had to finish her letter and get to bed. They must forgive her for running on so, but it was such a treat to chat with friends from home. She'd love to hear from them. And if they did have any plans to write, perhaps they'd do so on her birthday.

She woke early overwhelmed by a strange despondency as though she'd forgotten to do something important, but wasn't sure what. Her mouth was dry and a sour metallic taste clung to her tongue. Unable to go back to sleep she got up, lit the stove and heated some water. When it was warm enough she filled her jug and basin, pulled down her chemise and washed her breasts and under her arms. Perhaps it was Papi's letter that had made her depressed. Why was he so against her move, she wondered, as she dried herself? The old hotel had been filthy. Now, although she had very little, everything was spick and span. And there wasn't any difference in the price. By eating cheaply she could afford a *femme de ménage*. For thirty centimes the woman gave the place a good scrub every Sunday. In fact, Paula was becoming quite domesticated. Her second purchase, after her bed, had been a broom. She'd bought dusters and a dishcloth and all were in constant use. She was turning into a proper little *Hausfrau*!

As for Clara, well; she tried to reassure Papi that their lifestyles were very different and that they'd taken a conscious decision to pursue their own interests. Yet, she knew, no matter what she wrote, nothing would please him. What could she do? If only he would have a little faith.

The catkins and pussy willow were out in the boulevards. At least she was being spared the freezing Bremen weather. The rue de la Grande Chaumière was only a short walk from her room. It was there that Cola Rossi lorded it over this little fiefdom. Once a model, he'd transformed himself into a 'gentleman' and a 'Frenchman' to boot; though nothing could quite eradicate the suggestion that he'd once tasted the seedier side of life. Angelo, his underling the janitor, was a dirty, sly fox of a man who hired and fired the models, leering at them with a greasy lascivious grin. He was supposed to be in charge of the big iron stoves that heated the studios, but they were rarely lit.

Paula registered for the life-drawing class. At the beginning of each week Girardot and Collin came to criticise the students' technique, then on Fridays the senior tutor would discuss tonal values and composition. The rigour of this double-teacher method suited her. In the afternoon they drew from models. She had to work quickly and concentrate, as each pose lasted only forty minutes.

On her way home one mild spring evening she made a detour to Notre-Dame, curious why her Baedeker travel guide was so dismissive of the great building, detecting some incipient Franco-German rivalry. A service was in progress, so she slipped quietly into a side pew, drinking in the dark vaulted interior and pools of coloured light that bled onto the stone floor from the high windows in the incense-filled air. It was a long time since she'd been in a church and although her French was still far from fluent, she could make out that the red-robed priest was railing against Protestant heretics and the Russian Orthodox Church. Evidently there wasn't much Christian love here. She thought of Papi and his dislike of religion, and wondered how intelligent people could believe in this divisive mumbo-jumbo?

Slowly she was getting used to the French street life that assaulted her whenever she left her room: the man wrapped in a shredded blanket, accompanied by a dog on a piece of rope, who greeted her with a daily *Bonjour, Mademoiselle*; the *tabac* stands and flower sellers on every corner. Flowers were cheap here and, whenever she could, she bought bouquets of narcissi and mimosa for a few centimes to brighten her room. At times all this brash sensuality and wretched poverty were just too much. It was then that she'd sit on her bed beneath the skylight, covered in Milly's thick red blanket, and play her guitar.

She was to draw from a male model. She wasn't the only girl in the selected group, but the only foreign one. There were four from the advanced drawing class, a couple of Englishmen, some Americans, a Spaniard and a German. The girls were much more serious, drawing in silence, as the men tossed bits of screwed-up paper at each other, sniggering: *Est-elle gentille? Dites-moi!* Girls were all they thought about.

That afternoon, as she made her way home, she was surrounded by a jostling, jeering crowd. Unable to make out their taunts, she hurried on nervously looking at the pavement. Then it dawned on her that they were shouting: *Boer, Boer.* They thought she was English, and were protesting against the South African war.

'*Je ne suis pas Anglaise; Allemande, Allemande,*' she insisted, pushing her way through the throng, until they reluctantly left her alone and began to disperse.

There was no monetary prize, which would have been welcome considering the financial situation of most of the students, but still, it would be something if she won the college award and it would please Papi after the Fitger debacle. It would also give her a goal, for she was spending a good deal of time alone now. She wondered if she'd hear from the Modersohns before her birthday.

There were letters from Milly and the twins. Clara came round with a blue hyacinth in a green bulb glass and they went for tea and pastries in a rather grand café. Papi wrote urging her to take care of her health and not be stingy with fuel. He was glad that she had someone to scrub the floor and polish her boots; not that it did her any harm to attend to these things herself, but a little help would give her more time to concentrate on her studies. Did she have anyone to bring her bread and coffee for breakfast? He hoped that she'd abandoned her Worpswede habit of eating day-old bread. Frugality was one thing, but things weren't that bad! A good German breakfast of some cheese, smoked meat or a couple of eggs would set her up for the day. And she shouldn't spread the butter too thin. She must keep up her strength. After that, all she needed were some clean white cuffs, a nicely tied bow and, as cleanliness was her main luxury, she should find a good laundress. She should also take care on those slippery Parisian staircases. He remembered visiting the city as a young man, the heaps of rubbish and overflowing, stinking *poubelles* in every filthy courtyard. The French didn't have their German instinct for cleanliness and order. Also, he was glad to hear she was now doing landscape studies in the Jardin du Luxembourg. If she planned to earn her living with her paintbrush they'd stand her in greater stead than portraits. And, of course, he and Mutti wished her many very happy returns.

There was no word from the Modersohns.

She chose a postcard with a hand-coloured photograph of the Arc de Triomphe and on the back she simply wrote: 'Papi, I won.'

She hadn't expected it; but all four professors had voted for her. Of course it meant nothing and reflected little of what she'd learnt and was still struggling to learn. A few professors couldn't confer art's real prizes, but the accolade gave her confidence that she was making progress; that her struggles weren't in vain. The following day there was a letter from Otto Modersohn. He was delighted with her little sketch of the Seine. He regretted he'd not written before and was worried that his letter wouldn't arrive before her birthday, but he'd been very busy. Finally he'd taken the step to have a good clear-out of his studio and it had taken much longer than expected. He and Hélène had been discussing the possibility of coming to Paris for the *Exposition Universelle.* If they did, they hoped Paula would act as their guide now she was so at home in the city. He was sure that they would seem quite the country bumpkins. He'd love to hear which Rembrandts were in the Louvre. Were there any Velázquez or Turner?

Rousseau, Corot, Dubigny, Millet, Courbet. She copied a foot, a hand, a bowed head into her sketchbook, sitting on her stool in the Louvre. She was particularly taken by Puvis de Chavannes. It was harder, though, to find more contemporary stuff for most was being held back for the Salon and the *Exposition.* She wanted to see more Degas, something other than his ballerinas and absinthe dens, in which he seemed to strive too hard for a naïveté of line. Then there was Monet. She'd heard his name at home and had made a point of seeking out his work. But she wasn't convinced. She couldn't put her finger on it, but there was something too superficial in his approach.

When not working she met up with Clara. They took trips to the country, packing a picnic and sitting for hours under a line of poplars by the river, sketching. As they walked back into the city along the lilac-filled boulevards, the light was dazzling and she longed wistfully for darker, more saturated tones. Sometimes she missed Worpswede very much.

'Clara, Clara, put on your hat. Come quickly.'

'Paula. Why the rush? What's so important that I have to come this very minute?'

'Wait. Just come on. You'll see.'

Clara put down her spatula, washed the red clay from her hands, took off her chequered overalls and put on her hat, caught up by her friend's urgency. It was a clear, breezy morning as they hurried through the narrow streets towards the Right Bank. There, in a small square, where sparrows were pecking crumbs outside the restaurants, Paula stood with Clara outside a dark shop with the owner's name painted in gold lettering above the door. Monsieur Vollard was surprised to see Paula again so soon, but left the two girls alone to poke about in the dark interior.

'Clara, come here. Look. These are what I wanted to show you. Aren't they wonderful? Look at these apples, at the intelligence of the composition. I've never seen anything like this. Everything unnecessary has been stripped away. This is it, Clara. This comes closer than anything I've ever seen to what I'm trying to do. I thought I was dreaming when I found them yesterday. I had to show you. I was so excited. What do you think? I asked Monsieur Vollard who they were by and he said somebody called Cézanne. I've never heard of him. Have you?'

MATHILDE

A REFLECTION WITH a foam-filled mouth stares back at me from the mirror as I brush my teeth. I'm twenty-six today, only five years younger than Paula was when she had me, only five years younger than she was when she died. I woke early full of loneliness and dread. Last year, when I opened my eyes, you'd placed a vase of scarlet tulips on the bedside table so when I woke they would be the first thing I saw. Love consists of little acts. Later you brought me a tray with a pot of hot coffee and a chocolate cake decorated with one candle, and told me to make a wish. Then going to the phonograph, you wound the handle, took out Fritz Kreisler's recording of Mendelssohn's Violin Concerto from its brown-paper sleeve and placed it on the turntable, undressed, and climbed back into bed beside me. We sat propped up against the pillows, under the blue satin eiderdown, drinking black coffee with whipped cream and feeding each other cake, while listening to Kreisler's bow soar over the difficult stops of the slow movement. The cake came from the Viennese confectioner on the corner. It had two pink roses of spun sugar and my name written in icing. We often went to that cake shop after rehearsals, where we could be sure of a little privacy, and grab a snatched kiss in one of the wooden booths with its mirrored art nouveau surrounds.

After we'd finished the cake the bed was full of crumbs. You took my face in your hands and gently kissed me, parting my lips with your tongue. You tasted of chocolate and coffee. Then, slowly, ever so slowly, you licked the crumbs from between my breasts and went on licking until you got to my navel and thighs, until I thought I'd dissolve.

Shhh—you said, let me. I love you.

Afterwards we lay among the tangle of sheets, our eyes reflected back in the mirror of the other's gaze, listening to the sounds of the morning drift through the window.

As there's no chance of me going back to sleep I decide to get dressed and go for a walk. In the lane I pass a man carrying a bundle of wood, and a woman walking her small dog. I don't nod and keep my eyes firmly fixed to the ground. I feel more comfortable keeping to myself. I don't want to get too close and avoid everything beyond the necessary courtesies. It's started to snow again, not heavily, but a few fluttering flakes that leave a light dusting on the village gardens and melt as soon as they land on my face. It takes a while to find the house in Hembergstrasse. It's painted, as I knew it would be, yellow, and has a low-pitched red roof. There's a rambling rose round the door. In summer it must fill the house with its heady scent. This is where Paula lived with Otto; where I was born in an upstairs room decorated with sprigged wallpaper, in a big brass bed, the local midwife in attendance.

For a long time I stand at the gate. There's no one about and it's very quiet. I don't know who lives here now and don't have the courage to go and knock and ask to be shown around.

Other lives have flowed into the spaces we once inhabited. There are lace curtains at the windows, a brass bell on the door and a metal boot scraper at the threshold. I note all these small details with the objectivity of an archaeologist. In the snowy garden I sense the presence of that small child about whom I can remember almost nothing.

Could I have chosen differently? Perhaps. Though I couldn't have chosen not to lose my mother at less than a month old, though, maybe, I could have chosen not to love you, Dan. But only just. I loved you because you loved me. It was that simple. Love has always been more important to me than art or music. My mother's death ensured that. My whole life has been coloured by her absence. If Paula hadn't died, if my father hadn't married again, if I had felt that I belonged and had somewhere to call home, then, maybe, it would have been different.

And now? Will I have enough love to give to this child—our child—growing inside me? Enough strength to become a mother without ever having been a daughter?

I open the gate and it clicks on its hinge. There are the flowerbeds my mother created when she first moved here and the little summer house with its veranda where she and Papa must have sat on warm summer evenings, Paula reading her book, my father smoking his pipe. And there's the wooden angel, covered, now, in a light dusting of snow, next to the bench by the rose trellis, the one in the painting of Elsbeth, which Otto did just before he married Paula. Elsbeth must have been about five. She is dressed in a dark dress with a white lace collar, looking at the little statue. The garden is full of white flowers; alyssum perhaps? And pink geraniums.

Even though I never knew her, I've always felt as if I was primarily my mother's child. Of course my father tried his best after her death, but for him, I think, I was always a sort of changeling. The cause of his grief. After all, I'd pretty well killed her after such a brief marriage. Elsbeth was his real daughter. She was nearly eight when I was born and, I suspect, that he'd used up his capacity for child rearing on her. He read her bedtime stories, drew with her and took her swimming in the green pools on the moors. But he was too sad to do it again. Later the pleasure of having sons somewhat revived his parental interest.

My Aunt Milly did her best, taking me back to my grandmother's dark house in Bremen while my father mourned. I lived with them for the first few years until Milly married Hans and moved to Munich. It was too much for my grandmother, with her rheumatism, to look after me. So when my father married Louise I went to live with them. Dear Milly. I do miss her. I used to look at her face and hope I'd find a glimpse of my mother's. It was Milly who taught me the piano and, later, persuaded Father to let me learn the violin. I remember sitting on the long piano stool, the one used by my Aunt Herma and Uncle Henner when they were children, playing duets. Milly always made music fun. But it would have pleased Father more if I'd been an artist. He never had much feeling for music. But there's something about it that, for me, goes very deep. Even as a child I could feel it vibrating through my body. In that way music is like love. Painting is experienced with the eye and the mind, but music with the whole body. If I was religious I'd say that it touched my soul.

By the time I went to live with Papa again something had grown over the space in his heart that I should have inhabited. My presence must have hurt him. I must have been a constant reminder of Paula, when he wanted to forget. Elsbeth had his real attention and then, when my half-brothers came along, the house became more male, and he seemed to find a new lease of life. He enjoyed having a hall full of tennis rackets, bats and balls. I never quite fitted in; marooned and motherless in the middle. The violin became my companion.

I press my face to one of the downstairs windows afraid someone will see me. But there's no one at home. There's a large fireplace, shelves of books and a cuckoo clock. In the corner a wooden staircase leads up to the bedrooms. I'm not sure what I hoped to find; what I am doing here. All I know is that I had to come.

As I walk back down the path I click the gate shut behind me. Chicago seems a very long way away and your face is already fading; becoming a memory of a memory. But at least you'll be safe. You will start a new life and be a huge success. Everyone will love you. Everyone will want you to play.

PAULA

IT WAS TIME TO STOP WORK. The light was fading and her back ached. Paula sat by the window and listened to Paris. Outside, a blackbird was singing, and on her mantelpiece the green pot she'd bought in the flea market was filled with pine and scented stock. Today was Maundy Thursday and earlier she and Clara had been to listen to the *St Matthew Passion*. As they'd sat on the steps of the sacristy leaning against the pillars, their long skirts tucked under their knees, she'd been moved by the soaring voices of the choir lifting towards the vaulted ceiling and wished she could feel what she'd once felt, so easily as a child, an uncomplicated relationship with God. Easter was not an official holiday. Those who wanted to work could always find a model. But she chose not to. It was one of the few Christian customs she still observed.

After weeks of excitement the Salon was finally open, but what a disappointment. It wasn't better than anything she'd seen in the Munich Glass Palace; and that had been third rate. But the *Exposition Universelle* opened tomorrow and she had high hopes for that. The place was buzzing, though the sculptors' apprentices still hadn't finished rendering the stucco walls. None of the

Worpswede artists had sent anything in and that, she thought, was a mistake. It made them look parochial.

She received a letter from Heinrich. Worpswede, he complained, was changing, becoming petty. It was turning from a community into a cluster of separate houses. The Overbecks kept themselves to themselves and Hans am Ende, who had moved in next door, just sulked and complained endlessly about his work. Modersohn was always pleasant, but Heinrich couldn't see how he could be so oblivious to the demands made by his wife's deteriorating health. Or perhaps he wasn't oblivious and just saintly. Anyway, it was enough to try the patience of a saint. He wasn't sure what was wrong with her and didn't like to ask. Modersohn never referred to her condition, but these days she was more or less housebound and he had to attend to her physical needs, as well as to those of his small daughter. But the man was a painter, not a nursemaid.

As for him, well, he was beginning to feel quite isolated and wondered if he had it in him to go on being an artist when it yielded so few rewards. He hadn't meant to unburden himself, but he missed her company. Worpswede was much less fun without her.

April, and Paris was in bloom. Paula hadn't yet heard a nightingale, but expected to any day. That morning she'd jumped out of bed making sure to put her right foot down first. It was a childish habit, one that had started when she and Milly shared a room and Milly called out, 'Paula, right foot! Don't forget to put your right foot down first or the day will be ruined!'

Odd that such a small recollection could take her straight back to their old house with its high hall and big mirrors, where her father was about to leave for work in his navy railway jacket with the brass buttons, or back to the old garden where, on summer afternoons, bumblebees lumbered between the stocks and daisies. She loved that garden. It had been a sanctuary. For other people external events made the difference between happiness and sorrow, but not for her. Happiness came during those moments when she was approaching something new in her work. Then it felt, as it must feel for a believer, as if something had touched her soul.

To shake off the grime and stink of the city she and Clara took a walking trip out among the apple and peach orchards. She longed for light and air. Her mood swung between extremes. It was hard to keep faith, to believe that she was on the right track. She wanted to introduce more colour. To prevent her work from becoming muddy and predictable. More than anything she dreaded being charming or decorative. She wanted to embrace life in all its mucky splendour. Not for its own sake, but because that was the only thing that was truthful. And without truth, what was there? But to see was one thing and to translate what she saw, into paint, another. Sometimes she was convinced that a painting had a life; that, in some way, it knew more than she did, and if only she could listen to its demands it would lead her to what was significant. Other days she felt like a child banging on a locked door to be let in among the grown-ups. She knew that she demanded a great deal both of herself and her art; but what choice did she have?

In the warm spring air she wandered among the crowds on the boulevards. The horse chestnuts were in bloom and their pink candles had scattered petals onto the pavement like confetti. As she walked she felt something shift; as if the girl was finally giving way to the woman and she was seeing things in their unvarnished reality for the first time. It was then she understood that we're all, essentially, alone, especially at those significant moments of enlightenment and that, in order to find the strength she needed, she would have to dig deep.

But the truth was that she'd been depressed for days. She tried to accept these feelings as part of her development as an artist. Yet the world could be remorseless. She spent time wandering in the city, down the leafy boulevards and cobbled streets, window-shopping in the arcades with their glass roofs and art nouveau ironwork. In rue Saint-Denis she stopped outside a small shop selling umbrellas and canes, displayed in serried ranks like a phalanx of colourful crooks. In another window a group of mannequins sat dressed in orthopaedic belts while, opposite, the shopkeeper was filling the feeders of his canaries' cages with birdseed.

As she meandered through the covered glass passageways she felt like a fish in an aquarium, swimming among the bright green and coral-red shadows of the shops' illuminations. As people passed she greeted them with a nod, but mostly they ignored her, which made her feel even more isolated. It was as if there was a glass wall between her and the rest of the world. But she was good at keeping up appearances and kept her dark moods to herself. The iron pills Mutti sent helped and, occasionally, when she needed a lift, she treated herself to a bottle of red wine for sixty centimes. She knew that she just had to hang on and keep working.

She'd met a crowd of young German artists and most weeks she and Clara went with them on excursions to the country where they danced, went rowing and sang folk songs late into the evening. It was an effort to join in but, for a while, she'd forget her inner turmoil.

'Goodness, what an unsophisticated lot we are Clara, compared to the French!' But it did her good to be with her own, talking about history and politics. On Saturdays and Sundays they would still often visit the Uhlemanns in Joinville, where the deaf old lady always made them welcome, cooking special meals and making up feather beds, while they rowed on the Marne.

But Clara was slowly making her own way and Paula now saw her less often. Rodin had set up a school for sculptors and she had managed to secure a place.

'Paula, can you imagine having a critique from Rodin? I know it'll only be one or two a month, and that the rest of the time I'll be seeing assistants, but still, it's really something, don't you think? Imagine Rodin looking at my work!'

Yet Paula wondered whether Clara was thriving in Paris. There was something big and ungainly—inwardly and outwardly—about her friend. She was singular, German. Though Paula loved her, Clara was exhausting. There was an impending sense of melodrama around her. She seized on everything, worrying at things until she could make sense of them according to her own, sometimes, distorted lights. She reminded Paula of those women in Greek dramas for whom fate had already mapped out a path. But maybe this chance to work with Rodin was just what she needed.

The next day Paula received another letter from Heinrich about Otto Modersohn. Poor Frau Modersohn; her ill health must be such a trial for them both.

Clara's classes meant Paula spent even more time alone. She took her sketchbook to the Jardin du Luxembourg and drew the courting couples sitting on the benches. Courtship here seemed to be a very different affair to that conducted by young Germans; with more laughter and less formality. It was a game; with both parties still keeping half an eye open for the next suitor.

Taking a different route home after her class, she climbed up through the steep winding streets, past the women doing their mending in the late evening sun, to another painters' quarter where the young men sat in the pavement cafés, still in their splattered smocks, smoking, drinking absinthe and playing cards. When she finally got to the top the path opened out into a little marketplace full of scratching chickens, and there it was, the Sacré Coeur, bathed in golden light, gazing down over Paris. In contrast to the bright evening sunlight outside, the interior was dark and cold. Vespers was being said so she slipped quietly into a side chapel to think and sat beneath the candles lit in honour of the Virgin. She knew she wanted to paint the truth whatever the cost, but she had so little experience of life. She thought of Mutti and the love and loyalty she had shown Papi through all the family hardships and wondered if she would ever experience the love of a man and a family of her own. Wasn't art her religion and her love? But could that be enough? Sometimes it felt as though she needed the dedication of a nun.

There was no one else around, as she took a modest supper in the refractory, except for a couple of elderly sisters who decided that she wanted to become a novice. When she tried to disabuse them the elder of the two took her hands in her wasted freckled ones and announced that she'd pray for her soul.

Finally she was used to the city. There'd been some beautiful, rich days and she was rediscovering the tranquillity and pleasure of solitude. When she had first arrived so much had frightened her. But now she was beginning to sort out her impressions and make sense of things, learning to relax and be less introspective. Slowly she was growing into the place, making progress.

The *Exposition* was everything that she had hoped for. She spent the whole day there, hardly knowing what to look at next. The French were the most accomplished; indifferent to academic convention and daringly original. She was attracted to Cottet's triptych: *Au Pays de la Mer*, with its group of women and children at supper. Their faces in half-shadow from an overhead lamp, the evening sea shimmering through the window. In the left panel the crew of a small boat was being buffeted by the waves, while on the right, the women and children waited anxiously on the beach for their return. Paula managed to snatch a brief word with Cottet, with his wild hair and big beard. He was surprisingly friendly and suggested that she pay a visit his studio. When she got back to her room she wrote to Modersohn. He was the only painter she knew who would understand her excitement. There was so much to tell him. He really should be here. It was a unique opportunity. Maybe if his wife was a little better they could be persuaded to come.

It had been hot and sultry for days. That afternoon there was a thunderstorm. Now the air was fresh and clean as she sat in her wicker chair by the open window, looking over the rooftops, finishing her letter. There would be nothing like this again for a while. It was an important event. She would organise everything and show them around. She could rent a room privately from a painter she knew who would be out of Paris on a trip, so it wouldn't cost much. She could be their guide. She knew the inexpensive cafés where locals ate and where to get a good meal for less than a franc. She understood that Frau Modersohn had been ill again during the winter, but hoped she was sufficiently recovered to make the trip. If not, maybe she would consider sending her husband alone. Of course, he wouldn't want to come without his wife, but perhaps she could be stern and insist. One week would be more than enough. Paris made her realise what a backwater most German painters inhabited.

'It's really too bad, Herr Modersohn, that you don't have any paintings here. I think it could still be arranged. Honestly you're one of the few people I know who has sacrificed convention in order to say something original. I hope you don't think me too forward putting down my thoughts so directly on paper. But I'm so excited by what I've seen. Only you, of our little group, are really attempting anything new. Maybe I'm wrong and the others are too, but if so, I don't understand what it is they're trying to do. There's a seascape here that I wish you could see. It's full of energy and light, that shadowless light we have in Worpswede on certain autumn days. Oh, Herr Modersohn, sometimes I long for that deep saturated colour that's impossible to find here. For this is a brilliant, light-hearted, cruel city.'

It was getting dark. But there was so much she still wanted to tell them. She wanted to describe the scent of the lilacs and wallflowers, the wisteria and hawthorn and the bright torches of blossom that hung in the chestnut trees. But the daylight was fading and she had to light her lamp. Perhaps Herr Modersohn would tell Heinrich Vogeler and the Overbecks about the exhibition. There. That was the answer. They should all come.

'Please, Herr Modersohn, do write by return and let me know your decision. Tell the others there's a Hungarian band that plays waltzes in one of the small squares most evenings. Twice we've danced all night out on the pavement. Whenever people feel like it they just start dancing. You simply must come, and soon, before it gets too hot. I can't wait.'

Every spare minute was spent at the *Exposition*. How lucky she was to be in Paris now. Sometimes, on her rambles, she'd stand on the hill of the Trocadéro looking down at the Grande Rue and the Eiffel Tower reaching up into the sky like a beacon to the future, and feel anything was possible. And then it struck her; that she had grown to love this city. When she'd first arrived it had seemed so dirty and strange, but now Paris had seeped into her blood. Messy, smelly and excessive it may be, but she loved its vitality. Whatever you looked for you could find here. She still couldn't understand the French, but slowly she was getting there, even if her understanding was incomplete. Complete? Did one ever become complete? She hoped not. That's what she was learning; there are no fixed points.

He couldn't come. The letter arrived on a wet Monday morning. There'd just been a downpour, a break in the fine weather, and the cobbles were glistening as people rushed to and fro with dripping umbrellas. He had been tempted to telegraph her to ask her to reserve a room, but then, on reflection, had changed his mind. Pleasing as it might be to enjoy her company and for her to act as his guide, he was working well. His ideas were flowing and he was afraid of being torn away and over-influenced by what he saw. It was easy to lose one's sense of direction. Many of these new painters looked at too much and it threatened their individuality. No, what he needed was quiet and Worpswede. He sent her his very warm wishes, as did Hélène. She was terribly disappointed.

The paintings in the *Exposition* by the French were the most beautiful. They had a depth of colour that she hadn't encountered before. She would love to visit Brittany with its rugged cliffs and little fishing villages that so many of them painted. How bourgeois, how stolid most of the German artists seemed in comparison. That was because they didn't really look; except for Modersohn. What a pity that he couldn't come. She paid a visit to Cottet. He was generous and friendly and asked about her ideas as he showed her around his studio. A few days later he called on her, but she was out, so he left his card. She would go and visit him again.

That evening, as she walked back from her life class, the air was soft and warm. The fug of the recent heatwave had cleared after a morning shower. In the moonlight she could smell the damp lilac and the sound of a cello floated across the street from an open window. She stopped and bought a bunch of lily of the valley from the flower seller on the corner and everything seemed full of light: the bars, the cafés and restaurants. Paris was a shimmer and she was at its centre. At other times this excess was more than she could bear and she longed for the sepia tones of the north. Here, everything was exposed; nothing kept back or hidden. Soon she would be ready to go home.

The letter came unexpectedly on the last day in May. He had changed his mind. Otto Modersohn would be coming to Paris. Would she please rent him a modest room and another for the Overbecks who'd be joining him? They'd persuaded him. They would stay for ten days to make the journey and the disruption to their work worthwhile. His wife would remain at home. It would be too much for her after a winter of illness, but she sent Paula her very warm greetings and looked forward to seeing her soon. Her own return home was, he knew, imminent, so he'd like to suggest that she travel back with them so that she didn't have to make the journey alone.

Over the next few days she spent time with Clara. On the Thursday after Whitsun they went to a dance at Bullier, the big dance hall in the Latin Quarter. They spent all afternoon in Paula's room curling their hair in rags, and trying different blouses. She felt very French.

The place was packed with students, artists and hangers-on in velvet suits and slouch hats. Some of the girls even wore cycling bloomers. Others had freshly ironed summer blouses and a few had wonderful silk dresses. It was so noisy they could hardly hear themselves. All the men were smoking and drinking and in the corner an accordion was being played. At half-past midnight, as the gaslights were turned down, people drifted home through narrow streets, while the café owners stacked chairs and swept the pavements. By two, nearly everything was closed. Soon it would be Monday and Herr Modersohn would be there.

After the Worpswede group settled into the rooms she'd rented, they took a tour of the Louvre. Several of the galleries, which had been shut, were reopened. It was wonderful to have Otto Modersohn and Fritz Overbeck to share her enthusiasm for so many of the Old Masters, but the Rodin exhibition had the most impact. It was the first chance the general public had to see his work. She was taken by the bold sensuality of *The Kiss*. But, as for his head of Balzac? Well, though daring and modern, most hated it. Footsore and weary the little group crowded into a local bistro for lunch, then took a walk in the Jardin du Luxembourg as couples strolled in the sun and children played with hoops, watched over by their nannies. They even rented a boat on the lake in the Bois de Boulogne, and Fritz Overbeck proved to be an accomplished rower. Wandering back through Les Halles, past the piles of shiny aubergines, red peppers and courgettes, vegetables Paula had never seen, they stopped at a stall for bowls of steaming onion soup.

*

It had been quite sudden, but she could read on his face the horror. The terrible guilt as he scanned the telegram yet again, that it had happened while he was away. After all the years of care, how could he have been absent in her final hour? He was too calm as he gave instructions and made arrangements to return home as soon as possible; like an automaton. Thank goodness the Overbecks were with him to accompany him to Worpswede.

Had it been her fault? She'd persuaded him to come. Maybe if he'd been at home he could have done something to help his wife, even though the haemorrhage had been quick. What a sad little group they made, huddled in their funereal black on the station platform. How different it had all been a few days before when she'd come to greet them. Now, as she stood underneath the glass roof of the Gare du Nord, watching the train pull out in a thick cloud of smoke as they made their way back north, she was overcome with a sense of guilt. She would stay for a few days more to wind up her affairs and then return.

The sky was steely grey as she walked over the moors towards the mill. All day dark clouds had threatened a late summer storm, though there were still people out cutting peat—a girl hunched over her spade, an old man in clogs—as the twilight fell and thunder rumbled in the distance. Paula had rented a room with the Brünjeses just outside the village. It was quiet and would give her the chance to slough off her city skin and Parisian habits. That morning she'd spent drawing up at the abandoned barn where the roof had fallen in and the beams poked through like the ribs of some prehistoric animal. But it was good to be back beneath these wide skies, among the brown fields filled with tufts of cotton grass. How different the colours were to those of Paris. It was as if she was seeing the place for the first time.

She'd had a grumpy letter from Papi. He disapproved of her new domestic arrangements and made it clear that he thought she wasn't taking her future seriously. What was she going to do after her great-aunt's funds ran out? It was obvious she hadn't given the matter a second thought. From her last letter it seemed she intended to return to Paris in the autumn, but that was impossible. How could he countenance her borrowing money when she was in no position to pay it back? Debt was to be avoided at all costs. She must look for a position. He was sure, if she enquired, there would be something suitable. If she was lucky she might be able to save a little and continue her studies. Then, maybe, in the future, she could return to Paris and if not Paris, then, perhaps, Munich. But she had to come to a decision soon. That way she'd have some choice. The longer she let things slide, the more she'd have to take the first thing that turned up. She wasn't a child any more. She had to be sensible. As to the plan that she and Fräulein Bock had been hatching about earning a living in Worpswede from weaving, well, that was so much impractical nonsense.

During her first weeks back she was mostly alone, walking on the sandy heath or lying in the haystack reading. She'd grown thin in Paris and couldn't sleep. The Doctor ordered rest and a tonic, full of iron to help her regain her strength. She needed to eat well, be quiet and breathe clean German air. Slowly she improved and painted again, working outside until the shadows lengthened. Her sense of smell was keener. She could isolate different scents of ripening rye and hay. One evening, as she stood watching the willows turn black along the canal and the evening star appear on the horizon, a thought came to her that she didn't have long to live. She'd no idea why and didn't feel sad. It was just that she understood her life would be short and intense. And if that was the case, then there was still one other thing she wanted to experience, love. And if she could also leave behind three or four really good paintings, that would be good enough for one life, wouldn't it?

Clara was back in the village. She was bored, she said, calling in on Paula. She'd been working all day and needed to go for a walk. 'Let's go and find some music and dance.'

'And where, Clara, I'd like to know, are we going to find music in Worpswede on a Sunday afternoon?'

'Oh I don't know Paula, let's just go out and see. I can't stay inside a moment longer or I'll go mad.'

Leaving her sketchbook on the table, Paula quickly fixed her untidy hair. There was a wilful impetuosity about Clara that she loved. Slipping her arm through her friend's, they made their way through the village, up to the little white church. Finding the door locked, they climbed the narrow wooden stairs to the belfry where, before Paula knew what was happening, Clara had grabbed the rope of the largest bell and was swinging it until it lifted her off the floor. Laughing, Paula grabbed one of the smaller ropes, tugging it until she too was flying and the whole belfry resonated with clangs that rang across the fields.

Only the tall, thin figure, standing tight-lipped in the doorway, brought their escapade to an end. No doubt the pastor expected to find a couple of larking farm lads. He was taken aback by the sight of two young girls, in white dresses, dangling from the end of the bell ropes. Stifling their giggles, they followed the top of his bald head down the steep belfry stairs. When they reached the bottom the churchyard was swarming with people in their nightshirts and petticoats, laden with pots and pans. An old man standing in his socks was holding a birdcage. Hadn't they understood, the pastor chided, that they'd rung the fire bell? Someone had even rushed to the pump to hook up the hoses. Or had they deliberately engaged in a wanton act of desecration on the Sabbath?

'Oh Fräulein, we've been that worried,' Frau Brünjes said, wringing her hands. 'We thought they'd lock you up. What would I have told your mother if they'd put you away? Now that galumphing Westhoff girl, I've no doubt she could cope, but not our little Fräulein Becker. I don't mind telling you, I was at my wit's end.'

Even the kitchen maid with the crooked spine, morosely peeling potatoes into a pail by the hearth, couldn't keep the smirk off her face when she heard what Clara and Paula had been doing.

Despite the summer heat and swarms of flies Paula did nothing but work. She was trying to be more spontaneous. Though still weak from the physical collapse brought on by her time in Paris, she worked long hours in her new studio on a series of charcoal studies. When she finished her fingers and face were as black as a miner's. Yet, still, she felt like an incompetent novice.

Then, early one evening, he came, just as he'd done that time in the rain when she had dried his hat and coat and shown him her work. Otto Modersohn enquired after her health and asked if there was anything he could do. But, above all, he wanted to thank her for her kindness and for all the little notes enquiring after his well-being. It had been a difficult time. Elsbeth couldn't understand why her mama wasn't coming back and he still blamed himself for leaving Hélène alone. But the main purpose of his visit, and he should have made it weeks ago, was to exonerate her of the blame her notes implied she was heaping on herself. It was wrong of her. She was not responsible for his decision to go to Paris. She had merely extended an invitation, which he had accepted. She must never think that she was culpable. He alone had made the decision to leave his sick wife and had done so with her blessing. That the end should have come while he was out of the country was simply a cruel twist of fate. And he'd suffered, as no doubt she could imagine, a great deal of remorse. But it brought him comfort to remember their rowing excursion on the lake and their trips to the Louvre.

'I often think of you, Paula, standing there in your straw boater and chequered blouse, in front of Rodin's *Kiss*. And I've been thinking a good deal about the work you showed me the last time I was here and the talks that we had in the Jardin du Luxembourg. I'm convinced that what you're trying to do is innovative. I'd like to look at your new work, if you'd permit me.'

She went and fetched her sketchbook and watched, in silence, as he leafed through. Then, as he lifted the canvas of Annie Brotmann off the easel his hand, momentarily, brushed against hers.

MATHILDE

I WAS TERRIFIED. The violinist I was replacing had appendicitis. I was only twenty-three and hadn't been out of music school long. There were no full-time female members of the Berlin Philharmonic at that time, but I'd been recommended by one of the players in the small chamber ensemble with which I sometimes played. It had always been my dream to play with them, even as the most humble member of the string section.

Furtwängler was sitting in on the session, which scared me. I'd practised eight hours a day for a week and was worried about my shoulder. Every few hours I had to break off, stretch and do some deep breathing or go for a walk. I knew that I couldn't have done more. I'd studied the score until I was dreaming the phrasing. That morning I got up early, bathed and washed my hair, dressing in a white blouse and black skirt, putting on Paula's amber beads for luck. I've always loved those beads. On the way to the audition I had a black coffee and cigarette in the café on the corner to calm my nerves.

Afterwards I was exhausted. When they telephoned to say they wanted me I broke down in tears. The hours of work, self-doubt and discipline had paid off. I was, if only temporarily, to be a part of that amazing orchestra, one of the few women. I telephoned Otto and Louise. Papa was kind, but I knew it didn't mean much to him. He was busy preparing for an exhibition in Munich, but Louise was pleased. Then I telephoned Milly. She couldn't stop shouting down the receiver.

'Tille, Paula would've been so proud. The Berlin Philharmonic! Bruch!'

Dear Milly. Without her, where would I have been?

I only got to know you slowly. I was aware who you were from the start. Not only were you famous, but handsome, with dark mournful eyes, a kissable mouth and that shock of unruly hair. I hadn't realised that you'd also noticed me, though I'd wondered several times during rehearsals if you were looking in my direction. When you played I thought my heart would burst. I'd never heard anyone play the violin like that, with his whole body. One day, as I walked to the bus stop, I realised you were following. I thought it strange that someone as famous as you would travel by bus. When you caught up you invited me for coffee and cake.

In the dark booth of the cake shop you told me that you'd been playing the violin since you were three. You spoke a lot about your childhood. I was surprised at your frankness. As though, despite your fame, no one ever listened to you, Daniel, the man, rather than the celebrated musician. You'd been a child prodigy. Born in Vienna, your father was a doctor who specialised in nervous diseases and had studied with Freud. He was also a friend of Alfred Adler and Wilhelm Reich. In those days psychoanalysis was still considered eccentric. It was from Freud that he developed an interest in hysteria and wrote his student thesis on Charcot's use of hypnotherapy at the

Salpêtrière in Paris. Part of a small group who gathered around Freud—including Carl Jung and Ernest Jones—he'd just started assisting Freud when Rainer Maria Rilke turned up in 1915. It should have been a memorable meeting but, by all accounts, it was a disappointment. Rilke was a narcissist who didn't have time for psychoanalysis. He was worried that his neurosis was too closely linked to his poetry and that without it he might not be able to write, that analysis might erode his genius.

Your father sounds wonderful; compassionate, broad-minded and kind. He was part of the Haskalah, the Viennese Jewish movement that promoted secular enlightenment and included Gustav Mahler, Kafka and Arthur Schnitzler. He spoke five languages fluently and loved reading French poetry, as well as Shakespeare, in the original. I'd like to have met him. His own father had been a cantor in the synagogue in the Judenplatz and was renowned for his voice. You claim to have inherited your love of music from him.

One of the youngest pupils ever to have been accepted at the Viennese Academy of Music and Performing Arts, you studied conducting and the violin. Music, you said, seeped from the very stones of the city. It was, after all, the city of Salieri and Mozart. By the time you were fifteen you were giving solo recitals. People still talk about your first public performance of Mozart's Violin Concerto No. 1, particularly the Adagio.

It was on tour in Chicago that you met Lola. There was a civic reception after the concert and she came up and introduced herself. Her father is a bigwig in the city and she's used to getting her way. There's no doubt she wanted you. I gather she's beautiful; slender with blonde hair and milky skin and flashing

American teeth. When you first met you were smitten, flattered that this chic woman should be so obviously interested. You weren't able to see each other often because of your demanding schedule. There were lots of letters, telegrams and late-night phone calls. You met mostly in hotels. But once married, you realised your mistake. You always said it was ironic that your father had written a paper on hysteria and that you'd ended up marrying the world's most hysterical woman. Lola didn't have any real interests of her own and wasn't even that keen on music. What mattered was being seen with the right people, attending the right gala openings and parties. She loved the glamour and attention, riding in the back of chauffeur-driven cars to and from concerts in her haute couture dress and furs, being the Maestro's wife. But she'd complain bitterly every time you shut yourself up to practise or left to go on tour. She'd sit in your rented apartment, reading *Vogue* or making appointments with her dressmaker, drinking pink gin and tonics. You began to feel trapped. When you were invited to join the Berlin Philharmonic she made a terrible fuss. She'd had visions of staying in America, among the people she knew, where she mattered, where she could parade you as her own pet genius. She couldn't understand and didn't care what the opportunity meant to go to Berlin. But the Philharmonic was a great orchestra and you had to accept the chance to work with Furtwängler. I know you felt terribly guilty and almost didn't take the post. You knew you'd made a mistake marrying Lola; but she was your wife and your responsibility. There were rows and more drinking. Then she'd apologise and plead with you to forgive her, crying that she couldn't live without you, that she'd kill herself if you left her. When she's the centre of attention, I gather, she's bubbly, charming and attentive, but the minute the spotlight is off her she becomes morose and petulant.

I was in love with you. What I couldn't believe was that you were also in love with me. It was, you said, because I was so different to Lola. You called me modest. Perhaps it's just that I'm not very confident. I like to think I dress with a degree of style, but I'm certainly not chic. You said you loved the silences between us. Never felt compelled to fill the space with idle chatter because we both cared about the same things and were totally relaxed in each other's company. That's what I loved best, not so much the moment of passion, but just after. The familiar smell of your body as I nestled in the crook of your arm, your chest pressed against my spine.

When I worry that I'm beginning to forget your face, my body still remembers, holds it in my heart. I never had any doubt that I wanted to give myself to you. I hadn't had much sexual experience. Well, not much more than a few snatched kisses and an evening of drunken fumbling with Karl at the end-of-term party. Karl had been interested in me for several terms, but I'd always resisted. After that party he went home and became a piano teacher in Leipzig and I never heard from him again. But with you it was different. You were older for a start, a man not a boy. With you I was never embarrassed; in fact, I enjoyed it when you admired my body. You liked me to undress in front of you. You'd lean against the pillows, the lights turned low, and watch as I took off my stockings and brassiere, then hold out your hand and pull me towards you, kissing my neck and throat, and that special place behind my ear.

Occasionally you let me play for you. At first I felt self-conscious. But I learnt so much and you were always gentle when correcting my technique. You never made me feel inferior. In fact, it was less a case of correcting, rather more of helping me to discover my physical relationship with the violin and encouraging me to connect with that. I like to think that we both spoke the same musical language; just that you were more fluent than I. But you were a wonderful teacher. I suppose that's another similarity between me and Paula, her relationship with Otto and mine with you.

This morning I went out to buy some rye bread and smoked cheese from the village shop. I haven't eaten properly now for nearly two days. The woman who runs it was stout and dowdy, her hair pulled back in a steely bun. She kept asking me where I was from and why I'd come to Worpswede. 'Berlin!' she snorted when I told her, wrapping my bread, cheese and cuts of salami in wax paper, 'I wouldn't go to that cesspit full of Communists and Jews if you paid me a thousand marks.'

I was so shocked I paid and left without a word. Then, instead of going back to the guesthouse, I walked through the village in search of the Poor House where so many of Paula's subjects lived, half hoping that I'd recognise someone. But it's more than twenty years ago since she was here. Many of the inhabitants must be dead and the children long grown, so I took a track out over a humpbacked bridge, across a dyke and up onto the moors. It's the first time I've walked in this landscape that inspired my mother. A web of canals and ditches, fringed with silver birch, stretched out ahead, and on the horizon the black paddles of the windmill slowly turned in the wind.

Following the path, I came across two men dressed in wooden clogs cutting peat. One was slicing it into brick-sized blocks with a special spade. On the lower level, where the peat had already been removed, the other was stacking the blocks in a pyramid on a wooden trolley with iron wheels. As I walked back along the Hamme, the wintry sun sank below the horizon turning the water pink, then silver-grey. Until they built the canals and cultivated the fields, these wetlands were considered the ends of the earth. Picking up a stone, I threw it into the water and watched the ripples make concentric circles on the dark surface. Being here I can understand what Paula loved about this remote place. I wish I could find the same peace, but times have changed. I know too much. Mackensen, Vogeler, my father, Paula and Clara all came to this little Eden like innocents. But I can't forget what that woman in the shop said; her hatred and narrow distrust. The other side of belonging is that everyone else is always a stranger.

PAULA

THE APPLES RIPENED in the orchards and the corn in the fields was gathered into stacks. Violet clouds streaked the storm-filled skies and a sulphurous sun hung over the moors, as smoke curled from the squat cottage chimneys. What a gruesome place these artists had found, thought Rainer Maria Rilke as he climbed from the mail coach.

He was given the blue room under the gables. The one Heinrich Vogeler kept for special guests. Rilke had met Heinrich recently in Berlin and they'd liked each other immediately. Rainer Rilke enjoyed the company of artists and Heinrich had been flattered that the young poet had invited him to illustrate his new book. For Rilke, the invitation to Worpswede had come at the right moment. But to his disappointment the house was surprisingly full. He hadn't expected Heinrich's brothers or fiancée, Martha; for he knew that betrothal was not without complications. He'd hoped to have his friend to himself, to share the experiences of his recent trip to Russia and discuss his broken heart. He also wanted someone to listen to his grievances about what should have been his momentous meeting with Tolstoy, which had been marred by the old man's apparent indifference to the younger writer's work. Rilke had been offended. As he'd sped through the deep larch woods, towards the old writer's famous retreat, accompanied by the jingle of harness bells, he'd expected more. Now what he needed was a confessor, someone who would ease his restlessness, reassure him that his current lack of creativity would soon pass. Maybe out here on the moors he'd begin to write again; he had done nothing worthwhile during the months traipsing around Russia with his much older mistress, Lou Andreas-Salomé. And now she'd left. He had, she said, sucked her dry. He was insulted as well as hurt. No woman had ever left him before. He left, they always clung on. But Lou was different. She was older and independent. Wryly he had to admit that he'd come to need her more than she needed him. He was depressed. Maybe there would be something special about this rural community and the way these artists lived that would revive his flagging spirits. He had travelled too much, visited too many churches and galleries, climbed on and off too many trains. A home and a hearth were now very appealing; with a wife and, perhaps, a little daughter. A small girl in a white pinafore, who would hold his hand as they strolled through the rye fields on summer evenings. It was a dream, of course. His nerves would never hold; wet nurses, baking and laundry. The daily chores exacted by domestic life always proved too much. Poetry demanded extreme concentration, loneliness and isolation.

That evening they came out of their studios to greet him at dusk like a pair of pale moths: the two young women in white; the tall dark sculptress and the little, chestnut-haired painter.

Milly was staying with Paula. Paula was thrilled to have her sister with her again. In the early evening Clara cycled over and they all walked across to the Barkenhoff. Everyone was keen to meet the young poet, Rilke, and Heinrich Vogeler had organised a party. Paula was wearing her green dress. She was relieved that Milly had taken to Clara and hadn't been unduly influenced by Papi's negative attitude towards her friend.

'Don't take any notice of Papi, Paula. You know what he's like. He's just an old fusspot. He doesn't even know Clara. It's just that he worries about you.'

Everyone was there, the Vogeler brothers, Martha, Maria Bock, and her painter friend, Ottilie Reylander. Even Otto Modersohn had come and Mackensen put in a brief appearance. There was spiced wine, and bowls of candied oranges. There was also talk of another writer in their midst, Carl Hauptmann. Paula had seen one of his plays in Berlin and couldn't believe someone so famous should be interested in their little community. A stout middle-aged man in a frock coat, he had strong views on language and literature. Rilke with his wispy, boyish beard, in his rustic Russian tunic and sandals, was put out that he wasn't to be the centre of attention, though Paula was moved when he read his poem about a dying child. For in the flickering candlelight of the white salon with its prints and paintings, its Empire-style furniture, his quiet voice and intense blue eyes touched her. There was something in his disquiet she recognised; something of her own vulnerability. And was it her imagination, or did he keep looking in her direction as he read? But his performance wasn't to Herr Hauptmann's liking. No, the limp young poet, with the thin face and affected peasant clothes, didn't impress him. Realism, not sentimental twaddle, was what a modern German writer should be concerned with.

Milly attempted to apply a little balm by playing Schumann, though the competitive acrimony between the two men lasted until the last candles burnt low.

After Herr Hauptmann went to bed the evening continued until late and in a more relaxed mood. There was dancing accompanied by Heinrich on his guitar and Franz on the flute. When Rilke finally retreated to his room Clara and Paula followed, insisting that he recite more poems. As they sat on the bench in the bay window, their dresses luminescent in the moonlight, he read from his latest work. There, in the gloaming, they formed two sides of a single whole: Clara, shy, aloof and bohemian; Paula, alert and vivacious, with hair the colour of Florentine gold. Maybe he really would be able to learn something from these young women with their combination of sophistication and naïveté. What balm they were after Lou's cool, analytic mind.

He came often, now, to her studio. As she worked a part of her waited in anticipation for Otto's knock. He'd come in, hang up his brown felt hat on the peg behind her door and perch his gangly frame on the paint-covered stool by her stove. Sometimes he read to her while she worked—Goethe was a favourite—or he might discuss a painting he was doing, a large horizontal canvas full of sepia tones. He had been battling to capture the limpid opacity of the moorland dykes and pools and talked of what it meant to him to live in this wild place.

'What I'm striving for, Paula, is not some faithful reproduction of nature, not a description of the world or an illusion, but a parallel creation.'

There was no one else whose ideas about painting so profoundly echoed her own. Only Otto, for that is what she'd come to call him, understood what she was trying to do. She listened enthralled. He knew so much about the quattrocento, about Dürer and Rembrandt. As they drank tea from her blue-flowered cups, he talked of his feelings of remorse about Hélène and his worries about his little daughter.

'What do I know, Paula, about bringing up a small girl?'

Sitting with his head in his hands, his big red beard poking through his long fingers and his bony shoulders hunched in despair, she felt for him. She hated to see him distressed, closed in on himself like a shut book. Without thinking she got up and laid a hand on his shoulder. Then, as if it was the most natural thing in the world, he turned and buried his face in the folds of her woollen skirt. Suddenly she understood how much he needed her, and bent to kiss the top of his head as if he were a hurt child.

She sent him a note: he must take care of his health, eat well and not worry. Now that she was on the mend it wouldn't do if he became ill too. She would come on Saturday and they'd take Elsbeth to feed the ducks. Until then they must work, paint and attend to their art.

Elsbeth met her at the door, a small girl in a sprigged pinafore, her hair in blonde plaits. She stood on the step looking Paula up and down, before running off to tell her father that they had a visitor. Paula had been to the house before when Hélène was alive, but then they'd just sat in the conservatory. Now she saw how much of a real home this was compared to her modest room. There were rugs and paintings, books and prints. An antique bureau in the study on which stood a purple glass lamp. There were plush curtains and crocheted antimacassars. This was the home of someone who'd been married for ten years.

She and Otto took Elsbeth to feed the ducks and, when they got back, Paula read to her from *Hansel and Gretel*. 'I don't like the witch,' the little girl whispered, sticking her fingers in her ears and running from the room. After a prolonged search Paula found her hiding in the kitchen cupboard with her pinafore over her head. 'It's only a story, Elsbeth; it's only pretend. Come here, and sit on my lap.' Still distrustful the little girl climbed onto Paula's knee. As she began to relax, she laid her head against Paula's shoulder, counting the beads of her amber necklace.

'Fräulein Becker, Papa calls you Paula, doesn't he; can I call you Paula, too? And would you, if I'm very good, allow me try on your beads?'

Paula was learning to look at people in a new way. She wanted to see them as individuals, not types. She knew she had a tendency, inherited from her mother, to idealise and prettify. But now she was back in Worpswede and close to nature again, she understood that to generalise revealed nothing of what was unique about a subject. Peat, straw and cow dung, that's what she wanted her paintings to smell of. Slowly she was making progress. She painted her figures in brown tones as if moulded from earth. She was working on a picture of the sandpit and the undulations were beginning to resemble the curves of a naked body. Working on rough board, she stripped the landscape back to its loamy essence. On the hilltop she placed a single fir, suggested by a few quick marks of olive distemper, which leant into the strip of rain-filled sky like a lonely figure battered by the wind. After Paris she was beginning to find a new relationship with the sun. Not the southern sun that turned objects into a series of shadows, pulling the picture into a thousand pieces, but the brooding northern sun that turned things dark and weighty, linking them in all in their tonal greyness.

She decided to start a small vegetable garden. The Brünjeses were happy for her to have a patch down by the pigsty when she said she would contribute the produce she grew to their kitchen. She bought seed, planted potatoes, beets and radishes. She dug and raked her plot, tucking her petticoats into her belt, enjoying the feel of the lumpy earth beneath her boots. She planted the radish first, as that would germinate the quickest, pouring the shrivelled husks into her palm from the twist of brown paper, and then sprinkling them along the furrows. By the end of the morning her face was filthy and her nails filled with dirt.

She wrote to Milly. She was going through a difficult period; perhaps the most significant of her life and was aware her goals were taking her further and further away from her family.

'But Milly, what choice do I have? You do understand, don't you? All Papi says is I must find employment and some sort of financial security. He seems to have quite forgotten that I'm an artist.'

She knew that she had to remain steadfast, even if everyone else disapproved. There wasn't much to write about, she told her sister, because everything she wanted to say was too difficult to put into words. She was getting on with life the best she could. But she was still her old Paula, even if lots of things were changing. And if Milly didn't like this new version of her sister, then she could be certain that, in time, it, too, would be replaced by an even newer one.

'Dear God—or whoever's responsible for all this complicated mess—enough introspection! Tell me, Milly, how your singing lessons are going. I send you a big kiss.'

She was wearing her green dress and amber beads when he came to collect her. It was early evening and a red sun was sinking over the flat fields on the far bank of the Hamme. The canal was black as tar. As they walked along the towpath, moths darted in and out of the reeds and a wood pigeon cooed in the distance. Then Otto stopped and took Paula's hand, pushing back her white cuff, and lifting the inside of her wrist, with its delta of veins, to his lips. As he drew her close, she could feel the unfamiliar bulk of him pressing against her and the shock of his wiry beard against her cheek, as his wet tongue searched for hers like something living.

They all have the same face, Rilke thought. The hard, tense face of work. How downtrodden these moorland peasants seemed. How seldom they smiled. Like the Russian peasants he'd met between the White and Black Seas and on the shores of the Volga, these country people were rooted in the land. Turf ran through their veins. He envied their peace and tranquillity. He had suffered so much. Physical pain—though the doctors told him it was psychosomatic—along with mental anguish. His body continually betrayed him with its eruptions and erotic desires. How he'd like to eradicate all sensuality and exist only in the mind.

He had been thinking a good deal about the two young women, the tall dark sculptress and the little auburn-haired painter. One evening Paula stopped by his room to show him some Russian books. Later, at dinner with the Overbecks, he'd sat beside her and they had had an animated conversation and she'd invited him to her studio. When he arrived the following afternoon there was tea waiting for him, a poppy-seed cake and four tall white lilies in a stone vase that filled the room with their cloying scent. He was surprised by her paintings. With a few rough brush strokes she'd caught the bare trees, the hunched haystacks and the little vermilion house between two dark green horizontal slashes that suggested the far hills. They were not what he had expected. He had underestimated her.

Perhaps there was something he could learn from her approach that would help him out of his poetic deadlock. Something in the way she described this flat northern landscape and its peasants that might move him away from his confused lyricism and what he knew, in his heart, was a tendency to sentimentality. She had an uncontrived honesty he lacked. As they drank tea and ate cake, they talked of art and poetry, and the possibility of an afterlife, their words flowing like a stream around and over boulders, searching for new directions. And as the evening sun filled the studio with its honeyed light, he began to wonder if this young woman might understand something of his rootless despair. For she, too, had struggled, she told him, particularly in Paris, where she'd often felt lost and alone.

'Sometimes, Fräulein Becker,' he said, looking straight at her, 'I feel such dread. As though I don't belong anywhere and have no place to call home. Does that sound absurd?'

'No, of course not Herr Rilke; but we must never lose hope. Though hope must always be tempered, for sometimes we hope for the wrong things. We have to be patient. Only then are we likely to make art worthy of the name.'

Sitting in the growing dark amid the funereal scent of the lilies—the clock's tick measuring out the afternoon—she seemed to Rilke, with her eggshell skin lit by the dying sun and her copper hair glinting against her white dress, a Renaissance angel.

It always came down to money. Papi wrote again, asking Paula to outline her plans. She was in danger of becoming a dilettante. That was the trouble living among artists and poets. There wasn't a scrap of sense between them. But she couldn't exist on thin air. She had to make serious enquiries about finding a post as a governess. It was no good thinking that such practicalities were beneath her. If she wasn't going to find financial security in marriage like other young women of her age, then she would have to provide for herself. There was no alternative.

Nothing ever stayed the same. Since she'd been back from Paris something of the simplicity that had attracted her to Worpswede that first summer had gone. There were tensions and petty rivalries, coteries and cliques. A number of new arrivals had accelerated the slackening ties between the original group. When not working she spent most of her time with Heinrich Vogeler, Otto Modersohn, Martha and Clara. It was this little family to which Rilke attached himself. Occasionally Marie

Bock or Paula's older sister Milly would join them when she was able to take time from her music studies; she'd recently given her first public recital to great critical acclaim.

As Heinrich was often away helping his brothers set up their new chicken farm, an enterprise they'd been working on since they'd come back from America, Rilke spent more and more time in Paula's studio. He was aware Heinrich was in a state about his forthcoming marriage and wondered if that had something to do with his frequent absences. Martha had been a mere girl when they'd met; one of thirteen children from a poor family. After she'd joined him in Dresden, they'd become lovers. Now he was full of anxiety about the approaching commitment.

Rilke was thinking increasingly about Paula and she, too, looked forward to the regular visits from the young poet with the wispy beard and intense blue eyes. One evening, as she cleared her paints and washed her brushes, he called at her studio. The light had gone and she was about to go off to meet Clara. Would she permit him to walk with her? Picking up her shawl from the back of her chair, she went to tidy her hair in front of the small cracked mirror above the stone sink. As she stood pinning up a loose strand that had escaped its pins, he came up behind her and, without a word, ran a finger down her creamy nape. She didn't move and simply went on adjusting her hair as though nothing had happened; though her heart was pounding and she thought her knees would give way. But what could she do? Hadn't she kissed Otto Modersohn only two days before?

*

It was late when Clara rode over on her bicycle, knocked on Rilke's door and invited him to her studio in Westwede. He'd intended to spend the evening working, but the poem he had been struggling with all day wasn't going well. A stroll might do him good and take him out of himself. They ambled back along the canal and, as Clara pushed her bike, she walked so close to him that he could smell her lavender soap. But how different she was to the animated little painter; brooding and intense in ways that reminded him uncomfortably of himself. When they finally arrived at the studio she couldn't find the key. She searched in her pocket and under the stone by the door. She was worried she'd dropped it in the canal or shut it on the inside, but she had to show him her kneeling boy, now that he'd come all this way, she insisted, becoming visibly upset. Then grabbing a hammer she found lying in the grass, she tried to smash the lock, but the hammer slipped crushing her finger, and she let out a piercing cry. There was blood everywhere: on her face, her dress, her hair. Neither of them knew what to do. Rilke fumbled in his pocket for his handkerchief, attempting to wrap it around her thumb to stem the flow, but Clara brushed it away. It was nothing, she insisted, just a graze. Her only concern was to show him her work. She knew he had been spending a lot of time with Paula.

Having finally got the door open she struggled to unwrap the wet cloth from the clay figure with her good hand, while blood oozed from Rilke's handkerchief on the other. When, at last, it was uncovered he could see Rodin's influence in the naturalistic forms. But there was too much detail. It hectored and cajoled. He felt embarrassed and uncertain what to say, so talked of Rodin. It wasn't what she wanted to hear. It was five o'clock in the morning before he finally made it back along the canal, exhausted, to Worpswede and bed.

Everything was arranged. They would take the train from Bremen to Hamburg on Friday to attend the premiere of Carl Hauptmann's new play on the Saturday evening. Despite the rivalry between the two men, Rilke was keen to see the production. He didn't care for Hauptmann, but there was no doubt that he was a writer to contend with. Clara would join them on the Sunday, after a visit to her parents.

It was a bright clear morning as they clambered on the coach that would take them across the moors from Worpswede to the station. Paula was carrying a brown leather travel bag and wearing a smart little black straw hat she'd bought in Paris, her auburn hair piled beneath it in a French pleat. Rilke thought she looked lovely as he helped her up the steps and she settled herself in the corner. After an hour, when the coachman stopped to water the horses, they spotted a black figure in the distance furiously cycling over the fields towards them. It was Clara. She'd ridden from her parents' house and was waving a bunch of flowers, which she thrust, breathlessly, into Rilke's hands.

'Please Herr Rilke, give these to Herr Hauptmann and offer him my sincerest regrets that I'll be missing his play.'

Rilke took them without a word. But what a state she was in, wild-eyed and trembling. As the coach pulled off she stood in the middle of the far rye field, like Ruth amid the alien corn, her bike propped against her long skirt, waving. The irony that he was carrying a bunch of flowers given to him by Clara, whilst sitting beside Paula, didn't escape him.

Paula, and Milly—glowing after the recent success of her first public concert—Mackensen, Otto Modersohn and Heinrich joined the lunch in honour of Carl Hauptmann at the Hotel d'Europe. Clara arrived flustered and late, having hurried from the station after catching the morning train. A large oval table spread with a buffet of sausages, sauerkraut, a leg of pork, dishes of beetroot and potatoes glistening in butter, stood in the centre of the plush dining room. There was claret and sweet desert wine, dates and grapes, apple strudel and a big bowl of whipped cream. It was too much for Rilke's ascetic vegetarianism. As soon as the meal was over he invited Paula to slip away and take a walk round the city. They explored the park and the second-hand book-shops, stopping at a stall that sold exotic parrots. How easy it was to be with her, he thought. Her vivacity countered his gloomy introspection.

During the performance he was expected to sit with Mackensen and Otto Modersohn in the balcony, though he'd have preferred to be with the Paula and Clara in the orchestra stalls. But he hated the play. It turned out to be just as pedestrian as he feared. At the celebratory dinner afterwards he felt uncomfortable when commandeered to make a speech. What could he say? So he spoke of Worpswede, of the unique landscape and the art it inspired. It was, he said, as though he'd finally found a home: 'and it's as if those who live there have been expecting me all along'. At the head of the table Carl Hauptmann gave a tepid smile. He was not at all impressed by the young poet's sentimental solipsism.

On Sunday Paula woke to a blue sky flecked with white clouds. She and Clara were sitting on the end of her bed in their night-dresses planning a tour of Hamburg later that morning. As they chatted it felt as if they were back in Paris. It had been a long time since they'd been this close. Paula was pleased they'd decided to share a room. Not only did it save money, but it gave them the chance to talk in a way they hadn't for a long time. For Clara could be so brittle and aloof that Paula was often left perplexed, wondering if she'd, inadvertently, done something to upset her friend. But when they were together like this she felt a renewed faith in their friendship. Just as they were getting ready to go out, there was a knock at the door. It was Rilke, his hair dampened and combed, holding a bunch of white roses.

'For my two favourite young ladies in white,' he said with an exaggerated bow so that Paula burst into a fit of giggles. He really could be so pompous.

Two packed days followed: sightseeing in a coach-and-four, a tour of the harbour and trips to museums. She and Otto paid a visit to a private art collection before meeting up with the others to go to *The Magic Flute*. What bliss Mozart was. Paula was thrilled that Milly was able to join them. She was proud of her sister and her growing success as a singer.

Then it was over and Carl Hauptmann saw them off at the station. Paula travelled back with Rilke and Clara as Otto had to stay for a few days to attend to business. It took hours to get home. First there was the train and then the long drive by mail coach back to Worpswede. When they pulled into the village it was a still, starry night and the Plough and Milky Way were clearly visible. As they walked down the wooded lane in the dark September air, arm in arm, Paula on one side of Rilke, Clara on the other, Paula felt a surge of happiness. Then suddenly Rilke announced: 'I've made a decision. I'm going to stay. I'm sure I can work here. I want to be a part of this place, to experience the seasons and be snowed in with you and give my poems time to germinate. I need a proper home.'

It was becoming wintry, with icy rain and the first flutterings of sleet. All night the wind tore at the tall birches outside Paula's window. She tried to work but felt distracted. Otto came to visit and she regularly went to his house, sometimes staying for supper. She was becoming very fond of little Elsbeth. Often Otto would leave the two of them sitting by the fire and snatch another hour in the studio while Paula showed the little girl how to make papier mâché or stick pressed flowers in an album. One evening, after Elsbeth was tucked into bed and Paula was getting ready to go home, Otto followed her into the vestibule, kissed her gently on the forehead and said: 'My dear girl, you know, don't you, that you've given me a reason to go on?'

That this respected painter, a man ten years her senior, should need her, that she was able to ease his sense of loss and guilt and shield him from the world, was extraordinary. Yet when Rilke came unannounced at dusk and sat for hours by her stove, his face translucent in the dimming light, talking of religion, art and poetry, she felt an exhilaration she'd never experienced before. How badly she wanted him to reach out and touch her. That night she dreamt he was standing on the brow of a hill against the setting sun, beckoning her to follow. But just as she was about to set off she heard a voice telling her to go home, paint and love those who loved her; that if she did so, she would find peace.

With the onset of bad weather she didn't go out much and settled down to a period of hard work. There was so much over which she had no control, but she could, at least, make herself work. She started a new self-portrait, staring for hours in the mirror until her face turned into a mask and her eyes became dark holes rimmed raw from lack of sleep. Would she ever understand this person staring back at her? Dear God! If she couldn't, how would she understand anyone else? She was drawing a great deal now and painting on thin brown board. She'd start with a simple white chalk background and then add distemper to achieve a matt surface so the painting didn't look too finished.

But there was another letter from Papa insisting that she give him some indication of her plans. Her funds had all but run out and she needed to address what she was going to do over the next months. A post as governess with a respectable family would, if she was lucky, allow her time to pursue her own work. She had to stop being irresponsible and face facts. He was losing patience.

A vase of white autumn daisies stood on the table dropping yellow pollen onto the red cloth. A small fire burned in the grate. Clara was sitting in the rocking chair, a copy of the poem that Rainer Maria Rilke had sent Paula the previous day unfolded in her lap. She had just finished reading it aloud and now the only sound in the room was the ticking clock. It was Sunday and Rilke had promised to come, as he'd done the two previous Sundays, to take tea and recite his new poems. But now the seconds were slipping into minutes, and the minutes into an hour and still he hadn't arrived. Neither spoke as Clara continued to rock gently in the gathering darkness and Paula leafed through the notebook he had left, along with his red pencil, on his last visit. At nine o'clock, when he still hadn't shown up, and the single candle had spluttered and died, Clara got up, put on her coat and went home.

When she woke the next morning there was a letter slipped beneath her door. Putting on her bathrobe Paula hurried to the table in the window to read it.

'I had to leave unexpectedly for Berlin. We had urgent business there, which meant an early departure. Please keep the little notebook with my poems safe in my absence.'

Why Berlin? She couldn't make sense of it and who was this mysterious 'we'? Hadn't Rilke only, the other evening, announced he wanted to become a part of their little group, their 'family' as he called them, and spend the winter here and work? Hadn't he been making plans to rent the small timbered house up past the church, saying he'd done enough wandering, and needed a home? She was distraught. What had happened? Why had he left without saying goodbye? She thought they were friends. She carried his letter around in her pocket all day.

That night it rained. Outside it was dark and the only sounds, as she sat in the circle of light cast by her small lamp trying to compose a letter, were an occasional gust of wind catching under the wet thatch and the cow jangling her chain in the barn. She wanted to tell Rilke how much she loved his poems. That she cherished the chance to take care of his little book, which she'd return by registered post on the first of November, if only he'd tell her where to forward it, for she couldn't bear to part with it yet. There were so many things she wanted to ask him, so many things she wanted to say.

Instead, she suggested that while in Berlin he should contact her aunt. She was a highly cultured woman and her daughter an accomplished musician. Paula would like him to visit them as a special favour. For when she'd been nine years old, she and a group of children, including her cousin's elder sister, Cora, had been playing in the sandpit in the park in Dresden. She and Cora had only just met, as Cora had grown up in Indonesia, but they'd become immediate soul mates. She had been a sensitive and intelligent child. But there'd been a terrible accident. Cora had been buried alive in a sandpit and her death had haunted Paula for years. Rilke was the first person outside her own family she'd ever told. No one spoke of it. But Paula was sure that a visit from him would bring a little joy to her aunt and cousin. She'd send him the address soon. In the meantime, she hoped Berlin would give him all that he was seeking. She would miss his visits and their chats as she tidied her studio at the end of the day; miss the pot of tea that they shared as he spoke of the things in his heart.

When, eventually, she went to bed, she lay listening to the rain drumming on the cowshed. Then, falling into a fitful sleep, she dreamt of a pair of intense blue eyes staring at her from a cracked mirror.

She wrote to Rilke often over the following weeks, but had no idea, from his replies, when he might return. In the meantime she drew and dug her little garden plot. She enjoyed the distraction of physical exertion as she pushed the fork deep into the black earth and felt the honest ache in her muscles at the end of the morning.

Now Rilke had gone she hardly saw Clara and spent every evening at Otto's studio. He had three new paintings on the go, ambitious landscapes, and was always encouraging about her work. At dusk, they would meet to take a walk out past the clump of firs to their favourite spot and watch the fiery sun drop into the black peat bog. Whatever else, Paula felt comfortable with this tall gangly man with his russet beard and wire glasses. More than anyone else he understood her goals. They got into the habit of taking supper together. Afterwards, she would read to Elsbeth and wonder, if this was where she really belonged?

Then walking her home one evening, as the moon hung low among the willows, he asked her to marry him. And she knew, though she didn't answer immediately, that she would say yes; that this was her destiny, to spend her life with this calm, kind man.

When she got back to her room she lit her lamp and wrote to Rilke:

'I'm writing to tell you that I've rented the studio on the second floor of the house next to Otto Modersohn. I'm working now with great intensity, trying to listen to my brush. I want to paint the apple tree with its red apples set against the high blue sky flecked with wispy clouds. I think there'll be children dancing round it like a Maypole, but they will be scruffy village children. I've also started a painting where the chalky sky sets off the rust red door of the church. I hope it catches the mood of autumn; and another of the congregation leaving the service: the bent, black figures of the old farmers and their wives who I've come to love.

'But my dear friend, I'm not getting to the point. The real reason for this letter is to tell you that Otto Modersohn has asked me to marry him, and that I've said yes. It all goes back a long way, long before Hamburg, before Paris even. I've never spoken about it because I thought you knew. Now I want to ask for your blessing; for we're bound in friendship, you and I, for as long as we both inhabit this earth.'

He replied by return with a poem, which she folded neatly and put in the bottom of the little cedar box where she kept her hairpins, not daring to examine what lay hidden in the far reaches of her heart. For weeks she and Otto told no one of their engagement except her parents. Her father was keen to organise a little celebration, but she wanted to keep things simple.

'Papi, just be pleased for me. That's all I ask, pleased that at last my future seems settled, that I don't have to become, what I've never wanted to be, a governess to dull children. That I'm to be the wife of a good man and a great painter; and that I'll be free to continue—God willing—with the thing that matters to me most in the world, my work. You know Otto and I are both sensible people, so celebrations aren't really important to us. Anyway we're a little concerned that some of the others might think that it is too soon after Hélène's passing, though

Heinrich did bring round a bottle of wine to celebrate. He has only just realised what's happening, although Otto did drop a couple of hints. For now, though, both of us are busy with our work, which is how it should be. Otto has started three new paintings. Every evening I go over to his studio and we look at them together. I'm still working outside as much as I can, wearing my clogs to keep my feet dry and enjoying the wind in my hair. I so love these golden dog days of autumn.'

So it was settled. They would marry the following year. Sooner would not be respectful to the memory of Hélène. Now he'd found Paula, Otto insisted, he could wait. What was important was that they were of one mind, that she showed a mature appreciation of his work, and that he understood her hopes and aspirations. In many ways they were so different, but he loved her enthusiasm and her understanding of his occasional black moods. He would always remember the first time he'd seen her, with that mass of copper hair. The way she held her head on one side like a blackbird as she listened, or burst, for no apparent reason, into peels of laughter. Whenever she walked past their house accompanied by the old woman she was painting from the Poor House, he noticed how gentle she was with her. He loved the way she walked, with huge strides despite her diminutive stature, her toes always touching the ground first. When she'd visited him and Hélène she'd been so relaxed and natural. How could he forget the way she'd stretched out on the sofa, leaning her head back against the cushions, her feet in their little button boots, propped on the stool in front of her? Her informality had entranced him. She'd looked enchanting lying there in her white dress with its coral belt and her light purple jacket. It was only later that he realised how meagre her means were. Other people could wear new clothes and never look as she did. There was a natural grace about the way she did her hair, moved, spoke and ate. The day he'd taken her skating, she'd delighted everyone weaving around on the ice in her brown dress and fur jacket. He loved the way she sighed, covering her mouth with her hand when struck by a new idea. She even looked charming just sitting in a chair reading. But there was a dark melancholy within her that he found more difficult. It left him feeling alienated. But he had to count his blessings; she really did seem to love his little Elsbeth. He was a lucky man.

Paula went to give Clara the news. 'Married, I can't believe it; my little friend is going to be married!' Clara exclaimed, hugging her. Climbing onto the thatched roof they sat next to the chimney looking down over the ripening rye fields and apple orchard, as they wove lengths of ivy into a wreath for her door.

Making her way home beneath the full moon, she felt calm and happy. She was touched by Otto's kindness and his childish naïveté, which made her, young as she was, feel the need to protect him. But above all she had to work and make the most of these final months. Just because she was planning to get married didn't mean she had to become obsessed with trivia, with linen for her trousseau or new wallpaper for the bedroom. She went for long walks across the moor, collecting leaves, ferns and baskets of chestnuts, which she strung into long chains. She picked white autumn berries, the sort that went pop when you stood on them, and arranged them in a vase on her table. Then she wrote to Rilke.

'I'll be coming to Berlin after Christmas. Will you still be there? You're the only person I know there from Worpswede. I've been worried something's wrong as I haven't heard from you for a long time. I think of you often and hope you are well.'

Christmas was spent in Bremen. Otto went to Münster to visit his parents. She sent him a yellow nightshirt and hoped that he'd think of her when he wore it, just as she was thinking of him. On Christmas morning her brother Henner came to her room, bringing her Papi's heavy fur robe to put on over her nightdress and, together, they climbed onto the flat roof to feed the pigeons, and listen to the Christmas bells. As they sat, side by side, catching up on their months apart, the sun turned the door of the cathedral a dull gold and the busy market stalls in the street below, deep red.

'Think, Henner, this is my last Christmas at home as a single girl. Next year I'll be a married woman in my own house. I hope you won't have gone to sea by then and that you'll come and visit your big sister.'

Milly gave her a beautiful leather travelling bag and her parents an antique mirror. And that afternoon, Heinrich Vogeler dropped by. He was in town looking for wedding rings. He and Martha had finally set a date.

There was a poignancy about Christmas that she loved. The scent of the pine wreath on the mantelpiece, the thick curtains pulled against the dark, as Milly played the piano and they sang carols in the candlelight. But she knew it was a chimera, a fairy tale and that life's realities lay elsewhere, outside this warm circle with its smouldering Yule log, and scent of cinnamon oranges.

She wrote and asked Otto to join them for New Year's Day. Her parents would love to see him and then she would return with him to Worpswede in order to pack up her things ready for Berlin. She wasn't looking forward to these cookery lessons, but her parents had insisted. It was such a waste of time when she could be painting. Soups, dumplings and nourishing stew. You can't go wrong if you know how to make economic dishes like that, her mother insisted. A good wife should know how to cook. The way to every man's heart—even an artist's—was through his stomach.

'That's four pages you've written to Otto!' Kurt teased as he turned in for the night.

New Year's Eve and they all went skating to a lonely little church that could only be reached across the frozen lake. Carved gargoyles encrusted with yellow lichen decorated the arched doorway and a single candle burnt on the altar lighting up the stained glass windows. As they sped back across the lake she could hear the ice creaking beneath her skates under the winter moon, and the desolate cries of wild geese breaking the snow-filled silence.

After everyone had gone to bed she curled up in her nightdress beside the dying embers and wrote to Rilke. She would be arriving in Berlin on Friday or Saturday. Should she visit him on the following Monday in the early evening? He could write to her care of her aunt. That's where she'd be staying. For now he must excuse the scrawl. It was late—already the New Year—for which she sent him her heartfelt wishes.

She'd had enough stewing, poaching and baking. She felt like running away from this silly cookery school just to see a patch of blue sky. She didn't fit into city life, particularly this elegant neighbourhood with its school for young ladies preparing to become housewives. It wasn't her at all. She longed for the Latin Quarter in Paris. It was funny to think how afraid she'd been when she first arrived; afraid of the noise, the dirt, the sheer vitality. But she'd never felt so free as in Paris. It wasn't that the other girls here weren't friendly, just that she had nothing in common with them and their obsession with their future husbands' social status and income. How much more could she stand of bouillon and gravy, turkey and roast pork? Walking from her aunt's house, she tried to record the faces she passed: the road sweeper with the pock-marked skin, the old woman in the bread shop with warts on her face. If she kept looking she wouldn't forget how to draw.

She arranged her little room at the top of the house so she would feel at home, remembering how homesick she'd felt as a young girl in England. Her aunt had provided a desk, a washstand and a cupboard for her few clothes. She hung the sketch Otto had given her above the bed and, that morning, bought a pink cyclamen in a pot. But being with her aunt and cousin reopened the wound of Cora's death. They were good, kind women but they never referred to that past tragedy. It was as if Cora had never existed, as if that terrible day at the sandpit that had changed her forever, had never happened.

She tried to talk to them, but things would only go so far, then stop: like a steel door closing shut. The first few nights in their house she was revisited by the recurring dream that she'd had as a child: Cora with her white face and flowing raven hair. She felt vulnerable and missed Otto with his big red beard and comfortable, reassuring presence. He and Worpswede had become home. She took out his letters from the brown travelling case Milly had given her and sat reading them on her bed, listening to the woman four floors below, beating her carpet in the yard.

At dusk she caught a tram. Walking through the dimly lit streets, past the black-and-red-brick buildings that lined the misty canal towards his room on the outskirts of the city, she felt nervous. She didn't know what to expect. She had missed their conversations about Russia and the nature of God, the way he'd sat in her studio, deep in thought, waiting for her to finish work. Those moments had been some of the most intense of her life. When Rilke opened the door she was trembling.

As he read her his new poems she thought that he had never looked more beautiful, his thin face was white as porcelain in the candlelight of his modest room. She knew he wasn't happy, that he'd been working too hard. Yet it was as if they'd never been apart as they talked late into the evening, arranging to go to the museum the following day. As she stood on his doorstep taking her leave in the foggy night air, he took her hand, holding it a moment longer than necessary and drawing his finger slowly along the length of her cupped palm, before leaning over and kissing her. Not on the cheek as a friend; but full on the mouth, his tongue searching hungrily for hers. Back in her room she sat in the dark for a long time, disrupted and confused. She could smell his skin on hers, still taste his mouth and feel his fingers unpinning her hair.

What a noisy, busy place Berlin was, she'd forgotten. Full of clanging trolley cars, beggars and prostitutes, women in furs and businessmen in expensive astrakhan coats. When she wanted to be quiet she went to the museum. There she'd retreat into herself and think. She wrote to Otto about Rembrandt. At first, she had to confess, she hadn't really liked many of his paintings. But that was because she hadn't looked hard enough, hadn't understood what he was trying to do. It had come to her when studying his little sketch of Joseph and Mary visited by the angel in the stable at Bethlehem. The light on the angel's wings, the tilt of the cow's head and Mary's blue mantle with its touch of red, had moved her deeply. It had opened something in her, lifted a veil onto her real feelings. A painting had to infiltrate every fibre of one's being, like love.

She'd been looking at Velázquez, but found him too refined and cool for her taste. She had also seen some wonderful wood-carvings and portraits made of coloured wax from the period of Charles V, which intrigued her. Every time she went to the museum she discovered something new. She was invited to a literary evening with her cousin where there was a great deal of talk about Nietzsche and a reading from his work. Everyone was concerned with the present state of the world, though there was a good deal of chit-chat among these so-called artists and poets with long hair. And all the women wore too much powder and none of them corsets. Not that she relished that garment, but, still, there was no need to advertise that one went without.

Her aunt's house was far too warm. She longed to throw open the windows. If she lived somewhere like this she'd end up wearing silk stockings and ruche dresses and she didn't want to commit her future husband to trivial expenses like that! As to her cookery course, she had learnt how to boil potatoes, cook them in their jackets and mash them with salt and butter. She knew how to make gravy and roast beef, junket and sago pudding, so they wouldn't starve. Then she received a letter from Mutti. Papi was in bed after a bad asthma attack. Worried, she wrote to him straight away.

Sundays she visited Rilke on the other side of town. Often they just sat and read in his room, or sometimes they took a walk in the park among the bare winter trees. She was relieved he never attempted to kiss her again. They were friends; she was engaged to Otto Modersohn. And she was glad that Otto had been seeing Clara; that two of the people she loved best were getting along while she was away. She asked Otto to send her a photograph of Elsbeth. And she had another request. She'd like to have a new dress. Could he afford to buy her one? She hoped he wouldn't think her frivolous. It shouldn't cost more than about fifty marks. If he couldn't, well, it didn't matter. Also had he got the woollen undershirt she'd sent him? He hadn't mentioned it. She was sorry, too, that he thought she wrote too much about painting. Couldn't he feel her love emanating from between her lines? Maybe she simply didn't have the words to express her real feelings, but soon there would be other ways to show him how she felt.

But here, alone in the city, she tried not to dwell on such thoughts. Though, sometimes, in the small hours, lying in her narrow bed in the thin lemon light, her body ached to be touched and she'd slip her hand between her thighs, reaching for her growing wetness. Is this how it was supposed to feel? Her thoughts about this most sacred of acts were neither pretty nor pure, but she wanted, now, to become a real woman.

Clara came to visit and they went to hear Beethoven's *Eroica*. As the bass broke through the melody, Paula's blood stirred. If only Otto was here. She was determined that he should come for her birthday. And he had agreed to the dress. Clara would help her choose it. She was very happy.

On her birthday she received a long letter from Papi about her forthcoming marriage. She was leaving her father's house, he wrote, not only in fact, but also in spirit. For however close she was to her brothers, sisters, and parents, in future it would be her husband who had to came first. It would be her duty to dedicate herself to his concerns, to have his well-being constantly in her thoughts and not be guided by her own selfish wishes. Otto was a good man; so it shouldn't be too hard, as both of them already agreed on most things. He'd seen far too many marriages go wrong because the couple put their mutual shortcomings under a magnifying glass, turning them over and over, so their failings appeared to become bigger and bigger until they were insurmountable. She and Otto both had their strong points, but it was the wife's task to look for what was good in her husband and overlook his little weaknesses. She knew Otto loved her and would do his best to make her happy and comfortable. As her father, his concern was that her future husband was too good-hearted and being an artist, too impractical, and, therefore, might permit her too loose a rein. At present Otto was doing well and making a good income. But a painter was dependent on the whims of the public and she mustn't assume things would always be so easy. Also he'd not like to think that she had persuaded him to sell his family home and move into that old farmhouse, which she'd set her heart on them buying. It was true his present house was small, but it was important that Elsbeth didn't have too many changes. The child's needs came first. It was obvious that Otto adored her and it wouldn't be sensible for Paula to persuade him to do anything he might later regret. Just because Vogeler lived in a great rambling barn of a house didn't mean they had to too. He knew she was keen to do up the place with all the second-hand bits and pieces she'd found in Berlin, but Vogeler didn't have a child to consider, so rattling around in the Barkenhoff full of old country furniture was fine, but she needed to be more practical.

It wasn't that he wanted to interfere with their arrangements. The two of them must work things out between them, but he'd be failing in his duty if he didn't pass on his advice and experience. After all, much as he'd like to help with material things, that wasn't possible. So his advice and love were all he had to give her for her birthday.

Otto sent a little carved box, but she was taken aback by the enclosed letter. It made her realise that her recent dashed postcard hadn't taken sufficient regard of his feelings. But she was tired; sick of the city, the people, the cooking and the thousand trivial concerns that she was supposed to bear in mind. She'd never be able to make it past February. She wanted to breathe fresh air among the silver birch and heathland and walk freely over her beloved moors. Here there was nothing but overblown Baroque decorations and Rococo twirls. She longed for simplicity. In his letter Otto had called her complicated. Well perhaps she was.

For her birthday she and Clara took a trip to mountains. She loved the towering, snow-capped peaks and crisp fragrance of pine. When Clara went to bed she sat by the dying embers of the log fire, the tortoiseshell comb in her hair and silk kerchief around her shoulders that had been a present from her grand-father to Mutti when she'd been twenty-five and that Mutti, on this same birthday, had given to her. Then she wrote to Rilke to thank him for the book and chocolates: 'But most of all, for your friendship.'

Her father wanted to give her a thousand marks for her dowry, but she couldn't accept such a large sum knowing his strained circumstances. Two hundred marks would be more than enough and the rest could go on the twins' education. She'd already bought a few things for the house; a beautiful mirror she'd found in an antique shop run by an old Jewish woman, along with a glass tea tray and decanter decorated with turquoise and gold enamel.

As for the dress Otto was buying for her birthday, well that would do for the wedding. She'd already bought chemises, drawers and nightgowns, the prettiest she could afford, threaded with pink ribbon. She imagined her freckled skin set off by the fine lace in the lamplight as he loosened her hair. She was also planning a different layout of the furniture in the parlour, and new sprigged wallpaper for the hall that would set off their gilded picture frames. It would be good to be just the three of them again. Her red fox and new little daughter. She longed for the summer so they could just flop down on a haystack with a bottle of lemonade and a basket of cakes, listening to the skylarks. She wanted to do a portrait of Elsbeth. She'd grown to love her and it wouldn't be long now before the little girl found her lying on the pillow next to her father, wishing her good morning.

The next day she received a letter from Milly. Papi had had another severe asthma attack and the Doctor was insisting on complete bed rest. She wrote to Otto immediately. 'I've had enough. I'm coming home. Expect me on Sunday, on the eight o'clock train.'

As she sat on her packed trunk holding Mutti's telegram she wondered why she, of all people, was being so disapproving. Her mother didn't think she should leave before the end of her course. But how could she just go on cooking? She simply couldn't do it any more. She *wouldn't* do it any more. She was squandering the fine spring weather when she could have been outside drawing on the moors and she needed to see Papi. Something about this city depressed her. She felt like a prisoner in this stupid cookery school with the endless housekeeping lists and recipes for making blancmange. But she would *not* be ground down. From the outset she'd promised herself she'd stick it for two months and she'd done that. But enough was enough. She needed air and space, to reconnect. Why wouldn't Mutti see that she couldn't be held back from her real life any longer? If she could convince her, then Paula knew her mother would square her leaving Berlin with Papi. It made her sad to know she was upsetting her parents. She loved them and didn't want to let them down. But there was nothing she could do; she had to do what her heart dictated. She hungered for the peace she found only when she was able to paint. She would leave on Saturday. She hoped things wouldn't be too difficult with her parents when she got home. And on Sunday she'd go to Otto and Worpswede.

Otto and Clara had filled her room with vases of pussy willow and made her bed with clean white linen. For the next few weeks she was in and out of Otto's house, making plans to redecorate and arranging the bits and pieces she'd bought in Berlin, helped by Elsbeth.

'Mutti Paula, can I carry that jug? When can I see the new dress I'm going to wear when you marry Papa?'

They scrubbed and hammered and painted while, in the garden, the buds opened on the chestnut tree. At last it was spring, at last she was home. They would be married at Whitsuntide.

She was sitting in a patch of dandelions, surrounded by a flock of goats and geese, drawing, when a tall figure came across the field towards her. It was Clara. Paula hadn't seen her for a week. Since she'd been back she'd been so busy she hadn't had a chance to catch up with her friend. Gathering up her long dark skirts, Clara sat down on the grass beside her, absent-mindedly threading a daisy chain as Paula talked of Berlin.

'Honestly Clara, I never want to make beef stock again. But since I've been back, I think, I see this landscape differently. It's as if things are falling into place. Maybe that's just nonsense and nothing has really changed. It's not something I'd say to most people, but I thought you'd understand.'

'Of course you're not talking nonsense, Paula. You're just prepared to express what others won't or can't. You're more honest. But listen, I have something to tell you. I wasn't sure how you'd react. But now I can see how happy you are, I realise I needn't have worried. Rilke has asked me to be his wife.'

MATHILDE

I OFTEN WONDER what Paula's real feelings where when Clara announced that she was going to marry Rilke. Did she feel betrayed? Or was she so swept up with the arrangements for her own impending marriage to my father that she couldn't acknowledge how confused she must have felt? I know Clara saw much less of her from then on and that my mother took this as a rejection. But I don't think she ever realised how difficult things were between Clara and Rilke, almost from the first. As I understand it from Milly, it was Clara who more or less proposed to Rilke and he was so low, so convinced that he'd never write anything worthwhile again without Lou in his life, and, possibly, so disappointed at the prospect of Paula's forthcoming marriage, that he simply gave in.

I think, for a while, he thought life in Worpswede would save him. That somehow all of them would be close and he would be able to start writing again. But Rilke wasn't made for marriage; he was too solitary, too self-centred, too neurotic, and too incapable of earning a living. The only thing he was married to was poetry and the only real relationship he ever had was with posterity. There were tensions from the start. I think, honestly, that if he loved anyone, it was my mother. And then when Ruth came along nine months after the wedding he had no means of support, and he and Clara were almost starving, he just couldn't stand it. In the end he virtually abandoned them. I think Clara withdrew because she didn't want my mother to know, didn't want people to see that it had all been a terrible mistake. After Clara and Rilke married in the April, following my parents wedding, they cut themselves off from the Worpswede 'family'. Paula had visions of them living in each other's pockets, popping in and out of each other's houses and studios, borrowing cups of flour and tubes of paint. She had imagined them talking into the night, putting the world to rights. She needed a close female friend, someone she could confide in a way she couldn't with my father.

Sometimes I wonder if marriage is a state that's possible between creative people. But then look at Daniel and Lola; they couldn't be more dissimilar. She's not creative and yet he was unhappy. At first he thought he loved her. He's not an emotionally illiterate man, but, nevertheless, he is a man and was taken in by her elegant beauty. But they couldn't be less suited. She's not interested in music, just the reflected glory of being married to a famous musician. Would he and I have done better or was our love so intense because we knew we could never be together? If it wasn't for the threat of this horrible war, Dan would still be here, married to Lola. Would he have ever left her? It's not that he doesn't love me. I know he does. But he felt responsible, felt that he'd made his bed, so to speak. And me? What's my, no, *our* future to be? That I now have to make plans for someone else both consoles and makes me anxious. I wonder what Paula would have done?

It's been days since I've had a proper meal. My clothes hang off me as if they belong to someone else. I wash, put on a little lipstick and some face powder to cover the black rings under my eyes, get my hat and coat and, opening the door quietly, check that the landlady's not about. I can't face her intrusive interest as I slip out of the door and hurry to the inn, the only place where there's likely to be any food available.

As I make my way through the village it's quiet and the light has an eerie quality. Purple clouds hang over the moors and the air is damp with rain. When I get to the inn I find a corner table near the fire. I keep on my hat and coat. Light a cigarette, inhale deeply and watch as smoke curls towards the dark beams and yellow ceiling. Smoking gives me something to do. On the far wall there's a heavy oak dresser covered with blue and white dishes. They're decorated with windmills, cows and little figures in clogs—paradise on a plate. Beside these are a row of earthenware beer flagons. The room is empty except for a large man with a face the colour of boiled beetroot, tucking into a plate of pink frankfurters. He is sitting opposite an ample woman, her thinning hair pulled back into a tight bun. Neither speaks, the corners of their mouths turned down like glued envelopes. I wonder how long they've been married. The man has a white linen napkin tucked into the top of his waistcoat like an overgrown toddler, and there's grease on his chin. As he wipes his mouth I notice the tiny iron swastika in the lapel of his green Bavarian jacket.

A waitress in a black dress comes for my order. I choose a pork chop with potatoes. Anything will do. I'm not interested in food, but I know I have a responsibility to eat. I'm not sure when

I made the decision to go ahead with this pregnancy. Maybe I never decided, just relented. For a while I thought of trying to get rid of it. I considered gin and hot baths, borrowing money from the girl downstairs to visit the old woman who lives above the butcher. All I could think of was having lost you. I couldn't cope with, or imagine, anything else. I just lay on the bed in a grey haze, unable to image a future. But it's been more than a month since you left. You're in Chicago. Safe. And here I am in Worpswede.

The days flow seamlessly. But they pass. I'm terribly tired; for the last couple of nights I've not slept much. This morning I woke with a headache. It's much damper here than in Berlin. I hope I'm not going down with flu. I wonder if I should have come at all, what it is that I thought I'd find. The past feels so close, but always slips away, like water through my fingers.

I get out of bed and stand in the muddy light, naked, in front of the long mirror on the mahogany wardrobe. The room's reflected back in the glass: the brass candlesticks on the mantelpiece, the peeling wallpaper, the heavy linen cupboard and gilded mirror. I guess I'm about fourteen weeks pregnant. My breasts are tender, my nipples dark and distended as two prunes. I stand in front of the mirror noting the changes in my body, my hands resting on the unfamiliar swell of my belly, and think of the self-portrait Paula painted when she was thirty, on her sixth wedding anniversary. She wasn't pregnant then, though there's a distinct curve to her stomach as if impregnated with her art. It was done just after she left my father. She's wearing the amber beads.

PAULA

PAULA AND OTTO were married, not as they wished, in the little church in Worpswede, but at Papi's bedside. His health had been a matter of concern since the beginning of the year. There were no flowers, bells or music; just a simple exchange of vows and rings conducted by Otto's brother Ernst; a scrawny, black-clad Lutheran pastor, with a face like an untuned fiddle. Paula suspected that if Papi had been well enough he'd never have tolerated such dogmatic views being expressed at the end of his bed. But as it was, he smiled weakly and passed her hand from his now bony one, into that of her new husband's. Suddenly he looked very old.

She had tied her hair simply at the nape of her neck and wore the new muslin dress that Otto had bought. Elsbeth was dressed in one almost identical and carried a sprig of lily of the valley from the garden; the only concession to decoration, and a task she undertook with solemnity.

Afterwards their wedding trip took them to Berlin and Dresden, then to Schreiberhau, where they were guests of Carl Hauptmann and his wife for a week. After further short visits to Prague, Munich and Dachau, they returned to Worpswede at the end of June. By then Paula had had her fill of guesthouses and was longing for home and her studio. There were roses, forget-me-knots and sweet williams in bloom in the garden as Elsbeth came running down the path to greet them.

'Papa, Mutti Paula, you're home, oh you're home!'

She quickly fell into a rhythm. Every morning they were all up by seven and the few domestic tasks essential to the day were complete by nine o'clock. She'd no intention of spending her time as a conventional *Hausfrau,* and assumed Otto wouldn't wish that either. Tasks and errands finished, she'd head for her studio, bypassing the road and taking a shortcut across the rye fields to avoid inevitable encounters with people from the village. Increasingly she needed time to think. Lunch was at one o'clock, and then after a half-hour nap, she'd appear for afternoon coffee in the small conservatory, where she'd first sat with Otto and Hélène taking tea. At three she'd return to her studio and paint until seven. The evenings were devoted to Otto and Elsbeth. They would read and play dominoes. Sometimes they visited the Vogelers. When she could, Milly came for a few days.

But Paula missed Clara. She often imagined her tread on the gravel path leading to her studio and would wait in anticipation for her tall, angular body to burst in, breathless after her cycle ride, and sit down on the stool by her painting table. She tried to compose a letter; she couldn't understand what she was supposed to have done to alienate her friend. If she had offended her, why didn't Clara say? Couldn't she be forgiven for something that had never been deliberate, never intended?

It was as if Clara and Rilke had simply closed a door, shutting her on the outside. She thought of the months together in Paris, wandering in the boulevards, boating, visiting galleries and second-hand bookstalls, exploring the dark gas-lit alleys of Montmartre, where neither would have dared venture alone. They'd been in and out of each other's rooms like sisters, staying overnight when it was too late to walk back to their own lodgings. In the morning they'd lit the iron stove and wrapped in the feather eiderdown, dunked the stale heel of the previous day's baguette into steaming bowls of hot chocolate.

Apart from Milly, Clara was her closest confidante. Hadn't they struggled, side by side, to establish their artistic independence? As much as she loved her sisters it was Clara with whom she shared her innermost thoughts. Her battles with art and life. Why had she turned her back?

Alone in her studio she chewed over and over their past meetings, dissecting them with the precision of a biologist looking at a specimen under the microscope. She tried to talk to Otto, but he was dismissive. What did she expect from Rilke? Frankly, he'd always found him pretentious; too precious and self-consciously Slavic for his taste. The way he wandered round dressed like a Russian peasant. There was something suspect about him. Not quite solid, not quite German. And Clara, well, she had simply fallen under his spell.

Paula was surprised at his vehemence and wondered what Clara's response would be if she got on her bicycle and rode the three miles over the fields to see her, as if nothing had happened. Instead she wrote a note:

'Clara don't you ever feel the desire to come over to my little room at the Brünjeses' house in Ostendorf, where you'll find a new wife and young painter in need of her friend?'

But though she waited, there was no reply.

Slowly she settled into married life, waking next to a sleeping Otto, his bushy red beard spread on the white pillow beside her and his mouth like an open drawer. Each of them had their different habits; he drank coffee, she drank tea. He read the morning paper, while she read letters. After breakfast she'd borrow his thick scarf and overcoat, wrapping herself against the cold and set off for her studio.

She had dreamt, so often, of their wedding night, of lying beside him in the lamplight, her face reflected back in his hazel eyes as they snuggled beneath the feather quilt, exchanging endearments and kisses. When it actually came he was tender and kind, though she had expected something more. How strange his bony body had felt pressed against hers. Yet after he'd fallen asleep she lay awake with a deep ache in the pit of her stomach, remembering the feeling that had flooded over her in that narrow Berlin bed, the tingle and wetness between her thighs. And she tried not to dwell on how her heart had raced that foggy evening by the canal when Rilke had kissed her; how bright the stars had seemed in the inky Berlin sky. What was she thinking? She was a married woman now.

It was late November and there'd been gales and lashing rain for weeks that had turned to flurries of snow. The sky hung like a thick quilt over the village and no one went out unless they had to, hurrying between the squat houses with an umbrella carried like a shield against the driving sleet. Martha Vogeler had recently given birth to a little girl and Clara was about to be confined any day now. All this activity led Paula to think about a child of her own. Would that be what might bind her to Otto in a way nothing else quite had? Was she ready for that responsibility? She still had so much to do.

She was in Bremen visiting her parents when it happened. Papi was in his study reading. The familiar sliver of light escaping under his door that reminded her of her childhood when he'd sat in a fug of smoke writing furious letters, or reading a new book from England on bridge-building by Brunel. It was a relief that his health had improved. Six months ago he'd been bedridden with asthma. His face strained and blue around the mouth, as he wheezed and fought for breath. Now a little colour had returned to his pallid cheeks and he was back pottering about in his study. With luck he'd be completely better for her first married Christmas, perhaps even well enough to spend it with them Worpswede. It would mean so much to have him in her home.

Dear Papi. They'd not always seen eye to eye but he'd always been there, her compass and guide, cajoling, fussing and worrying. From him she'd inherited her spirit of independence and learnt to ask questions and not accept easy answers. He'd taught her endurance, to find the grit at her centre. He may not always have understood the direction she'd chosen, but he had never, seriously, challenged her right to choose. She wondered if she could talk to him about having a child. Would he understand her conflict; the pull between fulfilling her destiny as a woman and not wanting to waste the hard-won progress she'd made as a painter? Mutti always told her what she thought she wanted to hear and now she no longer had Clara, perhaps Papi would be able to advise her. He and Mutti had a happy marriage. She went into the kitchen and put a pot of coffee on the stove. She'd take it to him in his study. He had been working too hard and needed a break.

She placed a clean lace cloth on a tray, the little silver coffee pot, a jug of cream and bowl of sugar, and then carried it down the hall before knocking on his door. How typical of him to be so absorbed that he didn't hear. She knocked louder and wondered what he was reading. Many people of his age turned to the Bible, whatever they had believed in the past. Otto's brother, Ernest, was always chiding Papi for rejecting the true Protestant path. But he would just sigh, knock the ash from his big-bowled pipe into the fire, and turn back to his copy of *Zarathustra*.

She put down the tray on the hall table and opened the door. Inside the dim room the fire had died. She turned to his desk and there he sat—open-mouthed, his eyes blank, staring at nothing. She knelt down and put her head in his lap, lifting his hand, very gently, in hers, as if she feared waking him.

She'd bought him some coffee, she said. She should pour it for him? But it sat on the tray growing as cold as he was. She should call Mutti or Kurt. But what could they do? She'd wait. She needed these moments alone with him to say goodbye. His hand was icy and his face, though peaceful, not quite his face any more, as if he'd just understood something important. His lifeless fingers were stained yellow with nicotine and she could still smell the stale Turkish tobacco clinging to his jacket.

There was so much she still needed to ask. She wanted his advice and approval. He'd taught her not to fear the truth. And now he would no longer be here at the centre of the house, shut in his smoke-filled study reading books on genetics and plant propagation or writing irate letters to newspapers. Whenever she started a new painting it was him that she had in mind, imagining the conversation they'd have, the suggestions and criticisms he'd make. All she had ever wanted was for him to be proud. She picked up his papery hand, its freckled skin already cold, and held it to her cheek.

It ends here, childhood. Not with marriage, but here.

There was nothing that could have been done, the Doctor assured them, as he hurried to comfort his good friend, Frau Becker, in whose house he'd so often been a guest. It had been very sudden. His heart had simply given out. Herma and Henner were almost unable to bear it, this first great grief in their lives. Only now that he was gone was it apparent what they'd all lost; this father who had battled for his six children, who'd chivvied and chided and loved them. His depth could be measured first and foremost by his essential kindness and devotion. But he'd also been a man of principle, always prepared to stand up for what he thought was right and good.

Christmas was a quiet affair. Thank God she had Otto. Now she understood what he really meant to her. She was grateful for his tenderness and solidity, grateful that he'd known and loved her Papi. Together she and Elsbeth lit a Yuletide candle in remembrance of Grandpa Becker and placed it in the window, so it shone out onto the dark moors, the flickering flame reflected in the frosty glass.

The day after her birthday Paula received an unexpected note from Clara. She'd been reading her journal and had chanced upon the entry for the previous year when they'd been together in Berlin. It had reminded her that there had been two yellow tulips in a blue vase on the desk and a little painting by Otto above the bed and, if she wasn't mistaken, a bouquet of violets, and a bottle of champagne that had refused to go pop. Had a whole year really gone by since? She was so very housebound that it was impossible to get on her bicycle and ride over to see Paula as she'd done in the past. Now she couldn't go out in search of the world, but had to wait for it to come to her. But as she waited, she thought of Paula and her birthday celebrations in her new home with her new husband, and wanted to send her greetings.

Under separate cover Rilke sent an edition of his latest poems and asked Paula to pass on his good wishes to Otto.

It should have made her feel better. But it didn't, after the months of silence. Paula was none the wiser as to why Clara had been so distant. Why she hadn't answered her numerous notes or come to visit. Her letter hadn't taken away any of the sting of rejection. That morning Paula rose earlier than usual, lit the stove and put on the water for Otto's coffee, made him some toast and boiled him an egg. He didn't seem to notice that she wasn't in the mood to chat as he read his morning paper. Kissing her on the forehead, he disappeared into his studio.

Sitting alone in the parlour, she was in turmoil. She wrote and rewrote to Clara in her head, crossing out bits and then redrafting. She went into the study and got out a sheet of blue paper. Didn't Clara realise how selfish she'd been since that time in Berlin when she'd been so short of money that Paula had walked all the way across town to her room by the castle to advance her a loan? Paula had never asked when it would be paid back. She'd simply responded to Clara's request, given it freely, because Clara was her friend and needed help. Maybe they had different approaches to friendship, but why did love have to be so parsimonious? Rilke was Clara's husband, but did that mean everything had to be given exclusively to him? Shouldn't love be like the sun and shine on everything? Why couldn't they live, as they had always planned, as a community? Not just shut up in closed family units.

Rilke's voice, she wrote, had spoken too insistently from Clara's letter, as though Clara's own thoughts had been drowned. Surely the union between two strong people was rewarding because they were equal. Yet, it seemed, Clara had discarded a large part of her old self, spreading it on the ground like a battered coat for her husband to walk on. For the sake of their past friendship, wouldn't she pick it up again and wear it with pride.

'Yes, I admit it. I'm setting the dogs on Rilke. I'm hounding him for keeping you from me. When you wrote of my little room with the yellow tulips, didn't you realise how much you trampled on my heart? I don't think anything gives you the right to do that, Clara. Don't shut yourself away. Once we shared a vision. Can't we show the world that four people can love each other just as much as two?'

It was Rilke and not Clara who responded. She was stung by the way he addressed her as Frau Modersohn. He wasn't in Bremen or he would have come and spoken to her himself. He couldn't understand what she was making a fuss about. Nothing, as she suggested, had happened. Or rather a good deal that was positive and new had happened, which she was incapable of taking on board. Was everything, always, supposed to remain the same? If she really loved Clara, as she claimed, then her task should be to understand—what till now she had singularly failed to do—that her life had changed.

Clara had grown, but Paula stubbornly refused to accept that fact. People altered, but she wanted to keep Clara in a time warp, exactly as she'd been when they had first met, before she had been touched by life. Hadn't Paula once placed her trust in him when she'd given him her journal to read? Had she forgotten that she'd written how incomprehensible and strange Clara had seemed? Yet Paula had been attracted by those very qualities and the desire for solitude that she was now complaining about. If she were a little more astute, she would realise the enormous changes in Clara's circumstances. Did he have to spell out they not only had a child but, also, serious money worries that they could no more discuss in public than they could the few hours of intimacy that they shared? Why was she so surprised that the centre of gravity had shifted? Was her friendship so limited, so mistrustful, that she needed constant proof of others' affection? Why did she have to grab at what she already possessed?

If she expected things not to change, then she was bound to be disappointed. Clara couldn't be pinned down or owned. Couldn't Paula celebrate that? He, too, stood outside, waiting to be let in. Surely, the most valuable thing in any relationship was that each person guarded the other's right to solitude. The only true communication was to be found in those moments of closeness that punctuated periods of isolation. Couldn't Paula remember, before she and Clara met, how she'd simply been getting on with her own life? Now she was trying to force open a door, which could only be unlocked when the other person was ready; and no one knew when that might be. All any of them could do was wait.

It was snowing when she went to put a wreath on Hélène's grave. The woman Otto had once called his wife. The ground was brittle from the previous night's frost. It had been snowing for nearly three days. Worpswede was cut off from the rest of the world and the road to Bremen impassable. Goodness knows when it would be open again and safe to travel. Drifts covered the hedges, and piled against the side of barns. In the surrounding fields the tender shoots of winter rye poked green through the white blanket. How strange, how full of chance and uncertainties, life was. If Hélène hadn't died so prematurely, what would Paula's life have been like? She wouldn't be married to Otto Modersohn, perhaps not even living in Worpswede. Maybe she'd have become a governess as Papi had always recommended.

As she walked round the little snow-covered churchyard she decided she would like her own grave to be different to Otto's first wife. She didn't want a mound, but a rectangular bed with white carnations planted around the edge, and a modest gravel path framed by a simple wooden trellis that supported a climbing rose. And there'd be a small gate in the fence, so that people could visit her, and a little bench where they could sit and rest. She wanted to be buried by the hedge, in the old part of the churchyard. And at the head of her grave there would be two juniper trees and a simple black stone engraved with nothing but her name.

Otto was astonished by her progress that winter. Every morning he watched as she wrapped her shawl round her shoulders after her domestic tasks were completed and hurried off to her studio. It had been a while since he'd been there.

'Paula, what a development,' he said, hanging his hat behind the door. 'These are truly unconventional, unlike the work of almost all the other women painters I know. Look at these two girls' heads set against the sky. It's really fine; free, intimate and considered. I'd no idea, my dear, this was what you were doing.'

She hadn't dared ask him to come before, hadn't wanted to disappoint him. Was he being kind just because she was his wife?

'Paula, that's nonsense. I've always valued your artistic judgement, but now you seem to be reaching for something more profound. You know I don't always want to admit it, being a bit of a stubborn old fox, but you're usually right when it comes to artistic matters. You never liked those three paintings I sent to Bremen or the one I did last winter of that fairy dance.

'Well you were right, of course; it's too artful, too fey. I shouldn't listen to Heinrich Vogeler. He hasn't got your sensibility. He's too literal; sky, grass, flowers. Everything is filled in, highlighted in quotation marks, so there's nothing left to the imagination. But you've always had an eye for what's authentic. That's why it makes me angry that no one bothers to find out what you're up to. Admit it, even your mother, your brothers and sisters, don't really take what you're doing seriously. Even the Mackensens and the Rilkes. Their behaviour towards you proves my point. Clara Westhoff never visits, although she still claims to be your friend. And Rilke? Well, the arrogance of the man, writing that you're supposed to wait meekly outside the door until his lofty wife, the *great artist*, deigns to grant you an audience. Frankly, it's preposterous. And Heinrich drives me mad talking as if you're some sort of dilettante. For some reason it's all very different when it's Clara. *She* has to go to Florence. *She* has to have her works photographed, but he never bothers to walk over here and see what *you*'re doing. We've all done you a disservice; the fact is you *are* somebody and what you're accomplishing is important. I'm really impressed.'

As he walked back to his studio he considered how lucky he was to have a wife whose taste so closely mirrored his own. He'd paint her, as soon as the weather was fine, standing in the long grass in her wedding dress, or the pale pink one without sleeves, her bare feet in the long grass dotted with speedwell.

The catkins were in bloom, and the warmer weather had begun to melt the snow. There were snowdrops in their garden and outside her studio. Paula had been counting the different birds that visited the bird table she'd put up for Elsbeth; there were titmice, starlings, larks and finches. She'd even found clumps of yellow coltsfoot in the brickyard, which she picked and put in the green cup the old village weaver had given her. She had been touched. That small gesture made her feel as if she belonged in this community. She was enjoying her garden, slowly getting to know the different flowers. Now it was light until nearly seven, she would plant some seeds: blue love-in-a-mist, pinks and pansies. Elsbeth would help her, they'd do it together, hoeing the weeds and watering, tying up the weak plants onto sticks with bits of rag. Otto was planning a willow arbour under the birches for her to grow sweet peas and gourds. And in the middle of her miniature garden she would place a silver glass globe.

Yet despite Otto's recent endorsement of her work, she cried a great deal, alone in her cold studio, during that first year. Marriage, she now realised, didn't guarantee happiness as she had naïvely presumed. It simply took away the youthful illusion that one day she would find a kindred spirit, someone who would understand what was going on in her heart. Now she could hardly bear to listen to music or watch the sun setting over the black hills. For then a lump, like a great stone, would form in her chest.

And whatever Otto or Rilke said, neither understood what it meant to her to have lost Clara. Often she felt as lonely as she'd done as a child. Maybe it made her a deeper person, less concerned with keeping up appearances or gaining worldly recognition; for it was only when she was alone that she came close to her essential self. Once such feelings might have sent her scurrying off to a nunnery, but now they were the mulch for her art. Hadn't Rilke said that it was the duty of a husband

and wife to guard the other's solitude? But what was the point of solitude that someone else had to protect?

Looking back on her childhood, the future had appeared easy, promising; now life was a test and a struggle. Here she was sitting at her kitchen table, the sun streaming in through the window at three o'clock in the afternoon on this Easter Sunday in 1902, a married woman writing in her housekeeping book, tending to the roast veal. But there was really only one thing she felt compelled to do and that was work. She would go to the Poor House and get on with her drawing of Old Mother Schröder and the children who lived there. On fine days, she could, sometimes, hear them singing. They were the only singers she ever heard here except for the village drunks; for song didn't form part of the lives of these dour people she'd chosen to live among.

She was dreaming in colour now and enjoying the sensuality of her thickly applied paint and had begun to use different glazes, not only the single-glaze process that Otto had introduced her to. Perhaps she could glaze as many as ten times, one layer over the other, if she could work out how to do it. She wanted to create greater luminosity, to experiment with different types of underpainting, and might even try painting on a gold ground.

It was June and the rye was ripening in the fields. Mackensen, to everyone's surprise, had become engaged to a girl from Bremen, who might have been nicer if she wasn't so terribly bourgeois. He was working on a big canvas of the *Sermon on the Mount*, and Heinrich Vogeler was painting Martha with the new baby, seated beside a rose bush. Paula spent her days working, while Elspeth played in the sandpit, becoming as brown as a nut. It was hard to believe that it was a year now since Papi had died. Her childhood had ended then, and with it so many of the fantasies she had wrong-headedly cherished. Today would have been her parents' wedding anniversary. She would write to her mother sending her love for them both.

And Otto? He thought Paula had turned out very well. It was a pleasure to work beside her. Yesterday she'd surprised him with a sketch of the old woman from the Poor House, sitting amongst the goats and chickens. The colour was subtle and the composition unusual, for she'd done something strange to the surface with a series of swirls. He realised that no other painter in Worpswede interested him as much as his own wife. She had verve and imagination. When she disciplined herself a little more, she might be something special. They balanced each other perfectly. He was inclined to fuss so his work ended up too fiddly. She, on the other hand, was so free. He could provide her with ballast, while she stimulated him into taking risks. It wasn't easy for a man like him to admit, but he was learning from her. And, as if taken by surprise at his own thoughts, he realised he loved her more than ever. She was that rare thing; a natural artist, much more so than all the Mackensens and Vogelers. Only she, of all of them, had the mark of greatness.

She was sitting alone in her studio, writing to her mother. Everyone else had gone to church and she'd forgotten her key and been forced to climb through the window. She liked to keep to the routine of Sunday letters; since Papi had died it meant a great deal to Mutti. But this one was late as she'd been absorbed by her work. Recently there'd been a fallow period when she'd done nothing much except walk, read or tidy the studio, but something was beginning to stir. She'd had a sudden surge of energy, like a storm whipping across the mountain tops. It was as if something inside her had burst open, and its force was carrying her along. Finally, she knew that she was achieving something significant. If only Papi had been around for her to show him that his fears hadn't been justified; for her to repay him for that gritty, obstinate nugget that he had left her as an inheritance. Soon there would be a time when she'd no longer have to be embarrassed about what she did, but could say with pride: I am a painter.

She'd just finished a study of Elsbeth in the orchard, standing beside a giant foxglove. It had taken her a long time, but she felt that she'd achieved a greater control than usual. She was trying not to think too hard about the image in front of her, but to respond emotionally. Otto was encouraging, coming more regularly to the studio, and commenting enthusiastically on her work, joking that he'd have to watch out as she'd soon be painting better than him.

To become somebody was her goal. It wasn't fame, but a desire to reach a place where she no longer needed to apologise for who she was and what she did. She longed to look Mutti and her uncles in the eye. To satisfy all the members of her family who'd entrusted money for her education that she hadn't turned out to be such a bad investment after all, that she wasn't a dilettante but someone to be reckoned with, someone with a voice of her own.

Otto had gone to see his parents. It was the first time they'd been apart since they'd married. Walking by the canal as the sun set pink behind the distant chain of hills, she relished this chance to be alone, not only because it gave her time for reflection, but because Otto's absence allowed her to see him differently. There'd been doubts, there had been difficulties, but now she could feel her love for him growing. He offered her security. Wasn't he her beloved husband? During the past year hadn't they become more and more a part of one another? So why did he so often complain about her need for solitude? It was as though he was jealous. Surely he knew it didn't threaten their love.

That evening, as she was soaking in the bathtub, Elsbeth came in to scrub her back with the big sponge. As she washed her, the little girl leant over and touched her breast. 'Mutti Paula, what are those for?'

How should she respond? 'For milk, Elsbeth, you've seen the women in the fields feeding their babies, haven't you?'

Invigorated by her bath she took a long walk in the mild autumn air, breathing in the fetid scent of mushrooms and rotting leaves. A crescent moon hung among the willows and, suddenly, she felt like singing.

January went on forever. Long dark days when the clouds chased over the wetlands and the wind howled, rattling at the shutters. A silence descended over the house as each of them, wrapped in thick woollen jackets and scarves against the damp and chilblains, got on with their allotted tasks. She couldn't put her finger on what was different, but occasionally a shadow would pass over Otto's face as he came in, wind blown, from his studio. Was it something she'd said? He'd reacted badly when she had mentioned she was thinking of going back to

Paris; that she needed to expand her horizons and test herself against a wider world. She knew he believed that egotism was a contemporary sickness and that Nietzsche was its father. He railed against what he saw as a tendency to put the 'self' before everything else. For, fundamentally, he still adhered to the Protestant doctrine of duty and sacrifice, and 'modern' was a word that increasingly vexed him. In his eyes it denoted self-absorption and superficiality. That's how he saw Rilke and Clara, and he accused Paula of being infected by similar ideas. He made no bones about the fact that he considered her too dismissive of those who didn't live up to her stringent expectations; those who, in her eyes, weren't deep enough. She'd have to be careful, he warned her, or she'd soon find herself entirely alone. That she was gifted was all very well and hadn't he given her every encouragement? But it meant nothing if she didn't possess certain fundamental human values. He was beginning to doubt that modern women were capable of love. The husband was always portrayed as tyrannical if he expected his wife to consider his needs. All too often she gave the impression that she was sacrificing her rights, her freedom, and even her personality for their relationship. He was weary of such arguments. All this discontent just made people dissatisfied and miserable with their lot.

As to Paris, he was tired of hearing that infernal city's name. How could anybody with any sensitivity endure that stinking cesspit for more than a few days? The buildings and art were undoubtedly fine, but there was a decadence about the place he hated. Nothing was more important to him than peace and clean country air.

'Paula, I simply can't understand this obsession with return-ing to that city of thieves and bad drains. I'm sorry, but I'm not prepared to leave the quiet of my studio. I've everything I need here. I could never work in Paris, and I can't pretend I'm happy about your decision to go back, either. But however wrong-headed I feel you are, I'm a tolerant man and won't pre-vent you from spending some more time there if, as you seem to imagine, it is absolutely essential to your progress.'

He accompanied her as far as Münster, where they stopped to visit his mother. Paula could hardly refuse such a wifely act now Otto had, however reluctantly, agreed to let her go back to Paris. She wrote to Elsbeth from the train, hoping that her horrible cough had gone and urging her to be good for Papa and old Bertha. Elsbeth may not be her flesh and blood, but she'd become her own dear daughter and she knew that she would miss her. As Paula passed through Belgium she made quick sketches of the women scavenging for coal on the black slag heaps. What a grim place it was. When, finally, she arrived in Paris she settled into her old address in the boulevard Raspail. Room no. 53 of the Grand Hotel de la Haute Loire. And as she unpacked her brown leather suitcase in the cramped attic room, it came flooding back: the smell, the dirt, the noise, the vitality, and the reason for her return.

Her room was the same one she'd occupied during her last stay. Next door, in 54, she could hear the German accents of two women painters. She thought of Clara who'd lodged there; of the bed with the big red canopy where they'd sat huddled under the feather eiderdown talking late into the night. On her arrival she had been greeted by the same hostile stares from the concierge. It would take her a while to reacclimatise. She felt self-conscious among the arty crowd, in their paint-splattered smocks, when she walked into the local bistro wearing her fur jacket, to be greeted by a stocky Spanish artist and two Frenchmen, who called out from the other side of the bar: '*Aha, elle est rentrée la belle Allemande.*' Embarrassed, she ate her ham quickly and hurried back to her room.

She slept well, though still felt uneasy when she ventured out; as if everyone was pointing out she was too bourgeois, in her neat white collar and cuffs, to belong in this bohemian quarter. Yet it was no more than she expected. For she knew, from her previous visit, that if she relaxed her discomfort would pass. But what a city Paris was; she'd done the right thing coming back. She went to the market and bought a candlestick, a breadboard and a small mirror for her room, and was now drinking her breakfast *café au lait*, rereading Clara's letter. She was to meet her and Rilke for dinner that evening. They'd been in Paris for a while and Rilke was working as Rodin's secretary. Clara had organised an introduction and the job provided them with some much-needed income. They'd become very much part of Rodin's set, visiting him at home in Meudon and meeting up with other artists from all over the world who came to pay homage to the Master.

But they had been forced to leave their small daughter, Ruth, behind with Clara's parents. Paula wondered if she could have done the same if she'd had a child. She had been nervous of the response to her note announcing her sudden arrival in Paris for there'd been virtually no contact between her and Clara since their last awkward exchange in Worpswede. But Paula had missed her, though she was uncomfortable at the prospect of meeting Rilke again. Clara's reply was straightforward and friendly, giving her their address and a time to call.

The following evening they paid her a return visit. She arranged two small vases of anemones on the sill, bought some cheese and ham and a carafe of wine. Not the cheap stuff she sometimes purchased for a few centimes to help her sleep, but something that tasted of grapes. As they sat round her stove talking of old friends, the breach between the three of them seemed to have healed. But how nervy and drawn Rilke seemed, Paula thought, remembering how beautiful he'd looked in the lamplight in Berlin. And there was a palpable tension between him and Clara. She felt awkward when she realised that he was looking at her. His limpid eyes scrutinising her as if asking for something, until she was forced to look away, hoping that Clara hadn't noticed. Paris, it seemed, was a constant source of anxiety to them both and her small room soon became swamped with their melancholy. She hoped it wasn't contagious. After they left she drew five cats on a postcard and sent them to Elsbeth.

On St Valentine's Day she was offended when the concierge addressed her as Mademoiselle, so she made a point of showing off her wedding ring. It felt odd if she didn't wear it now, although it was so loose she was afraid of losing it. She'd already written three letters to Otto. She'd been spending a lot of time in the rue Laffitte where most of the important dealers were located. What he so often disparagingly called the French 'being artistic' was, she realised, their ability not to bring every painting to a point of perfection. What they omitted was as significant as what they included, whereas the Germans always painted their pictures from top to bottom, filling in every last detail. Their approach was too ponderous to do the little oil sketches that often said more than a finished picture. She was sure Otto would benefit from adopting a similar technique. Though he'd be unlikely to find support for it among the public at home and there certainly wouldn't be any dealers there who'd know what to do with them.

Slowly she was settling back into city life, but it was harder than she'd anticipated and would cost her more dearly than during her previous visit. Back then she hadn't had a husband tugging at her conscience. But distance allowed her to gain perspective on her relationship with Otto. The cliché about absence was true and there were moments when she felt like sitting down in the middle of the street and crying. What was she doing here when she had a home and a studio in Worpswede? Why was she pushing herself so hard? She was also looking for new lodgings and the process was proving bitterly frustrating. It wasn't that rooms were expensive; hers cost thirty-nine francs, about thirty marks a month. But she couldn't stand the clanging electric tram that rumbled all night outside the window disturbing her dreams. She longed to escape to the country at the weekend, but Rilke and Clara were insisting on seeing an exhibition of Japanese art.

Everything Japanese was the rage in Paris, so she decided to tag along. But she wished they could be a little more cheerful. Their gloom was exhausting and she was glad to escape to her life class where she enjoyed the challenge of being set a new pose every half-hour and being a student again. That evening she settled down to write to Otto. She'd just been to see Rodin's new sculpture, which had greatly impressed her, but she hated the boarding-house food and couldn't wait to move lodgings. She missed Bertha's cooking: her bacon knuckle and herring in cream sauce. Also, he must ask Herma to cut his hair and not go to that useless old barber in the village.

How conventional Japanese art made their work seem. The paintings were not framed, but executed on paper and silk scrolls. There were long-necked cranes, lithe dragons and little fishing boats floating on lakes beneath high mountains, which seemed to hover among the clouds. It was more direct and childlike than Western art, with no real sense of perspective and nothing extraneous or unnecessary. A single line said so much. As she watched the visitors come and go in the gallery, she realised how much more interesting real people were than most painted portraits. As she wandered past the galleries in the rue Laffitte, she saw that the French weren't concerned with making attractive pictures or wooing the public: it was truth that mattered.

But much of the time she felt lonely and wondered if she had made a mistake, whether Paris would really help her work. But it would. She was certain. She just had to hold her nerve. That evening an organ-grinder's cart, pulled by a moth-eaten donkey, stopped outside her window and everyone came out of their shops to dance. Even the little florist's assistant, bringing in the flower buckets, waltzed across the street with a pail of white freesias in her arms.

*

'*Travailler, il faut toujours travailler*,' Rodin had said to the Rilkes, and, now, they seemed be taking his advice quite literally. They no longer wanted to go to the country on Sundays and appeared to be getting less and less fun out of life. Recently Paula visited Clara's studio and found her finishing a clay sculpture of a girl's thumb that had shown real sensitivity. But, secretly, she was disappointed with her friend. She had hoped that Clara's invitation indicated that she wanted them to become confidantes again. Paula was pleased at the thought of seeing her alone, for she felt increasingly unsettled by Rilke's presence. She took her a bunch of snowdrops, but Clara barely noticed and left them to wither on the table. Paula longed to talk to her about the first year of her marriage. To regain some of the intimacy they'd shared as young, single women the last time they had been in Paris. But Clara was distracted and talked of nothing but herself, her work and Rodin. In fact, Paula wondered if she was in danger of becoming too enamoured with the great man. Recently she had met the odd little Welsh painter Gwen John, whose wild, handsome brother was the name on everyone's lips. It was rumoured, although half his age, that she'd become Rodin's new mistress. Paula wondered if she detected a hint of jealousy in Clara. A sense of being put out by the attention this new pupil was receiving. She was very glad she had nothing to do with the following at Rodin's studio.

She was becoming more and more attracted to Rembrandt's work, despite the fact that the varnish on many of his paintings had yellowed. She was also looking at other Dutch masters and had recently discovered the Venetians, particularly Veronese.

Where else but Paris could she indulge in such an artistic feast? And Rembrandt was teaching her about more than painting: she was learning about the vulnerability and intimacy of ordinary things. There was a particular nude—she didn't know its name—where he had painted the cushions to show the intricate detail of the lacework. But they weren't simply painted cushions; they were *real* cushions that *real* people had stuck under their greasy heads and stuffed under their buttocks.

She was waiting anxiously for a letter from Otto. Every evening when she came back from her life class she'd ask the concierge, '*Pas de lettre?*' and the old woman would shake her head and reply '*Rien du tout, madame.*' Then, just as she was becoming despondent, the *garçon* came running after her shouting: '*Voici, ma petite dame! Voila tout ce que vous désirez.*'

Slowly Paris was becoming more like the city she remembered. The same old woman sat selling violets on the Pont des Arts, and every morning the same booksellers set up their stalls along the Seine. But at the Académie they didn't seem to notice that she'd changed. Much to her annoyance, everyone continued to address her as mademoiselle. Couldn't they tell she was now a married woman? Even though she made her ring visible at every opportunity, no one took any notice.

Every morning she was up at eight o'clock, opening her windows onto the fragrance of lilacs. She would make cocoa or coffee with the milk left over from the night before, which she had with some of the bread delivered daily to her door. Then she would set off for the Louvre and spend the morning drawing, or sitting on a bench, looking at a particular painting until she began to understand how it had been put together. At midday she would eat an *omelette aux fines herbes* or some *pommes frites* at Duvals or fry a couple of eggs back in her room. Then at four thirty, after a short nap, she'd make her way through the Jardin du Luxembourg, swarming with children taking their daily promenade, to her life class. If she had time she'd drop into the Musée du Luxembourg, which had recently reopened, to look at Manet's *Olympia*. As for the Renoirs, well they were less to her taste. There was something too soft, too effete about them. It was the Cottet triptych that had so caught her imagination on her first visit that she returned to. The stoic patience of the women waiting on the beach for their men's boat to return moved her.

In the Louvre she copied from David, Delacroix, Ingres and Goya. What a sense of space and atmosphere Goya possessed and how brave his subject matter was. But until now she'd never been able to find a connecting thread between antiquity and modern art. Then she chanced upon the Fayum portraits from Egypt. The colour and detail of the painted faces on the wooden sarcophagi were so clear that they spoke to her across the centuries. Here, at last, was the directness she'd been seeking.

But the name on everyone's lips was Rodin. She wished she could persuade Otto to come and see his work. The previous Saturday afternoon, armed with a calling card from Rilke, she had paid him a visit. Saturday was his day for receiving people, so she wasn't alone. Half of Paris seemed to be there. He hardly bothered to look at the card; just nodded as if she was one of the crowd who had come to gawp. She was hurt by Rilke's introduction. His dismissive reference to her as '*la femme d'un peintre très distingué*'. Had it been a deliberate slight?

He knew she was more than the wife of a famous painter, that she was someone in her own right who wanted to visit Rodin for artistic and not social reasons. So why did he feel the need to goad her and undermine her confidence? She felt more and more uncomfortable in his presence. It was as though he was punishing her, though she had no idea for what. She tried never to be alone with him now there was no longer any possibility of them talking openly or intimately. He was tetchy and made little digs at her expense when the three of them were together so that she was forced to address her remarks to Clara in order to avoid speaking to him directly. What had happened to the young man who had sat in her studio, as the evening drew in and she'd tidied her paints, sharing notions about beauty? Now Rilke was forever dropping names, implying relationships with Tolstoy and Rodin that didn't really exist. Well, it didn't impress her.

As she was leaving Rodin's studio, she plucked up the courage to ask if she might visit him at Meudon. To her surprise he issued an invitation for the following Sunday. Early that morning she bought a third-class ticket and caught the train out to the little village, sitting on a hard wooden bench beside a couple of farmhands who were carrying a pair of squawking cockerels flapping inside a sack. Third class was a necessary economy now. She had to be careful with money. She had almost run out, and didn't want to ask Otto for further funds if she could avoid it. As she walked from the station through the little villages that bordered the Seine, Paris glinted in the distance bathed by the spring sun. How beautiful it looked: all the dirt and squalor hidden, and only the spires and domes of Notre-Dame, and the Sacré Coeur shimmering in the early mist.

As he showed her around Rodin answered her questions with kindness and interest. He always drew, he told her, direct from the model, working quickly in pencil, and then shading in with washes of watercolour. But his house was surprisingly modest, as though he couldn't be bothered with ordinary day-to-day matters. When she was saying goodbye she was struck by his remark—as if he'd been reading her thoughts—'*Le travaille, c'est mon bonheur, Mademoiselle.*'

Of course that was the point. What did worldly luxury matter when compared to the happiness that came from work? As the train left behind the fields and rows of poplars to approach her beloved city, she knew that she would keep coming back to Paris.

That night she sat by her open window, looking out across the rooftops, unable to sleep. The moon was full and cast silver-blue shadows among the chimney stacks and, in the street below, she could hear a pair of cats fighting. She had been alone a good deal over the past ten days. Rilke had a bad cold, his third this winter, so she'd hardly seen Clara either. Paris was, getting both of them down. Paula worried about her friend's nerves. Whenever they met she seemed more withdrawn, while Rilke held court. And it was hard to measure what effect being parted from her child was having, for Clara never spoke of Ruth or of leaving her behind with her parents in Germany. The pair were permanently out of kilter so that when they did meet it felt to Paula as if they were attempting to draw her into their emotional maelstrom. She tried not to take too much notice.

*

The following afternoon she was getting ready for class, pinning up her hair, and straightening her crumpled dress after dozing in the little wicker chair by the stove, when there was a knock at her door. It must be the concierge with the post. She was expecting a letter from Mutti. But it was Rilke.

'You?'

'Yes, it's me,' he said hunched inside his coat. 'Can I come in? I've brought you the monograph on the Worpswede artists I've been working on. It's finally been published.'

Paula was so surprised she couldn't speak. Did Clara know he was here? He handed her the brown-paper package, which she put unopened on the table. Then, without being asked he took off his heavy overcoat and hung it on the back of the door and settled himself in the wicker chair where she'd only recently been sleeping. She made tea and brought it to him in her best pale blue cup and saucer, then sat down on the stool opposite him and waited. His mouth was downturned under his boyish moustache, his eyes as intense as ever.

He gave no explanation for his visit other than the delivery of the monograph, but showed no signs of leaving. He didn't once enquire if she should be elsewhere or if she had other duties to attend, but talked, as he'd not done since the first time he'd visited her Worpswede studio, about the loss of Lou and his inability to write anything significant, and of his life with Clara and Ruth. As the afternoon wore on and the shadows lengthened, she realised she'd missed her class.

'Paula, you're my friend. I've come to you to unburden myself. You know,' he continued, 'I believe that intimacy between two people is impossible. No one can help anyone else live their life.

In the end, we're alone. Love is difficult, so fleeting and transient. Relationships aren't static. They change from minute to minute. No one expects a *single* person to be particularly happy, but if you marry everyone expects happiness to be automatic. But the truth that no one admits is that the physical side of marriage causes so much heartache. Why should sex be so difficult? It's not really different to any other physical pleasure—to watching a sunset or enjoying a glass of good brandy. We are so controlled by convention and guilt. Making love is like writing well. And marriage, well, Paula, marriage doesn't always offer that possibility.'

There was no comfort in his words and nothing she could say. Yet his confession unsettled her. For wasn't it also true for her. A fact that she'd not wanted to acknowledge, had tried to push away with work and the dutiful running of her new household. They sat in silence as the afternoon light drained and his expression turned from mockery to despair, and then entreaty. What was he trying to tell her? What was he asking? Why had he never spoken like this before? Why now, when it was too late? It was getting dark and she should light the lamp.

Then he got up, walked over and lifted her hand from the pool of her skirt, pulling her towards him. There, in her little room, in the fading light of early evening, his mouth was on hers, covering her throat, her ears and hair with hungry kisses.

'No,' she said, pulling away, he must not. Really he must not. But before she could say any more, he'd pulled the pins from her hair, so it fell in a copper cascade about her shoulders.

*

In the pigeon-coloured light of morning she reached to touch his pale face with the back of her hand. His eyes, reflected in hers, were so blue that she thought she would drown. How hungry, hard and light her body felt, as he ran his fingers down her spine. She took his hand, kissing the veins on the inside of his wrist.

'What are you doing?'

'Looking at your hands. I like your hands, they're like a girl's,' she whispered, interlacing her fingers with his; then laying her head on his stomach. 'Look how strong mine are in comparison. You'd never make a painter.' He was too thin. He'd not been eating and she could feel his ribs. She leant and kissed his navel, following the wispy line of hair along his white body with her tongue till it became a dark thicket. Then, removing her chemise, she climbed above him, fitting him inside her like a root, while he held her to his chest, rocking her backwards and forwards, grabbing her hair and pulling back her head until she felt herself tremble, as something in him broke against something inside of her.

When he left, climbing out of her bed without a word, without a goodbye, she sat still in the dawn light, her nerves frayed, her whole body alive. As she rose to wash herself a sticky trickle ran down her thighs. After her ablutions she pinned up her hair, put on her bathrobe and went to her desk where she got out a sheet of blue-grey writing paper, dipped her pen in the inkwell, and wrote to Otto.

'I'm coming home. Yesterday evening I suddenly knew that I had to come back to all of you and Worpswede. Dearest, Saturday evening, maybe even Friday, I'll be with you. I must see to it

223

that I leave Wednesday or Thursday evening. I'll stay a night in Münster and then I'll come to you as quickly as I possibly can. I can't stay a minute longer. I have no more need of Paris. I've just written to the Rilkes telling them of my sudden decision. A thousand kisses to you, my old red fox, and to Elsbeth. Has my little girl grown? More kisses when we see each other. Just open your arms wide and make sure that we're alone.'

MATHILDE

WHEN MY HALF-BROTHERS and I played hide-and-seek as children, I'd crouch in the linen cupboard among the steps of newly starched sheets or hide behind the big velvet sofa, frightened no one would bother to come and find me. I'd sit there in the dark listening, afraid nobody would notice I was missing, listening to the tick of the grandfather clock in the hall, willing someone to come, as the boys laughed and chased each other in another part of the house.

I never felt I belonged, but as a child I couldn't speak of such things. Who was there to tell? That's why I turned to music. The violin said the things I was unable to. The first time I picked one up I was seven. It was like cradling something living. It talked back to me, understood my moods. It was then I knew that music was capable of expressing every human emotion, from profound grief to joy. How else can one voice these things? Such feelings are too large, too abstract for words. There was that time when I was accompanying Otto to the opening of one of his exhibitions. I can't remember, now, why it was me and not Louise, Elsbeth or one of the boys. It was drizzling; a cold, dark November evening—that I do remember. We'd just stepped from the cab and were about to cross the road when I heard it, there on the corner of the street, the sound of a violin. An old man in a ragged coat, half-obscured by shadows from the street lamp, was busking in a doorway. What he was playing moved me so much I started to cry. I didn't know it then—I can't have been more than seven or eight as I was, I remember, wearing my grey angora beret—but it was a Yiddish folk song. I knew, then, that I wanted to play the violin. The long hours of practice suited me. Unlike other children I didn't want to play with my dolls or toys, but was happy working on arpeggios and scales. Music gave my life a shape. It was always there when I needed it. It never refused to play with me, cheated on me or sulked. If I gave it attention it would give back to me in return. Even at music school I was what, I suppose, others would have called solitary; though I did have my suitors. But mostly I wasn't interested. What could those young boys have given me?

I was happiest making music in small groups, in quartets, playing Schumann or Schubert, where there was a rapport between the players and each of us had to get to know the other's rhythms and silences. I'd watch across my bow, keeping eye contact with the cellist and then nod when we reached the bar where he had to take over the melody. After weeks of practice we knew one another pretty well. Katrina played viola, Hans played first violin, and Frederick played the cello. For most of my time in Munich they became my family. We'd spend afternoons rehearsing, have a beer and smoke cheap cigarettes in one of the dark student beer cellars. Although still in music school we were often invited to play recitals for visiting dignitaries or at the house of a wealthy industrialist where the women with bright red lips, dressed in crêpe de

Chine, fox furs and diamonds, thought we were sweet and romantic. Four fresh-faced young people playing music. They always wanted to know if Katrina and I were sweethearts with Frederick and Hans. I wonder what they'd have thought if they'd known that Frederick and Hans were in love with each other.

I miss them. Katrina ended up marrying a Swiss industrial magnate, who'd followed her around, coming to all our concerts for months and sending her flowers after each performance. Now she lives in Lucerne and has a child. A little boy. Fred and Hans moved to Amsterdam and started a quartet. So that leaves me. Mostly I play with small chamber groups, so I was exceptionally lucky to have the chance to play in those three concerts with the Berlin Philharmonic. It was a challenge to be part of such a famous orchestra, especially as there are no permanent women players. But it came at just the right moment, for all that previous summer I'd been attempting to give Karl the slip. He was always trying to get me into bed, but I wouldn't give in. At first it was funny, a game really, but then it began to annoy me. It's not that I'm a prude, not even that he wasn't good looking—he was tall and blond and well built—but he meant nothing to me. He was a nice boy. But he could never have given me what I wanted.

And then I met you.

There was a moment, a day or two at the most after you'd gone, when I considered giving up. I didn't think I could cope with the disapproval, the shocked looks and gossip, let alone the responsibility of an illegitimate child. At first the idea of being pregnant seemed completely abstract, an idea, rather than a fact. It didn't seem to have anything to do with me, with having a real baby. I thought constantly about ending things, but didn't know how or where. If I'd done it in my room, the girl downstairs would have been bound to come up to borrow some sugar or a bar of soap, as she does; really for a chat and a chance to gossip about the other people in the building. But I couldn't be certain she wouldn't find me. No, the fuss would've been unbearable and I couldn't think of anywhere else. The park, the library? That was impossible. Anyway I didn't have enough pills and I'm too squeamish to cut my wrists. There was the station, I suppose. I thought of Anna Karenina, but all I did was go there and spend the day watching the trains come and go until I got so cold I went home.

For a little while I imagined ending it in a hotel room. After all that's what people do in novels, isn't it? The anonymity appealed. It would have been comparatively easy. But then that evening I went to bed and when I woke the next morning somehow the moment had passed. What I realised is that I have a choice. That's what you don't have. For you and other Jews I know the choices are running out. God only knows what the future holds. But how could I take my life when so many others around me are threatened. So I came here. I'm not really sure why. Maybe looking for my mother is just an excuse. A reason to choose here as opposed to somewhere else. What I needed was to do *something*. This morning I walked round the village, out along one of the footpaths that leads over a humpbacked bridge onto the moors and stood watching the peat cutters piling up turf in the rain. It was then I understood that's what I have to do. Put everything back together bit by bit, like a pyramid of turf bricks. The only contradiction I can offer to these horrible times is to live as well as I can.

PAULA

WHEN PAULA CLIMBED from the wagon that had driven her home from the station Elsbeth and Otto were waiting for her in the garden. How clean and homely everything was after the dirt and stink of Paris—the fresh white counterpane on the bed, the mopped floors and the sparkling dishes on the kitchen dresser. That night Otto was tender. He said he missed her busy presence around the house, the smell of her soap after her bath, even her criticism. She was the only person whose artistic opinion he now valued. He knew, in general, she had a high regard for his paintings, but that sometimes she felt they lacked the pithiness that came from a close observation of nature. Hadn't he told himself that a thousand times while she'd been away? But he always made the same mistake, falling foul of his temptation to embellish. He could see it the minute she pointed it out, but he needed her eye. How right she'd been when she'd said art was like love; that the more you gave, the more you received.

She was getting close to the people of Worpswede again. The previous morning she'd sat in the warm April sun with Frau Schmidt near the canal, as the old woman told her how, one by one, she'd lost all five of her children and how the previous winter her three pigs had died, leaving her with nothing.

Then, taking Paula's hand, she led her to a cherry tree thick with white blossom.

'That's for my daughter, Frau Modersohn. I planted it for her. She was eight when she was taken from me.'

Paula wanted them to take a holiday in Friesland, to put as much distance between herself and Paris as possible. The sea air would do them all good. They'd go as a family, stay in a little inn on the coast and take trips to the Frisian villages where, on Sundays, they could paint the locals dressed in quaint silver headdresses and distinctive black-and-blue-striped skirts.

They sat on the wide empty beaches and drew the gulls and guillemots on the mudflats. While Otto remained in his deckchair sketching, Paula and Elsbeth explored the sandbar, collecting shells and examining spiral worm casts in the wet sand that squelched between their toes. But mostly it rained or was overcast and miserably cold. Fit only for the dogs that yapped and ran in circles across the flat beach. Yet even on stormy days Paula insisted on bathing. Plunging into the grey surf as Elsbeth, her dress tucked into her bloomers, and Otto in his rolled trousers, stood shivering on the shore, watching as she ran into the battering waves, washing away all memories of Paris.

Then the weather turned and they became as pink as lobsters. Otto got sunstroke and groaned and moaned all night that he was dying. When he recovered Paula bought him a bathing costume to encourage him to swim.

'Otto, don't be such a baby! It's not cold once you get in. You have to get it up past your knees. Come on. The salt's good for your health. Look how skinny you are. It'll put some meat on you and then you'll be as well padded and strong as me!' she joked, splashing him as the waves lapped round his white calves.

Then it was Elsbeth's turn to get ill. She woke in the night crying with a fever, her small face on fire, complaining of earache. In the morning she was covered in spots. Paula had no idea what to do and Otto was ineffectual, flapping around and getting in the way. But Mutti would know what to do with the measles. She'd nursed six children through a variety of illnesses. The next morning they packed up and headed for Bremen.

For several days Paula sat with Elsbeth, wringing out flannels and pressing cold compresses on her heated brow, as she screamed with earache. She would have no one other than Mutti Paula, not even Grandmamma Becker. Paula sang to her and read the fairy tales that she'd loved as a child, feeling a fierce protective love for the little girl. She knew how devastating these childhood illnesses could be. Sitting by Elsbeth brought back painful memories of Hans lying in the upstairs bedroom in quarantine, away from her and her brothers and sisters, with scarlet fever. How could she ever have considered not coming back?

After Kurt put carbolic drops in her ear the infection abated and soon Elsbeth was sitting up in bed, playing with the silk offcuts Mutti had found left over from the patchwork she was making. But just as the little girl was getting better, Kurt developed severe lumbago. Ever since he'd been a child he had suffered from rheumatic conditions. Now in pain and sleeping badly, he decided to go to Worpswede for the fresh air. Otto had already gone back to his studio, leaving Elsbeth in Paula's capable hands.

Otto had no doubt that Paula had more intellectual interests and a more spirited mind than anyone else he knew. She painted, read, played the piano and ran the household with great efficiency. The time spent in Berlin on her cookery course had not been wasted; she'd turned out to be a competent little cook. And it pleased him to see how well she and Elsbeth bonded. But he couldn't help feeling her heart was elsewhere; that her family was not the centre of her thoughts. Maybe things would improve, but she was very headstrong. When he'd last visited her studio he'd been shocked. He wondered if she did it just to be controversial. Perhaps it was a character flaw, this wish to be unconventional. Her paintings had become increasingly angular; often, quite frankly, plain ugly. That was the only word he could use. Her colours were certainly strong. But the form: hands like spoons, noses like corncobs, mouths like wounds and the faces, well, the faces were like the potato leers of cretins. Everything was exaggerated. Why did she have to cram two heads and four hands into such a small space? Hadn't she painted enough village children? It was as if she was being lured into the gutter simply to be fashionable.

Still there was no telling her. She wouldn't listen.

It had been freezing for days. Surely they'd be able to go skating soon. Paula loved skating almost as much as painting; speeding across the ice chased by the village lads with the wind in her hair. She needed to get out, needed exercise or she'd start to brood and think too much. She had so much energy she felt as if she would burst. But it was still too cold and grey, so she was sitting by the stove sharing a baked apple with Elsbeth who had come to the studio to do some potato cuts and stencils. The little girl got bored in the house with old Bertha and Otto had been unnecessarily short with her, complaining that she made too much noise when he was reading. Paula was endlessly pouring oil on troubled waters. Also he didn't like Elsbeth playing with the village children, but what was the child supposed to do? Paula thought of her own childhood. How lucky she had been. There had always been noise and someone to play with: dominoes with Günther, duets with Milly. In the summer they'd make camps in the garden, deep inside the rhododendron bush. She missed her brothers and sisters and wished Henner would write. No one had heard from him since he'd set sail three months ago on his merchant navy ship bound for Australia. She hated it when her family was out of touch. And now Otto complained she spent too much time in the studio or with Milly or Herma when they came to stay. And, if she was late for lunch, or painted through teatime, he sulked.

'Why's it so odd for a man to want his wife around, to know what she's up to? You're constantly disappearing. I never know where you are or whether you'll bother to show up for lunch or tea.'

He had been suffering from palpitations for weeks. He could have a heart attack at any moment while she was off somewhere and who would know? And did she really have to go skating with the village boys? She was a married woman, not a child. Look at the state of her clothes, she was soaking. And no, he didn't find it particularly funny that the ice had cracked and they'd all got drenched. She could have drowned. And what would have become of him and Elsbeth then?

She tried to calm and reassure, but there was something so dour and washed out about him. She bought birch tonic for his thinning hair, gave him a haircut and trimmed his beard. She brewed nettle tea for his digestion and made milk junkets because he was convinced that he was getting an ulcer and couldn't eat veal or pork. He always worried about his health and that his work wasn't going well. He'd leave the house, hunched inside his brown overcoat, flapping through the wind like a large heron, and go to his studio where he'd pace and get in a state. Over the last days he'd started to do small sketches. Paula was surprised how directly these revealed his feelings. He'd painted one after the other in a frenzy and had separated them into groups and was framing them. They were among the most immediate things he'd produced. Hardly anyone else had seen them except Heinrich and he thought they were rubbish.

She'd had a bad cold for weeks and painted little, but spent her time reading the letters of George Sand. What a life she'd had and how many great men had been her lovers. Paula couldn't judge her art, but she felt annoyed when Otto suggested that a little feminine restraint wouldn't have gone amiss.

For the last few weeks she'd been helping him choose works for a variety of up-and-coming exhibitions. Now his studio was practically empty. The paintings he'd produced had lifted his spirits, as had her help and undivided attention. He was less irritated by Elsbeth, and suggested they all take a short trip to Kassel to see the Rembrandts. For Elsbeth it was an excuse to experiment with new hairdos and make a list of things she wanted to persuade her papa to buy.

*

The larks were singing as Paula walked up over the hill and felt a heady sense of freedom. Otto was visiting his parents in Münster—it was his father's birthday—and she was able to do what she liked. Elsbeth's cough was better and, after an indulgent lunch of cold rice pudding, sliced apples and raisins, Paula left her with Bertha to play with her dolls. The laundry was snapping on the line and she had no more obligations. When she reached the top of the hill she flung herself on the grass and lay looking up at the wispy clouds chasing across the wide blue sky. She hadn't felt this carefree for a long time. Before making her way back down she dug up some anemones to plant outside her studio.

That evening she painted for nearly six hours at a stretch until the light faded. She was working on a still life of a pottery jug set among lemons when she thought of Papi's letter to her as a child, when she'd been staying in England. To her delight he had written to congratulate her on the beautifully proportioned fruit in the watercolours she had sent him, saying they were so real he wanted to eat them. But he obviously hadn't had a clue whether they were oranges or lemons! Dear Papi, he'd said he was proud of her. She hoped that was true. All she had ever wanted was his approval. To show him that she wasn't just a spoilt girl following her whims, but a serious artist. She could never rid herself of the image of him at his desk, his mouth dropped open, staring at nothing. Could never forget that moment when she'd reached for his hand, how cold and heavy it had felt against her warm cheek.

She was struggling, now, trying to break new ground. This time alone gave her the chance to focus. It was as though there was an invisible line she had to force herself to cross. On one side there were the society paintings at the Bremen Kunsthalle and, on the other, she couldn't be sure; something raw and dangerous. She felt fearful of crossing into this unknown territory, but longed to find out what lay on the other side; just as one day she'd find out what lay on the other side of death.

When she put down her brush it was already dark and she decided to sleep in the studio. The cockerel and the cow lowing in the shed woke her early. She didn't get up immediately as she did at home, but lay watching the branches dance outside her window. Once up and dressed she boiled two eggs on her little oil stove, just as she'd done before marrying, and sat in a patch of sun with the windows flung wide open, watching a robin eat the crumbs she'd put out on the sill. Later she walked down to the canal and sat sketching for an hour, enjoying the fine weather. In the distance she could hear two farm dogs barking. She was content. When Otto was away she valued him more. Things fell into perspective so that she looked forward to seeing him again. He gave her life ballast. But when he wasn't around she could do things he would never countenance. Eat what and when she wanted, picnic in her studio with Elsbeth. Her little daughter—that's how she thought of Elsbeth now—had become her accomplice. 'Mutti Paula,' she whispered, lifting Paula's hair and putting her mouth close to her ear, 'I promise I won't tell Papa that we had jam sandwiches again for lunch, sitting on your studio floor.'

Herma came to stay and she and Elsbeth practised country dancing with Martha in the white studio of the Barkenhoff, while Heinrich played the fiddle. Paula tried to teach them the

Gay Gordons, which she'd learnt as a child in England. But as they pranced up and down, their arms in a tangle, they fell over and ended in a giggling heap. Otto once owned a flute, but had pawned it for some much needed cash. When he came home she pleaded with him to redeem it and play for them, but he grumbled that he had better things to do.

Mutti was anxious about letting Herma go to study French and take up a post as an au pair in Paris and had sent her to Worpswede so that Paula could give her younger sister some tips. Paula hoped that Paris wouldn't be too tough for her. Now Papi was gone there was even less money and Herma would have to make her own way. Paula made lists of inexpensive lodgings, museums to visit, bistros and shops where food was cheap but fresh. She told her the best places to buy coal and the name of the baker where the bread was always several centimes cheaper than elsewhere and they didn't give you yesterday's loaf just because you weren't French. She also presented Herma with the little fur jacket she'd worn on her first visit as a going-away present. She felt responsible and hoped her host family would be good and that, with the right guidance, her spirited sister would blossom in Paris just as she'd done. She would like to visit, to show her all the sites and introduce her to the places that she'd discovered; the Sacré Coeur, the Jardin du Luxembourg. But it would be difficult to broach the subject with Otto. The very word Paris made him tetchy. No, he was not happy that she wanted to go back yet again. He had been reasonable the last time. How many other husbands would let their wives go off gallivanting to foreign cities whenever they felt like it?

But she longed for the place. It had entered her blood. Like the migrating birds that gathered on the barn roofs in autumn, she felt compelled to go back. It had been a bad time for her work. She'd hardly done anything and spent far too much time helping Otto, who had just shown nine paintings in Bremen to a lukewarm reception. She needed new stimulation. Fresh sights and sounds. She needed to look at great art and was hungry for Paris. In her mind she was already back there in her little attic room, her days measured out by small household chores and trips to the market, her life classes and visits to the Louvre. She was still too young to commit herself to the stifling domesticity of Worpswede. Paris was her city and it was calling her back.

This, she realised, was just the way her marriage had to be. She'd happily give in to Otto over a hundred little things—that wasn't hard—but over the issues closest to her heart she could never acquiesce, even if she had wanted. Otto was her husband and she loved him, but she couldn't deny what she'd fought to become. To paint wasn't a choice. It defined her; it was how she made sense of the world. When she painted it was as if she was trying to retrieve the memory of something she'd once known and lost. It was like entering a cathedral where she had to stand still and listen until her eyes became accustomed to the darkness and her ears began to hear what flowed from the silence. She thought of Caspar David Friedrich's paintings: his tiny figures perched on a precipice looking out into the landscape surrounded by lonely pines and towering mountains. Surely that's what Rilke meant when he talked of solitude. That only when solitude felt palpable was it possible to create anything original.

No, she hadn't meant to think of Rilke; to feel the disquiet that his name conjured. Only that morning she had picked up the paper to read that he was back in the country.

For the journey she wore her new velvet jacket and the jaunty grey riding hat Otto hated. As she waved goodbye, Elsbeth, Otto and her mother, who'd come to take over the running of the house while she was away, made a forlorn little group on the platform. Otto hardly bothered to conceal his annoyance that she was leaving again. But as she stepped into the carriage and leant out of the window to wave goodbye her thoughts were already running ahead to the Gare du Nord where the huge steam engines would be belching smoke into the vaulted glass roof as they arrived from Brussels, Dieppe and Calais. As she travelled through Belgium, with its flat potato fields, she watched the grimy, despondent little villages disappear one by one with a now reassuring familiarity. Soon she'd be back in Paris and Herma had promised to meet her at the ticket barrier.

The family, for whom her sister was an au pair, was cultivated and well to do. Herma was allowed a lot of freedom to take her small charges, two little girls, walking every afternoon. That meant she and Paula could see a good deal of one another. Her employers had also generously given her time off to meet the train and help Paula settle into her lodgings.

And how very French her little sister looked with her hair done up in a chignon. She was so grown-up Paula hardly recognised her as she hurried forwards, flinging her arms round Paula's neck. Together they managed to haul the trunk into the street and hail a hansom cab to take them to the rue Cassette, but Paula was distressed to find that her usual pretty room, with its view over the garden, was occupied. Instead, she was to be given a cramped, uncomfortable one at the back of the hotel that smelt of mildew and overlooked a noisy courtyard. It would be like living in a box and would mean she'd have to waste time searching for other lodgings. The noise and bustle in the street below got on her nerves, but she knew from previous trips that her low mood would pass once she was properly settled.

Each time she came back to Paris the transition between her roles as a housewife and, in effect, Elsbeth's mother, and city life as a single woman and an artist, was difficult. She loved Elsbeth, and although she couldn't imagine a future without a child, she wouldn't willingly have chosen the responsibility yet.

The next day was Sunday, so to raise her spirits she took a trip with Herma into the country and had lunch sitting in a meadow in the warm spring sun. Walking for miles down country lanes they passed farmsteads and haystacks and, on their return, that evening, made tea in her room, eating bread and butter with the apricot preserve they'd bought at a farm gate. The freshly picked pussy willow stood in a jar on the mantel.

As the museums didn't open until ten, rather than waste the mornings hanging around, she enrolled at the Académie Julian for a month's session of life drawing. It seemed that the Académie Cola Rossi had closed. She couldn't say she was surprised. She'd always thought Cola Rossi a bit of a crook and a charlatan with his exaggerated airs and graces. At Julian's she could start painting from the nude straight away. It was fun being in a class with other girls again. One of them, who was

Polish, had short cropped hair and dressed like a man. The French tended to be rather sloppy, although somehow they still managed to look chic. Julian also ran another academy on the other bank of the Seine, which cost twice as much. There you could see the marquises in their silk dresses climbing from their horse-drawn carriages, attended by their chaperons.

There were far more English women here than at Cola Rossi's, but how loud they were with their braying, haughty voices. Her Aunt Marie had always sung the praises of the English, but a young governess Herma knew had confided that, although they might seem very correct in public, they all had whiskey bottles hidden in their bedrooms and that she'd been propositioned by her employer's husband. As a result, she'd had great difficulty getting a reference and another job.

Paula loved her new room. It cost forty-five francs a month and was just what she needed. It was clean, bright and on the sixth floor of the rue Madame, with a lovely view over the rooftops. There was a four-poster bed, a wardrobe, a table and two wicker chairs in front of the fireplace, and big French windows that led onto a little balcony where she and Herma could take coffee and feed the sparrows. On her first evening she fried a mutton chop and some potatoes, then organised her pots and pans and other bits on the deal shelves. The day after tomorrow would be Otto's birthday and she was sending him a little Japanese book of prints. Remembering his hangdog expression as she'd boarded the train, she wished she could buy him something more extravagant to show that she hadn't forgotten him, but she didn't have the money. Maybe, one day, when she was famous she'd be able to do such things, but for now she sent him her love and suggested that Mutti make his favourite punch. They would find some pineapple essence in the wine cupboard in the dining room.

Also he'd be amused to hear that the little grey hat he hated had been a terrible flop. Everyone had stared at her. Even the coachmen had shouted out rude remarks and, one lunchtime, a group of shop girls and apprentices standing on a corner had sniggered as she walked past. Then, on the omnibus, she'd heard the conductor whisper that she was probably an anarchist. She'd been so mortified that she'd hidden in the back of the bus till the Bon Marché, where she got off and bought a hat that Paris would find more acceptable.

That should cheer him up. To know that he had better taste than her in hats!

But how ambivalent she felt about the French. They could be so good-hearted, but also infuriating. Only that morning, rushing to class, she'd dropped her paintbox and the tubes had rolled all over the pavement in the snow and slush. Suddenly an old woman appeared, scrabbling in the wet to help her pick them up. Yet when she got to her class the French girls did nothing but giggle. And the way they painted: as though they'd never looked at anything since Courbet; and she doubted whether they knew much about him. It was all so derivative. They were only interested in who'd won this year's Prix de Rome and gossiping about the best-looking man in class.

She found some canvas in the little art suppliers round the corner. She liked its coarse weave and had been working hard all morning. She was pleased with the results, but when she returned after her mid-morning cup of hot chocolate, she was disconcerted to find half a dozen girls standing around her easel sniggering: 'But look at the way she's painted the hands; they look like bananas.'

'Mademoiselle Paula, I hope you don't mind me asking,' a Russian girl in an old-fashioned blue dress enquired, 'but do you really see things like that? If so, who on earth was your teacher?'

'My husband,' Paula answered curtly, hoping that would put an end to the matter.

'Ah, I see,' nodded the Russian girl, as if that explained everything. 'You paint like your husband. Now I understand.'

How stupid they were that they couldn't imagine the possibility that she might simply paint like herself.

It was February, and in an attempt to stay warm she'd drop into the Louvre and stand with her skirts spread over the warm air gratings. When her legs and toes had thawed, she filled her sketchbook with pages of quick drawings. But on this trip she was less attracted by the old masters and more by the contemporaries she discovered. She visited Vuillard and Denis in their studios. Bonnard was in Berlin, but she'd already seen a couple of his works and hadn't liked them. There was something too dreamy about them. As for the Fauves, she wasn't sure whether they were mad or breaking new ground. She'd have to keep looking to understand what they were up to. But it was Gauguin who inspired. The solid, monumentality of his figures, as if moulded from the earth of Brittany and the tropical paradise to which he had disappeared.

She saw Herma whenever she was free from her duties. Together they went to the *Magic Flute* and Victor Hugo's *Hernani* at the Comédie-Française, as well as to a vaudeville act where, despite the children in the audience, the performances were a bit risqué. Paula worried that things might turn a bit blue in front of her young sister when the men came onto the stage in their underpants and the women in virtually nothing at all, but that was Paris and Herma would just have to get used to its bawdy side.

The following Saturday, as they walked down the Champs-Élysées, people were bombarding each other with confetti in a foretaste of the forthcoming Easter celebrations. One young man even emptied a whole bag over their heads so the paper shapes fluttered onto their hats like coloured snowflakes. As they ran up the avenue trying to catch the floating hearts and horseshoes they bumped into Cottet walking in the other direction. He raised his hat the way people do when they can't quite place someone, but think they know them. On her return that evening, there was a letter from Otto asking if she knew anything about the butcher's bill. It seemed very high. No, she wrote back, she knew nothing about it. She had always forbidden Bertha to buy anything on credit. There must be a mistake.

That week she paid a visit to the Bojerses, a Norwegian couple, who were friends of Rilke's. He had given them her address and they'd sent an invitation to call. Frau Bojers, who was expecting their third child at any moment, came to the door to welcome Paula with her naked two-year-old balanced on her hip, as if it was the most natural thing in the world to greet guests this way. The husband, a huge man with shaggy hair and a deep ringing baritone, asked straight out if Paula, like Rilke, was a vegetarian. 'Well thank heavens for that,' he bellowed amiably. Rilke's meatless diet got on his nerves. Paula was entranced by the way the two little boys, with their white blond hair, joined them at the table so that the meal was a family affair. After they'd eaten they played a riotous game of blind man's bluff, the small boys laughing and bumping into the furniture. When she went to put on her hat to go home the Bojerses insisted that next time she should bring Herma. They arranged to meet the following Thursday.

As she sat at her little table and reread Otto's postcard, she couldn't believe it. That his mother had been poorly all winter, she knew, but that she should have suddenly passed away over the weekend no one could have expected. Otto had rushed to her bedside, but had been too late. The funeral would be held in a couple of days. There was, he wrote, no point in her interrupting her stay to return for the service. After all she hadn't known his mother that well and, anyway, she would never make it back in time. Did he mean it? Or did she detect a tone of hurt martyrdom that she hadn't been with him? Only two days earlier she had received a letter saying that he and the Vogelers were considering a trip to Paris. Heinrich had thought it would be fun, but Otto had been less sure. He was in the middle of three new paintings. Now, it would be quite impossible.

That this had happened again felt like more than fate. She was overcome with guilt. The first time she'd come to Paris and persuaded Otto to visit, Hélène had died. Now his mother's death would remind him of that; take him back to those painful months and heighten the sense that she had deserted him in his moment of need. She wrote at once.

'If you think you'll be lonely without me you must tell me and I will come home immediately. I want to support you, but I've seen so many wonderful things and it's so rewarding that I really want to ask you not to give up your idea of coming here. Dear Otto, if you're not in the mood to come with the Vogelers, then come on your own. There's so much to see that I'm sure it will lift your spirits. I've thought about you a good deal today. Doesn't it strike you as odd that the two of us, who've been so very close, now have such different lives? There you are with your father in Münster, sad and grieving, while I'm in this great city, in spite of everything, full of hope. While your mother was being buried I climbed the hill up to Montmartre and stood near the Sacré Coeur looking out over Paris, watching the bustle of life below, very aware of the contrast in our situations. I tried to imagine you after the funeral, sitting quietly with your father beneath the large grandfather clock in the corner of the grey-painted morning room opposite your mother's empty chair. My dear, do write soon and tell me what you want me to do. Tell me whether I should come home to be with you or if you'll come to Paris.'

Spring was turning everything green. It was nearly three o'clock. Paula and Herma were waiting in the Jardin du Luxembourg for the two young Bulgarians they'd met at the Easter Parade. As they walked along the gravel paths they chatted in German, while the two young men spoke Bulgarian. When they wanted to communicate they did so in mangled French. Herma's beau, they decided, would be the law student, while Paula was to have the sculptor, who was studying at the École des Beaux-Arts. With his thick black hair and swarthy skin set off by a rough corduroy suit and knotted red handkerchief loosely tied round his neck, he was rakishly handsome. They went to the Louvre. Then, the following Saturday, to the Bullier, the dance hall in the Latin Quarter. It hadn't changed since the last time she'd been there. It was just as run-down, with the usual racy crowd of students, artists and hangers-on. They danced waltzes, jigs and polkas until they were breathless. The following week they went to the Folies Bergère where she was amazed by the dancers. She would never be able to get her leg up that high however hard she practised. There was one Spanish girl with a figure like Manet's *Lola de Valence*, and a little *chanteuse* who sang a risqué song about her navel. It was probably lucky that their French wasn't good enough to understand the *double entendres*. The young Bulgarians ordered champagne. Then, when the theatre closed they escorted them back, arm in arm, to Paula's lodgings. Because it was well past midnight Herma camped under a blanket in the wicker chair by the stove, creeping out at dawn to get back to her young charges. Paula couldn't remember when she'd last had so much fun.

They didn't even know the two Bulgarians' names; they simply addressed each other as 'monsieur' and 'mademoiselle'. When they next met in a little bar they attempted to introduce each other in halting French, trying out German and English, before writing their names on scraps of paper. Paula and Herma even dropped hints on etiquette, explaining that it was not done to eat garlic before they met or spit on the floor, but neither cared because their Bulgarians were so good-looking.

Paula was working hard. Every morning she got up early and flung open her windows to take an air bath. Standing naked in front of the mirror of her rosewood *armoire*, she checked to see if she'd put on weight eating so much French bread, before doing her stretching exercises. She wanted to be in good shape when Otto arrived. Yesterday a letter confirmed that he would be coming after all. She wasn't sure if that meant with Overbeck and the Vogelers, or alone. Perhaps Kurt might join them to celebrate his new medical qualifications. She would meet him in ten days at the Gare du Nord off the six o'clock train. He must, she wrote, make sure that his hair had been properly cut so he'd look handsome for her. If he did it now it would have a chance to grow back a little. And he should ask Mutti to go over his blue suit for stains. His favourite grey one would be too warm for the weather. She wanted him to look his best. She promised that in turn, she'd look as pretty as she could for him.

This was Paris. It was spring, and she needed someone to kiss.

When Otto arrived he was accompanied by Milly, Heinrich and Martha, who all stayed in Paula's hotel in the rue Madame. They went to see the Gauguins at Fayet's, and a performance of Buffalo Bill in a large tent where he was taming unbroken Arab stallions. As the horses thundered round the ring one escaped causing a commotion in the audience but with a single swing of his lasso, the cowboy caught it to thunderous applause. Still, the sun didn't shine and the weather stayed overcast. It was cold and Otto was miserable. He was critical of Paris and of French art, which he thought pretentious. He loathed the noise, the dirt and the crowds, even the food, which he was convinced was giving him an ulcer. He hated the boulevard Saint-Michel and, in particular, he hated the young Bulgarians. He decided that Paula was happier in Paris and didn't want to come home. He couldn't enter into the festive mood and was low and depressed about his mother's death.

What was he doing here? He should be at home quietly mourning and in the studio getting on with his work. He dragged round after the others; his shoulders hunched, hardly uttering a word as they climbed the Eiffel Tower and then caught a boat down the Seine. Every conversation with Paula ended in a misunderstanding and, instead of the kisses and caresses that she'd dreamt of, he slept on the far side of the bed in his heavy nightshirt, which made his legs look like white willow twigs. And she didn't like the way he'd cut his hair. It didn't make him look handsome.

The day after she got back she walked down to the village in the April sun to visit the children who had posed for her before she'd left. In each house there appeared to be a new arrival, another little Hans or Meta. Awkward and tongue-tied, they stood in dirty aprons and boots, picking their noses or twisting lank hair round their fingers, until she bought out a paper bag of gingerbread and they lost their reserve. Where's Paris, Frau Modersohn, is it far from Bremen? Do they speak German there? After they had eaten every crumb they all went to the brickyard to pick coltsfoot and sat on a mound of turf weaving it into coronets, which they placed on their lousy little heads.

But the spell of good weather didn't last. An east wind blew across the moors battering at the windows like a drunkard, followed by icy flurries of hail and sleet. And to think that in Paris the lilacs would be out and people sitting in Montmartre were drinking absinthe in the sun. So much had changed since her return. Mackensen had bought a white horse, which he rode imperiously round the village, and the Overbecks had moved to a new house some distance away and were cutting their ties with the community. Paula discovered that Lina, the kitchen girl, had charged unsanctioned and unnecessary items to various merchants' accounts, which explained the high butcher's bill, so they were forced to dock her wages. To her delight, the Brünjeses had whitewashed her studio and put a garden bench outside her window. But she missed Herma and the intimacy of those two months she'd spent in Paris with her younger sister. They were turning out to be much alike. Someday she was sure they would spend more time there together. Meanwhile, she was sitting at her little bureau writing to ask Herma to send her the catalogue of the Salon exhibition. Had she been to see it yet? If so, what did she think? Paula wanted to know who was in it and what the work was like. Would Herma also look out for the following articles and send them to her as soon as possible:

1. *Noa-Noa* by Gauguin, Éditions de La Plume
2. *The Biography of Gauguin* by Ch. Morice de France, Oct 1903
3. Study about Gauguin in the *Revue encyclopédique*, Feb. 1, 1904
4. *L'Occident* 1903, Nos 16,17, 18—Article by Signac

Also could she enquire about prices and availability? It was impossible to get such publications in Worpswede.

Elsbeth started at the village school. The first morning they were up early. She was very serious as Paula tied her hair in plaits and got her ready in her newly starched pinafore. As Paula left her at the schoolhouse door and watched her race in with the other children, she felt a lump in her throat and realised how much she'd come to love the child. While she worked in the studio she listened for her footsteps coming up the path so that they could walk home together for lunch. That afternoon Elsbeth was full of school: how she could now subtract 10 from 40 and tell the story of the Creation. Did Paula know that Eve was made from Adam's rib? Could she imagine that?

'Don't you think Adam would have missed his rib, Mutti Paula?'

After a lunch of bread and sausage they went into the garden to feed the rabbit and hoe between the carrots and onions. Elsbeth had the job of pouring salt on the slugs, which fizzed into a glutinous sludge beneath the lettuces.

Slowly Paula was readapting to village life. Otto was more cheerful now she was home. He was making a big effort. He had, he admitted, as they walked along the Hamme and the moths flitted across the towpath, realised that their life together had become monotonous. He knew she'd suffered and felt confined. He'd resisted thinking about it, but she was right. The things that had made their marriage enriching at the beginning—an active social and artistic life—had fallen away and they'd got stuck. However difficult it had been for him when he'd come to Paris, he had been forced to admit how vivacious she naturally was. Their life was in danger of becoming stale. When they'd first been together she had brought a much-needed vitality into his drab existence. There'd been skating parties in the winter, swimming and air baths in the summer, dancing in Vogeler's white room and midnight walks regardless of the weather. That he hadn't painted anything significant during that period was nothing to do with her. So he was determined, he promised, cautiously taking her hand like a young lover fearing rejection, to change.

'Will you help me, Paula, help your boring old fox to keep young and be a little more impulsive? I know I'll benefit, that *we'll* benefit and so will my work. And when we have a little extra cash there's no reason why we can't travel, if you still want to. I want you to be happy. We can start to plan a few trips. Apart from Paris, where else would you like to go?'

At the end of October they took a short trip with Vogeler through Westphalia. They visited the museum in Hagen with its fine collection of Rodins, Gauguins, van Goghs and Renoirs. As usual Paula sketched little holiday scenes on the back of post-cards to send to her family: Otto smoking his pipe and striding in his cape through a Westphalian village for her mother. Her naked, doing morning exercises—which she sent in a sealed envelope—for Herma.

But with their return Worpswede began to close in on itself. The moors changed from green to russet. Peat smoke curled from the huddled cottages and the air became thick with the smell of smouldering peat. Paula was nearly thirty and feeling a new urgency. There was still so much to do. She was running out of time. Time to make something of herself, to become someone significant. Otto had been good-natured lately. On a day-to-day level much had been resolved, the prickly antagonism abated. That he was a kind-hearted, gentle man, even if he did worry about money, his digestion and any change to his routine, was beyond doubt. He'd tried hard over the last few months to accommodate her and was, at times, touchingly thoughtful. Yet she still had longings for the wider world, which were impossible to express while fulfilling the duties and responsibilities of marriage. At times she found Otto's solicitousness even more difficult to endure than his grudging opposition. She felt as if she was being slowly smothered by a feather quilt. She missed Herma and worried that her sister was having a tough time alone in Paris. She wondered if she'd seen their Bulgarians again. All that seemed a long time ago; their trip to the Folies Bergère, dancing at the Bullier until two in the morning.

Paula had heard that Clara Rilke was back in the village, but although she'd paid a short visit to Worpswede in the summer, Paula had seen little of her, except for a dinner at the Vogelers, where the atmosphere had been cordial but formal. It seemed she was alone; that Rilke had left on a trip of indefinite length to study something or other. Paula wrote her a tentative note and the following day there was a knock on her studio door. There was Clara, her dark hair caught up in a severe chignon that emphasised her cheekbones, and the fine web of lines etched around her eyes and mouth that showed the strain of the previous months.

As she settled herself by the stove, just as she'd done so often in the past, Clara told Paula that as Rodin's secretary

Rilke was often away meeting the intelligentsia of Europe. He now had a new friend. An American woman called Ellen Key, she said, her voice tense and barely audible. She also spoke a lot about Rodin, so again, Paula wondered at the extent of his influence. But it was good to have her back. In spite of everything Clara was, of all her friends, the one she cared about the most. Every day after that Clara came to sit for her, bringing her small daughter Ruth, who crawled round on the floor playing with her brushes and tubes of paint. Every half-hour they would break off to give her some bread and milk. When Paula sat her on her lap and sang to her, she dribbled and clapped her hands.

Clara's tilted head filled most of the canvas and the tones of her skin mediated between the dark background and the luminescence of her white dress, which Paula had asked her to wear especially. Hadn't that been what Rilke had called them on that sultry summer evening of 1900 when he'd first arrived in Worpswede? The sisters in white? Paula painted her like a medieval saint, holding a red rose; that symbol of love, which had become so emblematic of Rilke's poetry. Her eyes fixed, not on the viewer, but on the window, as if she knew that the promise life had once offered now lay in the past. The down-turned corners of her mouth were heavy with disappointment. Yet there was a spirit of something strong and wild that Paula loved. A trace of the girl who'd swung on the bell rope of the village church, waking the whole community, which transcended her despondency.

There were subjects Clara found difficult to talk about. She wasn't comfortable discussing Rilke or with Paula's frank confidences about her marriage. So they chatted about day-to-day things and avoided the subject of Rodin and his influence on Clara's recent work. It was Ruth who gave them both a focus, while Elsbeth clucked round her playing the bossy big sister. But Worpswede was going into hibernation. Otto was painting frantically and quite content. Everything was just how he liked it: Paula at home, Elsbeth at school and, with the onset of colder weather, it would mean fewer tourists. He enjoyed nothing better than holing up against the world. For him the rest of life was only a remission from his art. But all sorts of longings were stirring in Paula. She felt unsettled, confined by Otto, Elsbeth and the house. She had come to consider such feelings as the onset of her winter sickness and hoped that if she could just hold on and get through the dark months, then everything would resolve itself with the better weather.

Then one morning, as Clara was taking a break from posing, Paula began to talk of Paris.

'Clara, I've got to go out into the world again. I have to go back to Paris. I feel,' she said, her voice cracking, as she threw piece after piece of turf into the stove, 'as though I'm suffocating.'

Outwardly things ran smoothly. They'd all become Thursday regulars at the bowling alley that had been set up in one of the barns. And, whenever she could, Paula met up with Milly in Bremen. They went to see *Elektra* and Wilde's *Salomé*. Though the lead actress was good, the rest of the cast was stiff and amateurish. She was reading a lot and had just finished Wagner's letters. But she felt little warmth for him. It had been the same when she'd heard *Tristan und Isolde*. Everyone talked of him as the quintessential German, but he wasn't for her. There was something in his approach that grated, something in her that resisted his hypnotising music.

Otto agreed to sit for Clara. Maybe it was the bad weather that made him out of sorts, but when he went to Paula's studio to pick up Elsbeth after school, he felt a familiar surge of irritation. Her work didn't please him as much as it had in the past. She was painting heads and life-sized nudes, which in his opinion she couldn't do. He noticed some sketchbooks lying on her work table. If only she would make proper drawings from those and improve her technique, but she had a stubborn streak and did things her way. Even her natural feeling for colour had become harsh. She had too much regard for the primitive, was constantly talked of uniting colour and form, in that louche, fashionable way he detested. Artistic women were all the same; arrogant and immodest. They would never achieve anything significant because they'd never listen and learn. It was just the same with Clara Rilke, for whom Rodin had become the only point of reference. She blindly copied whatever he did, to the extent that her drawings had become almost indistinguishable from his. Otto found himself increasingly irritable with Clara and wished that he'd never agreed to sit. And now Paula was thick with her again she was becoming just as bad. He'd hoped they'd overcome the difficulties in their marriage, but now he doubted that was the case. Paula would never shift her opinion, never budge. She was obstinate. They were back to their old impasse. It was sad, but her talent would simply go to waste.

*

She was cleaning her brushes after working hard all day on a still life of chestnuts. She'd been attempting to simplify the forms in order to find the intrinsic quality of each object—the flowered dish, the brown nuts and the knife—when the door opened. Paula expected it to be Clara, but it was Rilke.

And how different she looked to him. Older, yet more beautiful as she stood in the twilight, her hair falling messily about her face, her hands and apron smeared with paint. Her movements had lost their girlishness. When she spoke it was softly, deliberately, as if hauling up her words from a great depth. Without waiting to be asked he simply took off his hat and coat and hung them behind the door as he'd done in the past.

Her paintings were startling; personal and strong. They had something of that visceral quality he'd seen in van Gogh. She was painting Worpswede, but not as anyone else painted it. He saw that they were both trying to do the same thing. This was what he'd been struggling to achieve in his poems—a move away from the overblown and the general to the particular. Her bowls, jugs and fruit possessed their own unique character. As he walked round her studio looking at her work in silence, she busied herself cleaning her palette, trying to avoid his gaze.

He gave no clues about his life, about what he was doing or where he'd been, but simply announced that he had come to buy a painting. He'd acquired a little money and dearly wanted to own something by her. He was taken with the one she'd just been working on. He realised that the paint wasn't dry, but no matter. He would pick it up in a few days, before he left. He hoped fifty marks would seem a fair price.

Apart from that little more was said. Then, taking his hat and coat from behind the door, he turned to go.

'It's good to see you being true to yourself Paula, and good,' he said quietly, taking her hand, 'to see you again.'

What a maelstrom his unexpected visit had unleashed in her. But fifty marks. Her own money, earned with her brush. It was the first painting she had ever sold and who better to sell it to than Rilke? Despite everything, they were artistic soul mates and his approval mattered. She knew that, more than any other person, he understood what she was attempting; that he felt it in his gut, this desire to go within, to find a still point from which she could describe and mirror the world. Now, if she economised on the housekeeping—ordered belly of pork instead of loin, got Bertha to make nourishing casseroles with lentils, turnips and carrots from the garden—she might be able to save enough. Paris beckoned and she was determined to go back.

In January they took a New Year trip to visit Carl Hauptmann and his wife. There were dinners, luncheons and concerts. Otto was in his element, debating the nature of art and discussing the state of the world with Carl and his brothers, but Paula found it both exhausting and frustrating. It was always the men who had these interesting conversations, gathered at the dinner table with their port and cigars, while she was banished with the other wives to discuss domestic matters over coffee. After their stay they went tobogganing in the mountains and took a train to Dresden to see the Rembrandts. But what a contrast this social whirl was to the simple, rustic life they led in Worpswede.

As her birthday approached she had the sense that she was finally on the brink of something significant. Her family's greetings were arranged on her bureau and there was even a postcard from Henner, which he'd managed to mail when his ship docked in Jakarta. She was touched that he'd remembered so many months ahead to post it so that it arrived on time. She spent the day quietly with Otto and Elsbeth. Otto gave her a lacquer fountain pen, and Elsbeth a drawing of her in straw sun hat sitting beside Otto smoking his pipe. But that morning, unbeknownst to anyone, she had taken her clothes, her silver hairbrushes and the leather-bound copy of Browning her Aunt Marie had given her during her stay in England, to her room at the Brünjeses. The next day she wrote to Rilke. She'd been so happy that he'd bought the little chestnut painting and that he had liked the one of the young girl in the birch wood. His good opinion meant a great deal. It gave her courage and, at the moment, she needed courage to go back to Paris. Having made the decision, it felt as if a weight had lifted. She was grateful, too, for his enquiries concerning possible exhibitions that might include her work. But she'd no intention of trying for the Salon this year. She wasn't ready. Next year she might attempt the *Independents*. Would she see him before she left? Though perhaps, on balance, it would be better if she didn't, for nothing felt stable at the moment. She had decided to stay in Worpswede until the end of the month. It was Otto's birthday in a few days and she owed him that much at least, and her mother and brother were getting ready to go on a trip to

Rome. She had said nothing to Otto about her decision. Later, when they were apart, would be the time to try and explain her actions. She'd become fatalistic. She wondered if Rilke could do her a little favour and enquire among his colleagues to see if anyone was selling any household bits and pieces. That often happened at the Académie, she knew, as people left and moved on. It was a way of purchasing things at half price. She needed a good desk, an easel, a table and chair; preferably not one that was too ugly. She'd leave it up to him to decide whether to approach his acquaintances. She hoped she wasn't asking too much. She was looking forward to seeing him again soon, either during or after his tour, and to meeting up with Rodin and to a thousand other things that Paris had to offer. She was leaving on Friday night and would arrive on the Saturday. She hoped that he'd write to her c/o 29, rue Cassette.

'And I don't even know, my dear friend, how to sign my name at the end of this letter. I'm not Modersohn, and I'm no longer simply Paula Becker. I'm just me.'

It was a wet Saturday evening in February, as she stood alone on the platform of the Gare du Nord, halfway between her old life and her new one. She was thirty years old, had just left Otto Modersohn, and was waiting for a porter to help her with her bags.

MATHILDE

DEATH ISN'T GRADUAL, as the doctors would have us believe. However fragile the hold on life, one minute you're alive and the next you're not. As a child I devised all sorts of rituals in an attempt to reverse Paula's death. I'd imagine that if I folded my school pinafore in a certain way and put my stockings in the same position on the same chair at the end of my bed, that when I woke in the morning there'd be a knock at the front door and I'd run downstairs and find a woman with auburn hair and nut-brown eyes standing on the doorstep. For some reason she'd be carrying a wicker basket over her arm full of autumn fruit and vegetables, as if she'd just been to the market. She'd smile at me, wipe her feet on the mat and put the basket down on the kitchen table, laying out the turnips, the marrows and yellow pumpkins, as if she'd just popped out and been expected back all along. Then, kissing me on the cheek, she'd ask if I had been waiting long. I never knew what happened after that.

There were times when I made a pact with God begging him to give me back my mother. If I practised my scales and arpeggios for exactly two hours—not a minute less and without a single mistake—would he bring her back? But then, when I got them perfect, I'd convince myself that I hadn't performed them in the right order. So I'd invent more complex systems, then make a mistake and have to start all over again. Sometimes, in the cold music room at the top of the house, I'd see her sitting in the chair by the gas fire. She never spoke or did anything in particular, just sat with her eyes closed, listening to me play.

And now that you've gone, Dan, this, too, feels like a death. Though the grief is accentuated by the cruelty of knowing you're still alive, but out of reach. I wish nothing other than for you to fare well. For you this is not the end. And thank God for that. But for me your loss feels like a death without the excuse to grieve. However much I know that the world is on the brink of war, that I've no money, and that you're married, I still picture getting on a boat to Chicago, looking up your name in a yellow telephone book and picking up the receiver. I imagine you meeting me in a discreet bar where we sit on high stools and drink martini cocktails, while the barman in a dinner jacket and black bow tie polishes glasses and smiles because he knows we're lovers. Then you take me back to a hotel where we undress and make love very slowly. After, in the rose-coloured light, you lie with your chest against my spine, your arms wound round me, stroking my hair the way you always do that makes me feel so loved, so very special.

I've been through it so many times that it's like watching a film. I've imagined everything from the cabin I'd sleep in on the steamer crossing the Atlantic, to the shuffling hoards in the embarkation lounge. I've even planned what I'd wear to meet you: my grey silk blouse and little woollen bolero that you like, and underneath my best cream satin underwear. I've spent hours conjuring every detail. Love is every little thing that we ever do with someone, everything we know about them; the way they brush their teeth and scratch behind their ear or pour the milk into their tea or their tea into their milk. It's when you get caught in the rain together or share an apple strudel from a single plate. Love is the memory of time given and shared.

In my flat in Berlin I still have a pair of your gloves. They're leather, lined with sheepskin. You left them after a snatched visit when you promised Lola you'd be home for dinner with the Swiss ambassador. For nights after I'd said goodbye to you at the station, I slept in them, trying to catch your smell. They're miles too big for me; you have huge hands, which give you that tremendous reach on the fiddle. I must have looked like some sort of grotesque puppet, red-eyed from crying and lack of sleep, lying in bed in my pink nightdress with an outsized pair of gloves dangling from my hands. But I can't get rid of them because I keep thinking that one day you'll come back for them, complaining your hands are cold and that you won't be able to play that evening's concert unless you find them.

I've never spent so much time alone as here in Worpswede. When I'm forced to speak to the landlady or the woman in the shop, I'm surprised by the sound of my own voice. It's as if it belongs to someone else. The last few evenings I've just sat in my room wrapped in a quilt, staring out the window. The nights are very clear and the stars bright. I can see the Plough and the Pole star over the moors but can't identify the other constellations.

In the house opposite, the one where I've seen a woman in a black coat going up the garden path, there's a small boy. He can't be more than eight or nine. There's something wrong with him. He walks with crutches and has a white face like the heel of a clenched fist. But there's something sweet about him. Despite his useless legs, which he drags behind him in his big boots as he hauls himself along, he's always smiling.

PAULA

H ER NEW LIFE was beginning in earnest. This time she
couldn't afford the small luxuries she enjoyed on previous visits to Paris and, after a few days in the rue Cassette, she
moved into a draughty studio on the avenue du Maine. The high
windows were filthy and the glass cracked so that she couldn't
see the sky. Outside there was a courtyard, but she couldn't see
into that either, though sometimes she heard a woman screaming and the drunken voice of a man shouting back. But being
in a conventional rooming house depressed her. She needed
freedom to work. To come and go as she pleased and here, at
least, she could afford the rent more easily. She wrote to Herma
to let her know of her arrival, asking her to visit. But to Paula's
distress Herma seemed shocked by her sudden departure from
Otto and Worpswede.

It was the beginning of Lent and she remembered how this
time last year they'd just met their fun-loving Bulgarians, but
this evening she sat huddled in front of her stove in a sombre
mood. There'd been a stream of letters from Otto; pleading,
gentle letters asking her to return and professing his love:

'I love everything about you; you are my measure in everything
that has any meaning. Compared to you what is there, Paula? I
love your sensitivity, the way you've opened my eyes to things I

266

was simply too blind to see. You and your art have been, and still are, the dearest things to me. Until now I never realised—now that I've virtually lost you—how strongly I feel about you.'

But she couldn't answer, couldn't give him the comfort he craved.

She had little money and had to economise wherever she could and make do with next to nothing. She bought a minimum of furniture: a bed, an easel and a chair. Shopped at the end of the day in the market buying a few slices of sausage or half a cabbage to make soup, along with day-old bread from the boulangerie for a few centimes. She also tried not to light the stove, despite the freezing March weather, until her hands were so cold that she could no longer hold her brush. Then, one morning, on her way to enquire about classes at the École des Beaux-Arts, she bumped into her Bulgarian sculptor running, two at a time, up the school steps.

'Ah my little German, so you're back! How delightful,' he said, taking her elbow and steering her into a smoke-filled café brimming with market stevedores and students whiling away the morning. 'I hadn't expected to see you again. I thought you'd gone back to your husband for good. But how thin and pale you look. Don't you eat? Come on let me buy you breakfast. What would you like? An omelette? A bowl of *café au lait*? Have whatever you want. You look half starved. But it's good to see you again.'

As he watched her eat, he told her that he was making large sculptures, which he hoped to cast in bronze. In his improved French he suggested that she see them. And where was she living? In the same place as before? In a virtually empty studio, she told him.

The next morning she was woken by a loud banging, and there he was at her door with a load of salvaged wood. A friend had helped bring it over in a handcart. He planned to build her some shelves.

'No, it's nothing, but someone has to give you a hand *ma petite Allemande*. It won't be fine carpentry but I can sort you out something in a morning. Then with your drapes and rugs, and a vase of mimosa on the sill, it will soon feel almost like home.'

To thank him she cooked a rabbit stew and invited his young lawyer friend, along with Herma, to share it with them. It meant she could enjoy her sister's company without risking the dangerous topic of her relationship with Otto. Sitting in the candlelight, while the young men knocked back copious glasses of rough red wine and sucked the meat from the rabbit bones, picking out the bits stuck between their teeth with their fingers, it felt almost like old times. Even if their table manners hadn't improved, they were still as handsome and as good company.

But the next evening, after a hard day's work when nothing went well, she sat in the gathering twilight feeling sad. Otto had written to her almost every day, repeating the same heartfelt cry. When was she coming home? Would she ever come home? In pages of his neat crabbed hand he asked if she still loved him, what he had to do to convince her that he needed her. But she simply couldn't give him the reassurance he craved. She had no desire to hurt him and wished that her decision hadn't made him and her family suffer, but what could she do? Time was the only remedy; to let things pass. His continuous repetition would change nothing. It was like scratching at a sore so that it never had a chance to heal. It would be better if they didn't discuss the situation. There was nothing to talk about. If only he could believe that her decision was not due to cruelty. She was acting this way because she had no choice. If she didn't test herself, then after another six months in Worpswede she'd be in the same position, tormenting him again as she grew more resentful. However much he resisted the idea, he had to get used to the possibility that their lives would be separate. That didn't mean they couldn't care for each other as old friends. And she needed to ask him a favour. Could he go to her studio at the Brünjeses and look for six of the best nude drawings she'd done during her last stay in Paris, along with three more that she'd worked on for Mackensen. She needed him to send them if she was going to enrol in the École des Beaux-Arts. They were in her big red portfolio near the window. Would he roll them in a cylinder and post them as soon as possible. She'd be grateful and truly hoped he was well and beginning to work again. As always she sent affectionate greetings to both him and Elsbeth.

The previous year she'd written in her journal: 'the intensity with which a subject is grasped, is what makes for beauty in art'. Could that also be true of love? But now work was the only thing she could allow herself to think about. Finally she was beginning to settle and during the past week the weather had been warm enough for her to wander along the boulevards beneath the spreading chestnuts. And now that the evenings were milder she made a habit of sitting on the step after her drawing class, looking out over the city, spread out like a cloth, embroidered with rows of flickering street lamps, in the blue dusk.

The previous Sunday she and Herma had been to hear Beethoven's *Eroica*, and afterwards Herma invited a few friends that Paula hadn't met for a modest meal in her little room. But Paula hadn't enjoyed it and for the next few weeks saw little of her younger sister. She knew that Herma was struggling to understand her decision to leave Otto and that she didn't approve.

While she'd been away Otto had been granted a professorship. It made him sound terribly grand. Perhaps that's what he really wanted, though it wouldn't do for her. Recognition as an artist didn't come from academic accolades. She was upset that he hadn't bothered to forward her work in time to enrol in the École des Beaux-Arts, so that she was forced to join a private school that was more expensive. All she did was work. She was becoming more and more involved with her drawing, though her paintings remained obstinately dark and muddy. She knew that she needed to achieve purer colours. At times she was sure she was getting nowhere and felt defeated. She'd given up so much, risked everything. She enrolled on an art history course, joined an anatomy class and made a promise to spend every afternoon drawing from plaster casts in the Louvre. But to get permission she had to have an identification card from the German ambassador and for that she needed papers, but she'd taken all her possessions to her studio at the Brünjeses. Although it made her uncomfortable she'd have to ask Otto for a copy of their marriage certificate; he must have it somewhere. But the hardest thing was to ask him for money. She was broke.

He sent her the funds she requested by return. In the circumstances it was good of him. But she still couldn't bear to read his letter. It wrenched at her heart as she sat in her cold room, her head in her hands, and wept. His words moved her deeply, but what could she do? She'd loved him once, her red fox, but it was not the sort of love he needed from her. However much he pleaded, she couldn't go to him; she simply could *not*. Neither did she want to meet him in Paris, nor anywhere else. She no longer wanted him as her husband. She simply couldn't bear any more nights lying beside his bony body. His cold hands fumbling under her nightgown, feeling the desolation that washed over her as he rolled over and went to sleep, leaving her to watch the shadows on the bedroom ceiling, before falling into a fitful slumber, broken by dreams of sand and suffocation.

'Otto,' she wrote, 'I know it'll hurt you to say so, but I don't want your child, or any child. Not now. Once you were a significant part of my life, but that's no longer the case. That time's over. You have to accept it. Wanting it to be different won't change anything. I simply can't manufacture the feelings you want from me. All I can do is wait and see if they ever return or if something else appears in their place. I can't force them. I've gone over and over what's best; sat up night after night in this draughty studio, unable to sleep, worrying. Do you think this is easy for me? I know I'm causing you pain, but I'm not a cruel person and I feel desperately uncertain and insecure. I've walked away from everything I know, everything that was my life. But whatever you think of me I have to live out in the world, where I can test myself, for a while longer. And the most difficult thing is that I'm now going to have to ask you to send me, at least for the immediate future, one hundred and twenty marks a month so that I can live. I've rented out my studio at the Brünjeses so that should help a little and you know my needs are very modest and that I'll do everything I can to economise. But I have no choice. But please, can you do it automatically so that I don't have to be in the humiliating position of asking you every month? If I could do otherwise, you must know that I would. I thank you for the anatomy book and the pressed coltsfoot from the brickyard that reminds me of happier times. In fact, I thank you for everything you're doing for me. You're a good man. But then you know that I'm grateful and, however it may seem to you, I'm not bad or heartless. But whatever this is that I have to go through, there seems to be no other way that I can do it without hurting those closest to me. It upsets me a great deal to cause all this suffering, but I must follow things through to one conclusion or another. Stay close, my dear, to Elsbeth and to your art.'

She'd been working on a new painting, a self-portrait in oil distemper on cardboard where she had placed herself against a mottled sandy ground broken by olive dots. Her hair was parted in the middle and loosely looped at the back of her neck, while her head was tilted to one side like a blackbird's, listening, and her eyes looked straight ahead. Round her neck she wore her string of amber beads, which hung over her naked breasts as far as her navel and emphasised the curve of her lower abdomen, around which she'd wound a length of blue cloth like one of Gauguin's Tahitians. Standing in front of her long mirror she thought of the young breastfeeding mother she'd painted in

Worpswede who had been little more than a vessel to provide food for her children. She was a vessel of sorts too, wasn't she? Not for the child that Otto wanted, but for her art. Through a different sort of love she would give birth to paintings, nurture them and bring them to fruition. After working quickly and with determination she turned over the board and wrote on the back: 'Painted at the age of 30 on my 6th wedding anniversary'. She then signed it 'PB'. She'd dropped the Modersohn and felt a weight fall from her. From now on she would find her way in the world as Paula Becker.

There was a letter from Carl Hauptmann. He had already decided where his loyalties lay, making it clear that he thought her leaving was a selfish act of egotism. He wrote that no doubt, in time and with the application of her husband's firm hand, she'd come to her senses. She was incensed. What did he know about her real feelings? At the start of their relationship Otto had been a sanctuary. She'd learnt from him, but then it had taken five years to extricate herself from his tetchiness and melancholy rigidity. She had not left lightly. She was not trivial, but struggling against the odds to make something of her life.

She and Herma took a short trip to St Malo, but walking from the station through the suburbs, past the filthy railway sheds and torn billboards, she was disappointed. She'd expected a wild, windswept coastline, but it was a stinking, gloomy place. They found themselves out on a rocky headland dotted with old fortifications. Hitching up their skirts they clambered towards the ruins of a military watchtower and stood in the wind as their skirts puffed up like balloons. Away from Paris they managed to recapture something of their old intimacy if they avoided talk of her separation. They made their way down through clumps of yellow gorse, past gooseberry-eyed sheep vacantly chewing the cud, to the black rocks, and sat in the April sun with their sketchbooks.

From St Malo Paula sent Rilke a postcard. She'd not heard anything from him for some time. He had a way of vanishing. She also wrote to Otto. She knew that her words wouldn't heal his hurt, but urged him, as he'd often urged her, to work. More than anything she wanted to know that he was painting well. But in truth, these few days were simply a distraction. For much of her time in Paris she was lonely, her means strained. This was not the reckless Paris of her girlhood where everything was exotic, from the entertainers and ragged acrobats on each street corner, to the bloody carcasses hanging on large iron hooks in the butcher's shop. On their return to Paris Herma seemed withdrawn and Paula realised that she couldn't possibly understand her reasons for leaving Otto. But she hoped that her sister would come to forgive her. There was also a note from Rilke. The familiar handwriting unsettled her. He was depressed and needed company. She'd not allowed the thought of him to play any part in her decision to leave Otto; though she knew that for much of the time he and Clara now lived apart and that their relationship was fraught with tension. It seemed that they could neither be together nor separate. Nevertheless he was Clara's husband and she was still Otto's wife.

She woke early, the thin dawn light making a ghost of her dressing gown on the back of the door. She was at the beginning of her third decade, having chosen art above everything and facing an uncertain future. Would she be forced to grow old alone, dressed in dusty black like the widows of constrained means who passed their afternoons on the benches of Paris' parks and gardens? She felt so desolate, afraid of the choices she'd made. She remembered how inadequate she'd felt among the older students at The Wood as a young girl in England. How she'd so nearly given up for fear that Papi was right, that she'd never amount to more than a governess, never find it in her to become an artist in her own right. All these years later, she hardly felt any different. But now, being a painter was not some adolescent dream; her present life was the result of choices she'd made that had wounded her husband and hurt her family. Would she be able to see it through and have the strength to continue alone without love and the intimacy she craved? There were times, in the middle of the night, when she woke sobbing, longing to be held, longing to reach out and find someone on the other side of her bed. She wrote to Rilke. She'd be free the following Thursday. She suggested a walk. That would be safe. She'd meet him in the Luxembourg Gardens at three o'clock by the fountain.

He was waiting for her on the wrought-iron bench next to a bed of scarlet and yellow parrot tulips. She noticed him before he noticed her, huddled in his heavy coat, his shoulders hunched, despite the weak spring sun. As he turned to greet her she was struck, again, by the intensity of his blue eyes and his pale face that looked as if he'd spent too long out in the moonlight. He stood up, clicked his heels and greeted her with a formal little bow. She wasn't sure whether he was being ironic. Then he kissed her, in the French style, on both cheeks. His face was cold. He must have been sitting on the bench a long time.

'It's good to see you'.

'I wasn't sure whether to come.'

'I thought you might not; but I'm glad you did,' he said, taking her by the elbow and walking with her beside the lake where children were sailing their boats, so that for a moment she thought of that distant day in the Dresden sandpit.

As they strolled down the gravel path he told her that it had been a difficult time. He was no longer working for Rodin. They'd had a row. While he had been on a trip to Berlin he'd come to realise how untenable his position was, how much his secretarial duties were eroding his creative energies. He was a poet, for goodness sake, not a clerk. Rodin spoke no German, but had been furious when he'd replied to letters from German clients without prior consultation. Rodin had been particularly irate when one of the letters had been to the wealthy collector Baron Heinrich Thyssen-Bornemisza. Also, the two hours he was supposed to work for Rodin each morning had gradually extended to become an unbearable burden. There were sales, bills and endless lectures. He had brought with him many of his important contacts, but had been dismissed like some thieving domestic servant who'd filched the silver. Now he was back where he'd started, without resources. Life was uncertain, his wife and child elsewhere, and poetry eluded him. He was sure he was ill. He couldn't sleep. He had problems with his bowels, poor circulation and toothache, as well as a permanent sore throat. He'd tried steam baths and had resumed walking barefoot, but nothing helped. And the poetry he'd written recently? He had to admit, as they made their way past the empty bandstand, it amounted to little.

'One has to be patient, Paula, and get on with life and then, if one's lucky, one might write ten good lines. Poetry isn't just a question of feeling; it's a distillation of emotion and experience. For the sake of a single poem you have to visit numerous cities and know the names of different birds and flowers. You have to remember roads travelled down, meetings and difficult partings. You must return to your childhood and to those experiences you still don't fully understand, to the parents you've hurt, and those childhood illnesses spent in quiet rooms smelling of liquorice and rhubarb with the curtains drawn against the bright sunlight. You have to remember mornings convalescing by the sea, and those uncomfortable journeys travelling on trains under a starless sky to god knows where; and all those nights with different women whose faces you no longer remember. And still,' he said, taking her hand, 'to have memories isn't enough. Then you have to forget everything, and wait for it to return, like a ghost, in its own good time.'

A peal of bells was striking the hour as he walked with his collar turned up against the torrential Sunday morning rain to Paula's studio. He still wasn't sleeping and had taken to strolling through the city to calm himself. Past second-hand bookstores on the rue de Seine and antique shops crammed with engravings and tarnished silverware, which nobody visited and never appeared to do any business. He walked around the Faubourg Saint-Germain, past hotels with their pale blue shutters, set in secluded gardens and courtyards with bolted wrought-iron gates and heavy wooden doors. Past grand houses where he tried to imagine the small rituals of unknown lives—a husband expecting

277

his wife's return from Mass or a *grandmère* waiting for her favourite grandson—as a marble clock ticked out the long minutes and the ormolu mirrors reflected back the dove-grey light.

Over the past few days he'd been thinking about Cézanne. He was the central influence that bound him to Paula's work. She'd discovered him on her first visit to Paris when, in her excitement, she had run all the way to Clara's studio to persuade her to come and look at the canvases she'd found at Vollard's. And now he, too, was beginning to understand something of the way Cézanne reduced reality to its colour content, so that objects achieved an independent existence. When he looked at Paula's work he could feel her striving for the individuality of each thing or person she painted. It was there in the smudged moss green dress of the little girl with dark hair and her sister, painted against a chalky white background, and in the reddish brown of her earthenware wine bottles. There was an honesty, and humility in the way she painted a withered orange or a broken baguette that touched him. He wasn't well versed in painting and was slow to learn how to distinguish the good from the merely competent, always mixing up early and late works. But he could see that she was striving to describe what she saw with objective clarity. That what she was seeking was the innate being of her subject. He knew she was struggling and wanted to encourage her, for he could still discern something of the girl he'd first met that balmy summer evening six years ago, when she'd come out of her studio like a pale moth in her white dress with that halo of auburn hair. Art without pain, without sacrifice, without loneliness, he constantly reminded her, was impossible. Yet he was impressed by her courage and determination, though it was, in his view, the courage of despair; she was nearly destitute. He gave her whatever support he could and lent her, despite his own constraints, one hundred francs to get settled.

After a day's work it was their habit to meet in one of the cheap workers' bistros where the wine was sour, but the onion soup excellent.

'I hope there'll be asparagus the way you like it,' he said, pulling out her chair as they took their usual dark corner amid the stink of garlic and unwashed bodies. Invariably he ate the same thing: a mushroom omelette with spinach. He needed the iron and cheap French cafés weren't good at catering for his vegetarian diet. Afterwards they walked and talked. Then, one afternoon, he introduced her to his new friend Ellen Key and, together, they attended the unveiling ceremony of Rodin's *The Thinker* at the Panthéon. It was a big event. There was a band and speeches. On the pedestal Rodin's bronze figure sat in brooding contemplation, the muscular body contorted to suggest its internal struggles.

Strolling through the Tuileries at dusk, her arm through his, Paula stopped under a lime tree to straighten her little straw boater and said, ' I'd like to do a portrait of you. You will pose for me, won't you?'

In the following weeks he visited her studio and sat in quiet familiarity as she painted him. He wondered if she ever thought of that night they'd spent together. She never made any reference to it even though he often dreamt of her auburn hair falling over his chest in the moonlight.

*

The toothless concierge peered from her cubbyhole to ask her business before allowing her to go up. The gloomy stone stairwell, like much else in Paris, stank of drains. Although they'd never met, Paula knew Bernhard Hoetger's work from Bremen. Hearing that he was in Paris she had dropped him a note. He'd written back by return inviting her to call. She was delighted; she needed new friends and allies. An architect and a designer, as well as a painter, he was a dapper man with a fleshy face, polished forehead and bushy eyebrows. When she reached his apartment his wife ushered her into a small salon, hung floor to ceiling with paintings. Frau Hoetger was wearing a blue-spotted dress with a rope of coral round her throat and a warm smile accentuated her strong chin. She told Paula, with an indulgent sigh, that her husband was something of a collector. Paula liked them both immediately and enjoyed their easy manner and the chance to chat about Bremen and mutual acquaintances. She'd been uncertain about making contact and, not wanting to appear presumptuous, hadn't mentioned that she was a painter. She assumed Herr Hoetger had agreed to see her because she'd signed herself Frau Modersohn; naturally, he knew Otto's work. It was only when they were talking about Cézanne that she let slip that she, too, painted.

'What fascinates me, Herr Hoetger, is Cézanne's less interested in the fleeting impressions of light that seem to be the rage among every two-penny painter aspiring to be another Pissarro or Renoir, but is more concerned with the structural analysis of nature. It's the sparseness of his compositions that so attracts me. Everything is stripped down to its essence.'

'But Frau Modersohn, how interesting, I knew, of course, of your husband's reputation, but are you telling me that you paint, too? I'd no idea. I'd very much like, if I may, to come to your studio.'

When he reached the top of her stairs he was puffing and sweating profusely.

'But my dear young lady, these are quite magnificent,' he said, mopping his brow with a silk handkerchief as he walked round looking at her canvases and drawings. 'I congratulate you. You have a great talent.'

A great talent! Could he have any idea of the importance of what he'd said? She'd been so low, lonely and uncertain, but he had given her courage. Here was proof that she was amounting to something. Someone she didn't know, someone who had no reason to be nice to her, had told her that her work was magnificent. *Mag-ni-fi-cent*, she shouted, waltzing round the room, *mag-ni-fi-cent*, she called out of her little window to the astonished draymen below. That evening she sat down and wrote to Otto.

'I'm getting there at last! I'm working tremendously hard and believe I'm finally achieving something important. Would you send me, by return, the oil paints that are on my table at the Brünjeses? Also please give them notice about my studio. Otto, I'm very happy about your recent success. Herma tells me you've sold five paintings. That's wonderful. No one deserves it more than you. I send my greetings to you and Elsbeth.'

Then she sent a card to Milly: 'My darling Milly. I'm finally becoming *somebody*—I'm living the most intensely happy period of my life. Pray for me, dear sister, and please, *please* send me sixty francs for models' fees. Never lose faith in me. I thank you with all my heart.'

Something had opened inside her and she'd found a new strength. Her work was frenzied. In the middle of the night she'd get out of bed and stand barefoot in the moonlight to look at her paintings. She thought of little else and worked all the time. In April alone she'd done nearly twenty large nude drawings and filled her sketchbooks with studies. But she still had to push herself. Her colour was too sludgy. She needed to find a greater clarity. But slowly she was moving towards her goal. She had never felt so free; so truly herself.

The next morning there was another letter from Carl Hauptmann who seemed to be acting as Otto's emissary. He urged her to return to her husband. He had no doubt that her artistic destiny lay with him in Worpswede. Not in the lonely life she'd chosen in Paris. Lonely? What did he know? There was nothing so lonely, so suffocating as a marriage where she couldn't express her true nature either as a woman or an artist. It was pompous of him to make assumptions; to say he'd continue to hope that she'd come to her senses; and imply that she was simply being wilful. There was also a letter from Mutti who had just returned from her trip to Rome. As she opened it, sitting and looking out over the rooftops and chimney pots of Paris, she cried. Mutti had received Otto's letter the other morning informing her that Paula had left again for Paris. Naturally she'd been concerned, but his restrained tone led her to assume that it was something they'd agreed. She had not guessed the true disruption in their relationship. How things must have built up, how painful the situation must have been for her to take such a drastic step. As her mother she couldn't bear to see the two of them unhappy. She'd been looking forward to coming home—and by home she didn't mean Bremen, there was nothing there for her now her Woldi was gone—by home she meant Worpswede.

'My beloved child, it was your house and your garden with everything that you've planted in it that I thought of in the baking Rome heat. I imagined you running down the path in your white dress, your eyes shinning, your lovely hair lit by the sun, to welcome your old Mutti. I've never known anyone create such warmth at her table or put her guests so at their ease. Why didn't you come to me, or speak to Kurt or Milly and let yourself be cared for until all this had passed and you felt better? You must have suffered dreadfully going through this alone. Perhaps you're ill. Can't I come to you? Just say the word and your Mutti will be at your side. My dear child, your husband is in a dreadful state. He's dragged your paintings into his studio. Heinrich Vogeler wants to buy your *Apples*, but Otto won't part with it. He's taken some of your oils from the Brünjeses and is painting extraordinary things with them—stuffed birds and old jugs—which he's placing next to your canvases to see whether he's managed to replicate your colours. Paula, he wants you back. He's been staying here with me in Bremen for three days and has talked of nothing else. The man loves you; he's wasting away. He keeps saying, "When she's back, things will be different. She can have anything she wants, anything. There'll be no more depressing winters here. She can even go to Paris if she wants to, if only she'll have me back." Paula, as I write the trams are clattering in the street below and a nightingale's singing so loudly that it's almost drowning them out. Otto says it's a male serenading its mate. Then he turned to Kurt and said: "The moon's full and the trees are in blossom. If only our Paula was here."'

That her mother wasn't angry was a huge relief. Not only would it have devastated her, but it would have hardened her heart. But how could she explain, after her mother's loving words, that she'd not been able to endure any longer, that she would never be able to again. She remembered how, as a student, she'd gone with her old teacher Jeanna Bauck to see *The Doll's House.* How little she'd understood that play until now. She must write to Mutti. She had to make her understand that she was beginning a new life and that she mustn't interfere. What she was experiencing was important and she was on the verge of accomplishing something real. 'Don't be sad for me. Even if my life might not lead me back to Worpswede again, the eight years I spent there were very beautiful. Let's wait calmly for time to pass. It will bring what's right and good.'

The city lay stretched out like a cat in the balmy evening air. The pink candles of the chestnut trees were in full bloom and as the petals floated down to the pavement, she thought of the previous spring with the handsome Bulgarians and the Easter streets filled with confetti. It was a welcome break to sit in the sun, as though she had just crawled out of a dark dungeon. For the last two weeks she'd worked day and night on a number of life-sized nudes. This afternoon, she'd just finished a still life of a clay jug with three pink peonies and two oranges on a white plate. Painting was the only thing she thought about. The rest was too painful. She was short of money. Otto had sent her allowance by telegraph, along with the paints she'd requested, but the post office wouldn't let her have them, even when she had gone back with her documents. So she'd had to ask the concierge and her husband to vouch for her identity.

Then there was another letter from Carl Hauptmann. She was angry. What right did he have to interfere and make judgements about her life with so little insight or information? Why couldn't he understand that she didn't go back to Worpswede because she didn't *want* to? If Otto thought asking him to intercede on his behalf helped, he was wrong. The truth was staring them both in the face. Even so it didn't make her position easier. Did they believe she was so frivolous that it didn't pain her to reject Otto's obvious love? Martha Vogeler made contact and asked to buy three paintings, including the little girl in a black hat. It was a warm letter, which gave Paula heart, for she'd just had another row with Herma and they had parted acrimoniously at the Pont Neuf. She knew her sister was upset, that she didn't know how to handle her split with Otto and that if Paula gave her time she would come round. But it was good to receive Martha's friendly words, to feel that she hadn't listened to gossip and sided with everyone else. She and Heinrich were now keeping horses, two big roans. Many other things had changed in the village. Paula replied thanking her for the news and saying that if she would send one hundred francs for all three paintings that would be perfect. Otto's money went on paying for models, paints, brushes and canvas, but what was left barely covered food and lodging. So if she could earn a little in her own right she might just be able to survive. And, despite what Martha had heard from Otto, she wasn't ill. In fact, she was on top of the world. Although she worried about him and Elsbeth, not to mention her own family, for they all seemed to be suffering. The thing was that they weren't getting anything out of this arrangement, whereas she was living through the most exciting period of her life. Her recent paintings were strong and she was working hard; she had always promised herself that she would amount to something by the time she was thirty. And if Martha and Heinrich should decide to visit Paris, it would be wonderful to see them.

But, in truth, she was fighting to survive. When Otto's allowance was held up at the post office, she had nothing to eat for three days except a heel of stale baguette and a lump of old Gruyère. She ran out of coffee and fuel and, though it was spring, her studio was still freezing. It never got direct sun and the walls retained the damp. And then there was Rilke. From time to time he still came to sit for his portrait or read her a draft of a new poem he was working on, but he was spending a good deal of time with his new friend Ellen Key, who seemed to be acting as some sort of amanuensis. Yet, when they sat in her studio, Paula felt the unspoken bond between them to be as strong as ever. They never mentioned Clara, never made reference to the night they had spent together. On Saturdays they often strolled in the parks or wandered along the banks of the Seine. One afternoon they went to Chantilly. When Rilke invited her he asked her to wear the white dress and little straw boater that he liked so much. They visited the collection of Poussins, Ingres and Delacroix, but it was the Fra Angelicos, with their economy of drawing and composition, that moved her the most. They took a boat down the Grand Canal, where the fountain jets made prisms in the sunlight, and walked arm in arm through the English garden with its curves of natural planting, so that the world must have thought that they were lovers. Otto's pleading letters seemed far away.

Then, at Whitsuntide, he arrived in Paris. She hadn't wanted him to come, had tried to dissuade him, but he had insisted. What could she do? She was dependent on his goodwill for her survival. She pleaded with Herma to come with her to the Gare du Nord to meet him.

'Herma, I can't go alone, I just can't. Please don't be angry with me. You're my sister and there's no one else to ask. I'm begging you to accompany me. It's just too much for me to do by myself. I know you don't approve of what I'm doing, but I'm asking you as a favour from the bottom of my heart.'

But Herma refused. When Otto got off the train carrying his small bag, he was wearing the same suit he'd worn the last time he'd come to Paris. He looked older, she thought, hunched under the weight of his grief.

They made an uneasy trio during the course of the week as they wandered in the Luxembourg Gardens and lingered, uncomfortably, over cups of coffee in pavement cafés. Otto tried everything and was touchingly decent, while Herma urged and disapproved in equal measure.

'It's not fair, Paula. You just don't seem to care that so many other people have to suffer on your account. It's not only your happiness or even Otto's that's at stake, but Elsbeth and Mutti's; even mine.'

But these were familiar arguments and the Worpswede Paula once loved was now little more than a joyless prison. She hated to see Otto suffer as he sat nervously chewing the stem of his pipe, but she couldn't relent. There was too much at stake. She was working so well, she couldn't give up now. Why couldn't they understand the willpower it took to keep going instead of seeing her as weak and selfish? And besides, how many more ways were there to show Otto that she didn't want him? By the end of the week there was simply nothing more to be done. Everything had been said a thousand times. They'd talked in circles, only to return again and again to the underlying problem. She didn't love him any more. Herma wouldn't come with her to the station to see Otto off. They made a forlorn pair as they waited for the train on the platform. She felt like a mother saying goodbye to her child as she watched the train pull out of the station. They agreed he should come again in the autumn. That would give them a bit of breathing space, and a chance to see if anything changed. As she made her weary way back to her room, two stray mutts were snarling over a bloody carcass in the gutter.

During Otto's visit Rilke had made himself scarce. It wasn't until he received a letter from Clara telling him of Otto's return to Worpswede that he wrote to Paula.

'I hear you're all alone again. I wish you everything good and that your work will nurture you and compensate for much.'

He knew that now she'd made a firm decision to separate from Otto she'd turn to him, but he didn't want to become entangled in the Modersohns' affairs, or to be seen by Otto as

a rival. He knew she would consider him wavering and incon-
sistent, see his behaviour as a betrayal of their friendship, but
he couldn't articulate the dread he felt at the prospect of deeper
intimacy. He couldn't risk anything that might cause emotional
disruption and take him away from the solitude he craved. He
sometimes considered how things might have been different,
remembering her wet mouth in the rose lamplight. How much
he'd wanted her. Sometimes, at night, he still dreamt of her
and would wake, his body aching for hers.

She had written and asked him to come for another sitting
and, rather reluctantly, he agreed; though as he climbed the
stairs to her studio the misgivings were revealed by the heavi-
ness in his steps.

She'd done a good deal of work since he'd last been there.
Though she looked thinner, there was a new calm determination
that he had not detected before. On previous visits he'd not
asked to see his portrait, but this time he did. She had painted
him in tones of pastel grey, with a high forehead, his eyes like
dark cut-outs edged with red, as if he'd not slept for weeks, his
mouth, framed by his moustache and beard, slightly open like
a wound that wouldn't heal. He didn't know what to make of it
and felt hurt, though he wasn't sure why. When she asked him
to come again he excused himself, saying that he was too busy.
The following day she sent a note asking him to accompany
her to the theatre. By return he replied that, sadly, it wouldn't
be possible. He was preparing to leave for the Belgium coast on
a family holiday with Ruth and Clara. She wrote, immediately,
asking to join them. She'd been writing to Clara regularly and
they'd become intimate again.

'Think how lovely it would be to walk barefooted on the sands, to collect shells and take Ruth shrimping. We could spend mornings drawing and writing. All of us together again, just like old times.'

But, no, he answered, that wasn't possible.

Hurt, she wrote again, but he didn't reply.

Later she heard that he'd left Paris.

For weeks she couldn't eat or sleep and was plagued by head-aches, and a general sense of lassitude. Her mouth was full of ulcers, her skin dry and flaky. The tension of Otto's visit, the disharmony with Herma, Rilke's rejection and the constant worry about money played on her nerves. Otto wrote to say that he'd sold one of her paintings, but as soon as he forwarded her the money, she sent it to Rilke to repay the one hundred francs he had lent her. She couldn't bear to be in his debt. It was June and, although the weather was fine, she could do little more than lie exhausted on her bed and listen to the starlings outside. Worst of all she couldn't work. There was a plague of fleas in her building and her legs were covered with livid bites, the air so dry and full of dust that she thought she'd suffocate. Did she really have the strength to continue? Or was she, as Otto insisted, simply obstinate? There were days when she longed for a downpour of rain to wash away the stench of Paris; heavy grey rain that would soak into the cracked earth and clean the filthy pavements. She didn't miss Otto, but she did miss the moors and waking in the moonlight after a storm, or lying in bed listening to the wind in the wet birches and, then, the hoot of a barn owl as it swooped to snatch a mouse in the log pile.

Her mood changed daily. Sometimes her painting went well, on other days it felt like a bitter, pointless struggle. She was trying to spend longer on each canvas now and follow them through to some deeper resolution, but the more she worked the greater the opportunity there was to bungle them. The weather was growing terribly hot. Often, after a day's painting, she found that she was stinking with the sheer physical exertion of it all, but as she had to go down two flights of stairs to fill her water jug, she often felt too tired to wash. She had no money and couldn't be bothered to cook, so simply opened cans of sardines, which she ate straight from the tin with a bit of old bread. She longed to get out to the country and paint under the shady branches of a poplar in some little village where she could sketch the locals. The previous night had been the most sultry she'd experienced, the air charged with electricity. Just before midnight there'd been a tremendous thunderstorm. She'd sat at her open window watching the blue flashes zigzag across the city until the rain came, soaking her face and hair like a baptism, turning the dusty cobbled streets below into rivers so sewage belched from the inadequate drains. But when she woke the air was fresh and clear and her resolve to leave Paris had weakened.

Milly wrote. It had been a long time since they'd met. She was worried about Paula in the heat. But it was over now and a little bit of heat wasn't the end of the world. She also hated to think of Paula struggling alone so far from home without any support. But 'struggle' sounded a bit melodramatic. She just did what she could and then rested. That was the only way she could accomplish anything. Guilty or not of hurting others, this was now her life and there was little point trying to change it. She'd chosen her path and was following it with determination. By nature she was optimistic and loving. She'd never meant to harm anyone, never set out with the intention of causing grief or hurt. Recently she had become more resigned and philosophical. People were different. The important thing was to be consistent and to hold on to her integrity.

Her new friendship with Bernhard Hoetger was a source of strength. There was something solid about him, with his fleshy face and bushy eyebrows. Although a sculptor, she was learning a good deal from him about weight and form. Since he'd taken her under his wing she felt more stable. He and his wife regularly insisted that she should eat with them and fussed about her health. They fed her fried liver with spinach to build up her strength, and soft-boiled eggs. He invited her to his studio where he was working on a large sculpture that he complained was going very slowly because his model was always ill. One day Paula took him some of Otto's work, and the little painting of a man throwing his hat in the air particularly impressed him. Paula urged him to visit the next time he was in Worpswede. She may not want to be married to Otto, but she still respected him as a painter; still cared for him and what he'd taught her. She knew she owed him a great deal. Last week he'd sent her a package containing some paints and the thin muslin blouse she'd requested, along with a new photograph of Elsbeth. She missed the little girl. What a heavy price art exacted.

Paris was dissolving in the heat. The streets were dusty and everything blowsy and overblown. The agreed time for Otto to come back, ostensibly to work things out, was getting closer and Paula was becoming more and more anxious. She'd been working very hard and not sleeping. At night she wandered round her studio, sitting for hours looking out at the moon that hung over the churchyard. As the warm breeze from the open window cooled her hot skin she thought of all the other artists and writers awake across the city, worrying about whether they'd ever make a mark or simply be swallowed up by the callous indifference of history. She'd been affected, the day before, by a knackered dray horse, its mouth frilled with spittle and its coat soaked with sweat, that had fallen to its knees in the gutter under a heavy load of wine kegs and was being beaten by its driver to get up. She had watched appalled and angry, wondering whether to confront the man. Then the horse had let out a strange gurgling noise from deep within its chest and its head had dropped to its chest. She felt pity for the dying animal and wished she could have done something to ease its pain. It was the same emotion she felt towards the peasants in Worpswede who stuffed straw into their clogs to keep their blackened toes from freezing in winter. It was a love of sorts, wasn't it? Even if not the kind a woman was supposed to feel for a husband.

That night she wrote to Otto.

'The time is getting closer and closer for you to come here. But I have to ask you, for both our sake's, to spare us the ordeal. Let me go, Otto. Let go of the past. I don't want you as my husband. Nor do I want your child. Please try and accept it and don't torture yourself any longer. As for any other arrangements you wish to make, I'm more than happy for you to organise things however you think fit. But please, I beg you; don't continue to take any further steps to engineer a reconciliation. It will only prolong the torment. Also, very reluctantly, I have to ask you to send me one final instalment of 500 marks. I'm going to the country for a while, so could you please send it to B. Hoetger, c/o 108, rue Vaugirard. I intend to spend time trying to take steps to secure my own livelihood from now on so that I'm no longer a burden to you. I thank you for all your kindness. There's nothing else left to say.'

She thought the letter would alleviate her anxiety, but it only made it worse. After Otto's money was spent how would she live? She could give private drawing classes or teach German, but all that would take energy and time away from her painting, and still it wouldn't provide enough for her to survive on unless she did it full time. She couldn't eat and when she worked her hands shook. After her letter to Otto she saw no one for the rest of the week. She was closing in on herself. Then she received a note from Bernhard Hoetger. He and his wife were concerned. They hadn't heard anything from her for days. Would she come for dinner that evening? Seven o'clock would suit them perfectly.

After a coq au vin, eaten in the candlelight of their little salon, Bernhard's wife excused herself saying that she had a number of domestic tasks to attend to. Pouring them both another glass of red wine, Bernhard turned to her and asked, 'Paula, honestly, how are you? You can tell me that it's none of my business, if you like, but I ask as your friend. It's not easy for a painter to survive in Paris without a dealer or a rich patron, and even harder for a young woman to do so on her own. Am I right,' he asked, breaking off a bunch of black grapes, 'in thinking that Herr Modersohn is due here any day now?'

She took a slow sip of wine before answering.

'I wrote and told him not to come. I hadn't meant to discuss this with anyone. But as you've asked, I'll confess, but it's very hard. Perhaps it sounds ridiculous to you, but I have to live in my own way and get on with my work. Maybe it's just the wine talking or the relief of being able to share what's been weighing on my heart. But I don't want to continue with this marriage. I don't love Otto in the way he wants me to love him and now I have,' she said, bursting into tears as if the confession had broken down her defences, 'to find a way to support myself or I won't survive.'

'My dear girl, this is a momentous thing you're considering. No wonder you look so pale and thin. Paula, it's not that, for one minute, I doubt your talent. You know that. It's what drew us to become friends in the first place. I've nothing but the greatest admiration for what you're trying to do. But although I'm an artist, I'm also a man. I can't, of course, discuss what's in your heart or how you really feel about your husband; that's for the two of you to sort out. All I can say is that I don't believe the world is yet ready for a woman artist to make it alone. Talent isn't enough; you need a dealer, connections and a good head for business. I'm rare that as an architect and an artist I can inhabit both worlds. Of course it's much easier for me being a man. But you, Paula, aren't tough enough to survive unprotected in this harsh environment. I'd worry about your health, as well as your work. No one can produce good work under such difficult circumstances. Also I'm very lucky in my marriage. There's friendship, love and, if I don't embarrass you by saying so, my dear, sensuality. But we're blessed. Not everyone can have everything with one person. You have a husband who loves you. A respected German painter. From what you tell me he wants you back, wants to encourage you to paint. But he's older than you and set in his ways. You challenge the very foundations of his world, Paula. These are radical times and we Germans are not radical people. We like order and what's familiar and knowing where we stand. You've a great gift for both art and for life; don't throw it away. Don't become bitter and ground down. You have to be practical. You're a young woman, but in a few years what will become of you? Where's the dealer who'll take you on so that you can make a realistic living? Do you really want to end up alone, your health broken, your means meagre, giving drawing lessons to the daughters of tradesmen who think that such skills will make a plain girl more marriageable? Write to your husband, Paula. Make it up with him; ask him to take you back.'

As they sat beneath the guttering gas lamp she felt the tears begin again; tears of frustration and disappointment. Ahead of her time? She'd never thought of herself like that. She had simply followed her heart and done what she loved and felt compelled to do. All she'd ever wanted was to paint; but she had always wanted to be something more than just another 'lady' painter in a straw sun hat who did pleasing watercolours to pass the time. She wanted to get to the heart. To paint life's raw realities, to show the world little Meta's crooked louse-ridden body and Mother Schröder's legs stunted and bent from rickets. She wanted to paint the drained light of the moors on a late November afternoon or a Paris street stinking of bad drains. What she was trying to explore wasn't to be found in any drawing room, but in the pitiful rattle of a broken dray horse.

'Paula, my dear, listen,' Bernhard said, as she wiped away her tears with the back of her hand. 'I hope you trust me and believe that I'm your friend. But I advise you, both as a man and an artist, to go back to your husband. You won't survive alone in Paris. Make what you can of your life in Worpswede. There are people there who love you. You'll take what you've learnt here back with you. You'll never forget. Your heart and vision remain yours alone, but your physical well-being, well, that has to be cared for by others.'

'It's so hard, Bernhard. I've tried with every bit of my body and soul to keep my integrity and follow my heart. I've never thought of what I'm doing in terms of history. All I've ever wanted was to paint the world, honestly, as I see it. Will there ever be a right time, do you think? Or will we women always experience this conflict between the need for security and children, and the hunger to express ourselves? When I was little, sitting drawing the cat by the fire, how could I have imagined where it would all end? But you're right. Otto does love me and maybe I can find a way of loving him again. Not as he wants, perhaps—as you say, life's a compromise—but as a painter and friend. But it's late. I have to go home. I need to think. Thank you and your wife for the delicious dinner, but most of all,' she said, kissing him affectionately on both cheeks, 'for your advice and friendship.'

As she made her way through the dimly lit streets, down the narrow alleys with their peeling posters advertising absinthe and cigarettes, towards her lodgings, she could hear feral cats fighting for scraps under the café tables. As she walked she felt she was seeing the city with a new clarity. Paris had given her so much; had opened her eyes and shown her the power and poignancy of the ordinary. It had become a part of her now. When she got to her room she lit a candle and got out a sheet of writing paper.

'Otto, my last harsh letter was written when I was terribly upset. It's been a testing time. I know I've said some very hurtful things, including that I didn't want to have your child, but it was said in the heat of the moment and I now regret having written something so absolute. If you haven't completely given up on me, then come here soon and let's see if we can try and find a way back to one another. I expect this sudden shift will seem peculiar to you, but all I can say is that I've been so buffeted by my emotions that I'm no longer sure of the right path. I've had so many conflicting thoughts and feelings, but I can't feel guilty; for this is who I am and how I learn. All I can promise is that I never meant to cause you pain.'

So it was arranged. She'd rent a studio for him near hers. It would be more comfortable than some dirty *chambre garnie*. He would send his things ahead, including bed linen and her favourite feather quilt. She wrote that she wanted him to meet the Hoetgers who were spending the winter in Paris. She hoped they'd become friends. Bernhard had spoken of him with high regard. After she sealed the letter to Otto she wrote to Herma. Despite the antagonism between them during her young sister's last weeks in Paris, Paula missed her now that she was back in Bremen. She loved her and knew that one day they would be close again, that it was only a matter of time and that Herma had to follow her own path, just as she had.

She didn't meet Otto at the Gare du Nord but waited for him to come to her. It was a dark November afternoon full of wet fog. When she opened the door to him he was standing on the step beside his bag, clutching a bunch of white roses. His face and beard, as he kissed her cheek, were damp. She took his things and hung his heavy woollen coat by the stove so that it gave off a smell like wet sheep, and she remembered, all those years ago—when he'd still been married to Hélène—how he'd sought shelter in her studio from the rain. How much had changed. As he took off his hat and straightened his hair she noticed that it was receding; he needed a haircut.

'Thank you, Otto,' she said, putting the flowers in a vase. 'I'm glad they're white. That somehow seems appropriate. Did you have a good journey? How's Elsbeth?'

'The journey was fine, though Belgium, as usual, seemed to go on forever. Elsbeth's well, though I expect you'd think she's grown. She drew you some pictures; one of her rabbit and another of your mother. It's a little less than flattering, I'm afraid, but I had express instructions to give them to you as soon as I arrived. Your mother and Elsbeth have become as thick as thieves.'

'I'm so glad. It's good for Mutti, as well as for Elsbeth. I've missed them both very much. Thank you for the drawings. I'll pin them on the wall. But you must be hungry. I bought some bread, and a little pâté and wine. I wasn't quite sure what time you'd get here.'

As she busied herself setting the little table with a gingham cloth, her two glasses and white plates, Otto opened the wine. She lit a single candle and then laid out the baguette and pâté. Everything between them was deliberate, guarded, as if each was measuring the other's words and actions, so as not to give away too much. After they'd finished eating Otto lit his pipe.

'I promise Paula, I won't get in your way. I don't want to stop you working. I want to get settled into my studio and start on a series of drawings as soon as possible. I have no intention of disrupting your regime. Also, as you know, I've been trying to promote your work. I was sorry that the North-west German Artists' Association decided to reject your *Still Life with Apples*. But the four canvases you suggested for the Bremen Kunsthalle have been accepted. I hope you're pleased. I think it's wonderful and it seems that the director intends to write the catalogue himself.'

Apart from that he assured her everything at home was going on as usual, though he'd been worried about Elsbeth's health. Mutti had been wonderful, but Elsbeth had so many earaches and sore throats that she'd missed a good deal of school. He'd been considering letting her drop back a year, but wanted to consult her first before making the final decision.

'Your instinct for these things is always so much better than mine.'

Paula was happy to discuss Elsbeth. She loved the little girl and it was a concern they could share. When they'd finished the bottle of wine and the candle had burnt down low, Otto got up and took his hat and coat from the hook behind the door.

'I'll say goodnight then. I need to go and get settled in,' he said, kissing her gently on the cheek.

She was touched by his delicacy, grateful that he was giving her time and not forcing things.

Their days were filled with work and reading. Sometimes they spent the mornings in the Louvre or visiting one of the small galleries on the Left Bank. But Paula was not ready to compromise her art to either social or domestic routines, so everything else had to fit around it. Otto was amazed at the intensity with which she worked and did as little as possible to disturb her. At the end of the day they would meet, mostly in her studio, to eat together and talk, then he would return to his own lodgings. He knew he couldn't push her and that things had to evolve slowly, in their own time. One evening, after they'd finished eating and he was helping her with the dishes, they started to discuss how it might be possible to live in a similar way in Worpswede. If they had more space they could live more open lives, together but separate. He'd heard, he said, handing her a dry plate, that old Brünjes might be selling his place. Perhaps they could buy that. After all she had her studio there already and he had been selling well, so the money shouldn't be too much of a problem.

'And the garden is lovely, Otto,' Paula offered cautiously, stacking the clean crockery on the shelf above the stove, 'and there's my little blue bench outside the window where I love to

301

sit and draw. And, who knows, we could keep some goats and chickens there. You could build Elsbeth a run for her rabbit and I could plant fruit bushes—blackcurrants and raspberry canes—and extend the Brünjeses' vegetable garden. Do you remember how I used to grow vegetables there when I first moved in?'

'Paula, I think it's a wonderful idea. This is the first time I've heard you talk about Worpswede with anything like enthusiasm since I've been in Paris.'

That evening he didn't go back to his studio, but how strange it felt to lie beside his long, bony body again. He was like a young boy in his eagerness to please. He wanted her so much that it was all over in a matter of minutes. She accepted that this, with its disappointments, frustrations, tenderness and familiarity, was to be the rest of her life. As he lay stroking her hair in the moonlight, whispering over and over again, 'Paula, oh, my Paula, you are so beautiful,' she couldn't find the words to answer.

The next morning the concierge brought her an excited letter from Mutti, which included a cutting from the local paper. It talked of the cruel treatment meted out to Frau Modersohn by one of the city's other distinguished newspapers a few years ago; and went on to describe her uncommon energy and strongly developed sense of colour. The vitality and attention to quality that characterised her work. Bremen, the piece concluded, was fortunate to be able to lay claim to so powerful a talent as that of Frau Paula Modersohn.

'Otto, you see, there *is* justice in the world after all! This puts egg on Arthur Fitger's face! Now I *can* go home. Not just as your wife but as a painter in my own right.'

*

They would return in the spring. There were still things to do. She wanted to see the Cézannes in the Pellerin Collection. But Elsbeth was missing her and Paula wanted to sort out her school. She wrote to Clara. It was a great solace that they were in contact again for she couldn't imagine Worpswede without her. Whatever the tensions between them Paula loved her. Slowly she was accustoming herself to the idea of returning to her former life. But this year in Paris had changed her. She was more independent and no longer so full of illusions. During the course of the summer she had realised that Bernhard Hoetger was right. She couldn't survive alone. She couldn't cope with the eternal money worries. The freedom she needed was the freedom to cultivate her talent and paint. Was she being brave or simply making a compromise? She was unsure, but life wasn't as black and white as it had seemed. The main thing was the peace and quiet to work she'd have if she returned to Otto. It wouldn't be easy. Artists tended to live alone because it was hard to balance the demands of work with domestic life and the needs of another. But she'd made the decision to go back and would have to make it work. She'd caused enough pain and disruption, and Otto had been nothing but solicitous over the last weeks. If the dear Lord would only allow her to create something worthwhile, something powerful and honest, she'd be happy. And if she had a place to work in peace and could remain strong and healthy, then she'd be grateful for the portion of love that had been allotted to her.

They spent her birthday quietly enjoying their last few days in Paris. Otto gave her a white shawl and a book on Egyptian statues and Mutti sent her a little gold-beaded bracelet in a leather case. There were cards and letters from the rest of the family and from Milly the money to buy a Turkish shawl. In the enclosed note her sister confided that she was concerned how unhappy Henner had seemed since his return from sea. Paula wasn't surprised. She'd been struck last Christmas by how shy her younger brother was compared to his twin sister. Herma had acquired all the panache and Mutti didn't always handle him well; one minute indulging him, the next making unrealistic demands so that the poor boy never knew where he stood. Paula remembered her own ambivalence towards her mother when she'd been younger, for she had a tendency to fuss and smother which, since she'd become a widow, had become more pronounced. It must be hard for Henner not having Papi around. Paula wished they'd talked more the last time they'd met. She was fond of her brother and didn't like to think of him struggling.

She was also concerned to hear from Kurt that Mutti had a nasty skin condition. He and Henner had been taking care of her, but Paula was anxious that she and her sisters were all so far away. She remembered, when she had been a child— the only time her mother had been sick in bed—how lost and despondent Papi had been. Mutti had always been the calm centre around which the house revolved and now she was ill. It was time to go home.

Elsbeth had grown. As they climbed from the mail coach she came running down the garden path to greet them with a bunch of anemones in one hand and a coronet of primroses in the other. As they walked back to the house, arm in arm, the little girl bubbling with news, Paula could smell peat smoke and see the black sails of the windmill slowly turning in the distance. Despite the February sun it was still very cold, though the first pussy willow and catkins were just beginning to come into bud along the lanes. How neat and clean the house seemed. There were all her books and the mirror and the little tumblers she'd bought in the second-hand shop in Berlin just before she got married, gleaming on their glass tray. The stove was lit and Mutti had arranged a large bowl of forsythia on the table and put new patchwork cushions on the chairs. Everything was pristine after the muck and grime of Paris.

As soon as she could she went to her studio. Walking down the path, she was filled with a sense of peace. This was her real homecoming. Her return to this room with its pale green walls and blue door, its jars of feathers, and stones arranged along the sill. She longed to get to work; she'd done nothing during her last month in Paris. Time had been taken up with packing and tying up loose ends, though she had made a point of seeing Cézanne's early work and been touched by its angular peculiarities and vulnerabilities. She wished that she could have stayed to see his exhibition at the Salon d'Automne. But she would have to accept that Paris would go on without her: the flower sellers with their little bunches of fragrant *muguet*, the pavement book dealers laying out their rare editions, the *chanteuses* and entertainers plying their trades on the street corners, would all continue their lives and she would no longer be a part of it. She had loved it all—the rawness, the depth and vitality. But that period of her life was over. No doubt, from time to time, she would go back, but she knew that she'd never live there again as an independent woman. Things were about to change in ways she hadn't anticipated. In October she was going to have a child. Yesterday, sitting over a mug of milky coffee at the breakfast table, she'd broken the news to Otto and had been touched by his response. He was elated. She realised it was easy to make him happy. She had always imagined having a child of her own. Yet knew that she wouldn't have chosen to have one now or in these circumstances. But everything had its price, she mused, as she rolled up her sleeves and set about priming a fresh canvas. If she could only go on breaking new ground and say something important, she'd accept fate.

But the paintings she'd done in Paris now felt too cool. She knew she was overreacting against the ubiquitous influence of Impressionism and that she was trying to find something more visceral, which plumbed the depths. Now she was home it would be easier to be true to her own voice. Here she could listen to the wind moaning in the silver birch, or walk alone over the moors feeling the heavy peat cling to her boots, as it did to the hooves of the ploughing carthorses. As much as she loved Paris, it was here, in Worpswede, that she felt connected to the earth. As she worked there was a tap on her door. It was Clara. For a moment Paula hardly recognised her. There were dark circles under her eyes and threads of grey in her tightly knotted hair. What had happened to the wild girl who'd clambered into the church tower to ring the bells over Worpswede? She seemed to be subsumed beneath this nervy-looking woman for whom life had become a painful disappointment. Yet she was delighted to see her, the only one with whom she could truly share what was in her heart.

'I'm so glad,' Paula said, hugging her friend tenderly, as if she might bruise beneath her touch, then leading her by the hand into the studio, 'so very glad that you've come.'

'It's Grandmamma, Grandmamma's here.'

There was a clatter of cartwheels and Elsbeth, who'd just gone to bed, came dashing back downstairs in her nightdress. It was a glorious May evening and Paula and Otto were working in the garden planting lettuce and spinach. Paula, her skirts tucked up into her belt, her cheeks streaked with soil, ran to greet her mother. Now she was up, Elsbeth was allowed to join the adults as they ate supper on the white veranda in the mild evening air. Next morning, as she attempted to attend to her chores, Paula felt overcome with nausea. Otto was solicitous, rushing round with cups of camomile tea, plumping up cushions and even agreeing to forgo his pipe because the tobacco made her feel sick. As she rested on the chaise longue in the conservatory, she watched him walk round the garden with Mutti. It was good to see them so happy and absorbed in each other's company.

A bicycle flew round the corner and on it was Kurt, wearing a newly laundered panama hat.

'As your elder brother, and now,' he announced with a funny little bow, 'a fully qualified doctor and a potential uncle, I felt duty-bound to come and check on my little sister. Paula,' he said, flinging his bike in the grass and giving her a big hug. 'This is such good news. A baby, I'm really happy for you both.'

As she sat at the lunch table, amid the warmth and love surrounding her, it was hard to believe that anything had been patched and glued back together. The shape of things may not be what she would have chosen; but somehow it fitted and was all of a piece.

The next day she received a letter from Rilke with a copy of his new book. She was happy he'd sent it, though she wouldn't read it for a while. The time for such things had passed. He was in Paris and she wrote to offer him the use of her studio, which her landlady hadn't rented yet. In return could he possibly dispose of her furniture and her other bits and pieces: the daybed with striped mattress, the large looking-glass and chair and table she'd left. Also, she had lost her carved mother-of-pearl brooch. She had looked everywhere. It had been dear to her, a present from her cousin Cora. Could he, perhaps, find something similar and buy it for her with the money her furniture raised? She'd be grateful. She knew he would choose well. And as she wouldn't be able to see the Cézannes at the Salon d'Automne, would he send her the catalogue? Since she'd dragged Clara to Vollard's all those years ago, Cézanne had meant more to her than any other painter.

She was kept awake by the jabbing of fists and elbows. She felt like a whale when she turned over. Her nipples had grown as brown as conkers and her belly button was distended. But it only made Otto smile. Everything about her pregnancy made him happy. It was a guarantee she wouldn't stray too far from home. She hoped that she wasn't putting on too much weight and weighed herself every week; standing in front of her long mirror. She didn't want to be one of those women whose body collapsed just because she had a child.

In answer to Milly's postcard, she wrote to her sister, that she would simply refuse to answer any correspondence that mentioned nappies or her 'blessed event.' She wanted to be like the woman in Frau Brünjes' story. A neighbour had called to speak to the local farmer; his wife, who was making soup by the hearth, told him that he was resting. 'You see we had a bit of a sleepless night last night. I just gave birth to my fifth!'

Elsbeth was staying with Herma and Paula was trying to take advantage of the last few weeks before her confinement to paint. She wrote to Clara, asking if Rilke had sent the book on Cézanne. She'd give anything to see the exhibition. If it wasn't absolutely necessary for her to stay put, nothing would have kept her away. And would Clara be able to come over soon? Could she come on Monday? She'd love to see her.

It was nearly midnight when the midwife hurried, hot and flustered, into Otto's room to ask him to fetch the Doctor. The child's heartbeat seemed to have stopped and she feared it might be dead. Dr Wulf arrived in the early hours with his brown Gladstone bag, took out his stethoscope and listened to Paula's stomach. She was wringing with sweat, but determined not to make a fuss as she smiled weakly at the midwife, who sat mopping her hot face with a damp sponge.

'It won't be long now, young lady. Slow deep breaths—that's it. This little one just doesn't want to come out into this big bad world. Come on, push; that's it.'

Paula had never experienced such pain. She tried to focus on the crack in the ceiling above her bed, but felt as though she was being split in two like a carcass on a butcher's slab. Was this right? Was this how it should be? She lost all sense of time and only knew that it must be morning by the thin grey light seeping beneath the curtains. Then the contractions stopped. The Doctor placed a chloroformed cloth over her face and as he drew out the baby with forceps, she lost consciousness.

Outside Otto could hardly bear it. He paced the garden sucking the end of his empty pipe, waiting for Kurt. He had no idea what was going on. The house was in chaos. People running to and fro with boiling kettles, fresh towels and linen. Finally, flushed and streaming with sweat, and barely able to conceal his blood-spattered shirt, Dr Wulf came out of the labour room.

'Congratulations, Herr Modersohn,' he said, extending his hand. 'It's a little girl.'

'Is she alive?'

'And how. She's roaring like a lion.'

'I've never seen you so happy, Paula,' Clara said, standing at the end of her bed with her daughter Ruth.

'Is she real?' the little girl asked, unwrapping the tiny fingers from the swaddling. 'Look at her little nails. They're like shells.'

'Yes, she's quite real, Ruth. Come here, and you can hold her if you climb onto the bed next to me. Very gently now, that's it. You have to hold her head. It's all wobbly, see. She's too little to hold it up alone. But you should see her in the nude. She really loves her bath, and waves her arms around as if she's swimming.

She's very strong and keeps trying to grab things. Frau Brünjes says that shows she's going to be a painter.'

So this was happiness: a shaft of autumn sunlight pouring through the white curtains, her baby daughter at her breast smelling of milk and a vase of late dahlias on the mantelpiece that Mutti had cut from the garden. At the end of her bed Otto had hung a copy of Franz Hals', *Nurse with Child*. The nurse looked like Frau Brünjes, and the little girl, in her stiff baroque dress, like Mathilde Modersohn would, no doubt, look in just a year. Mutti had been touched when they announced she was to have her name. It was easy enough to make other people happy.

Otto kept popping in to see how she was recovering, as if he couldn't quite believe that she'd survived the ordeal and they now had a baby daughter. He sat on the end of her bed full of plans to buy more land so Paula could paint in the garden while Mathilde slept in her straw bassinette under the apple tree.

She wasn't afraid of anything now. Everything seemed possible. She was full of energy and would have got up if it hadn't been for the stupid pain in her leg. But she wasn't allowed out of bed and had to be content, for the moment, to make plans. Things had become clearer and the sense of struggle and existential anxiety had dissipated. Perhaps the truth was that life had a way of sorting itself out. It was hard to stand outside and see a pattern. Maybe there wasn't one. Maybe things were simply arbitrary and random, and we just chose a fork in the road and pitched our tent beneath a tree for a while to take shelter, waiting to see what would happen. No one could guess what was round the next corner. She thought of Cora, but she brushed the thought away. She wouldn't let anything spoil her happiness.

She was sitting in bed nursing Mathilde and looking at the Cézanne catalogue that Rilke had sent. The delicate watercolours and landscapes had been executed with the lightest possible pencil lines. Here and there, for emphasis, he had added a hint of colour or a row of dots to suggest a distant line of trees. They appeared simple, yet she knew that to touch others like this was a gift. A combination of fortitude, dedication and sensibility. She was bursting with ideas and couldn't wait to get back into the studio. Her still life of sunflowers and hollyhocks was waiting for her on the easel. She knew it was good and that she'd caught something of life's fullness in the radiant rusts and purples of the late summer flowers. What had Rilke said in his letter? That even though her life had turned out differently to the way she had imagined, she had found a *raison d'être* and the possibility of true freedom.

'For freedom and solitude are what we hold inside us, Paula. The most valuable thing is to realise that, and to live accordingly. Success comes in many different forms; often we have so little control over it. As for the rest, my dear friend, I have great expectations of you. I know that I'll not be disappointed and hope, from the bottom of my heart, that everything will go well for you. It isn't possible for me to wish for more—though sometimes I do.'

She folded the note, refusing to be drawn in by his seductive ambiguity, and slipped it in her bedside drawer beside her amber beads.

*

The photographer from Dresden was well known for his studies of fashionable figures in the art world. After photographing Otto in his studio, he came to take pictures of Paula and Mathilde. Propped up in bed in a clean white blouse, her hair caught loosely at the nape of her neck, she couldn't get Mathilde to smile. Each time the bulb flashed the little thing burst into tears.

But Paula was bored lying in bed. It had been eighteen days. She wasn't ill. She had simply had a baby. The women in the fields were back at work cutting peat and tending their animals within hours of a delivery. She hated this mollycoddling and wanted to get back to the studio. Mathilde was feeding well so there was nothing to prevent her from getting on with her work. Seeing how restless she was, Mutti promised to ask Kurt to come and examine her. If he said she could get up, then she and Otto would agree.

At mid-morning she heard a cheery 'Yoo-hoo' outside her window, and her brother came bounding up the stairs.

'Well, my little sister. Let's take a look,' he said, feeling her pulse. 'I know you're champing at the bit to get back to your easel. Well, everything seems fine to me. I can't see any reason why you shouldn't get up. That's if you promise to be sensible and not try to paint the Sistine Chapel before lunchtime.'

That evening Frau Brünjes brought her the long mirror and placed it at the end of her bed. Paula shook her hair loose from its pins, brushed and plaited it, and wound the auburn braids into a coronet round her head, before pinning the two white roses Otto had given her that morning into the belt of her dressing gown. With Otto and Kurt supporting her on either side, she climbed out of bed. But she hated this fuss. She wasn't an invalid and could walk on her own, she insisted, slipping her bare feet into her satin slippers.

They moved the big wing chair into the middle of the room so that she could look out at the garden, with its autumn dahlias and purple Michaelmas daisies, while she nursed Mathilde. Mutti had lit candles in the angel candleholder, so with the heavy velvet curtains drawn against the rain it felt just like Christmas. Although Mathilde was sleeping peacefully next door, Paula asked Frau Brünjes if she would bring her in so they could sit together in the candlelight.

That there should—after everything—be so much love in her life was more than she could have hoped. No happiness lasted, she knew. Rilke talked of the freedom to be found in solitude but, she wondered, if he had ever known real joy.

Wrapping her green shawl round her shoulders, she held out her arms for her child. Cradling her head in the crook of her arm, she breathed in her sweet milky breath as she listened to the wind and rain outside banging a lose shutter. Sitting there in the candlelight with her sleeping daughter, she wondered what the future held for her. Would she become a painter too? If not, then Paula would encourage her to follow her path wherever it led. She knew her daughter would have her own struggles, but hoped she would be able to support and guide her. She tried to imagine her a year from now, walking and learning to talk. As Mathilde grew Paula would read to her from her favourite Hans Christian Andersen tales and sit by the stove in the studio, making potato stencils and eating baked apples, just as she'd done with Elsbeth. She wanted to show her the secret places she loved on the moors. The green pools and dykes where, on summer evenings, the bats flitted over the dark water and the moon hung low in the silver birch. She was sleeping so soundly that Paula decided to have another look at the Cézannes. But just as she stood up to put Mathilde back in her bassinette a spasm, like an electric current, shot through her leg that felt as heavy as lead. She staggered back to her chair and managed to call Frau Brünjes, though her voice sounded like someone else's calling through water. And then it went dark, and she could feel it all slipping away: like the pull of the outgoing tide, which left nothing but an empty beach.

This was it; her allotted span. She had always known she wouldn't have long; but now there was her daughter with her little crumpled face and her painting of hollyhocks and sun-flowers waiting on her easel in the studio...

Clara was in Berlin. When she received the news she thought her heart would break. How could her friend, who she'd last seen sitting up in bed in a roomful of dahlias, holding her beautiful new baby girl, her face radiant with love, her friend with whom she'd shared so much, who had such a hunger for art and life, be gone?

Bleached with grief she went straight to Worpswede and, on the last day of November, walked, in the fine rain, down the alley of silver birch where she and Paula had so often walked, with a bunch of autumn leaves in her hand. Then, crossing the bridge, she made her way up to the village and the yellow house with the red roof—but it was empty.

Otto Modersohn had gone. Milly had taken the child and nothing of Paula remained.

MATHILDE

I'M STANDING AT THE WINDOW wrapped in my coat. It's half-past five in the morning and still dark outside. I've been here, now, for three days, existing in a sort of limbo. I feel nauseous and I'm unable to hold down my food. The snow outside is bathed in moonlight, the frost-covered trees white as bones. The temperature is falling and it's started to snow again. I get back into bed and try to sleep, but I'm too cold.

My nights here have been interrupted by dreams. Sometimes I dream of Paula; sometimes of you. Last night I dreamt you were performing Bruch's Violin Concerto No. 1, at the end of the bed. The second movement with its rich melodic line. It was the last thing I heard you play. As your bow soared over the frets your eyes searched out mine, as if to say, this says everything, my darling. It affirms that as long as there's music, as long as there's art, but most of all as long as there's love, the threat to civilisation will somehow be held at bay. I know it was a dream, but it made me feel better.

I can't stop shivering so decide to get up and go out, hoping to avoid the landlady. Yesterday she asked how much longer I'd be staying. It's still early. As I walk towards the Barkenhoff leaving footprints in the fresh snow, I try to see the village through Paula's eyes. The light is pearly grey and an icy wind is blowing off the moors. Across the fields the black sails of a peat barge, carrying its cargo downstream towards Bremen, floats past.

At the Barkenhoff a group of gaunt-faced children are already out digging in the front garden. They look frozen and blow on their chilblained fingers and stamp their feet in their thick black boots. When Heinrich Vogeler came back from the front in 1918 he turned this place into an orphanage for children suffering from malnutrition and TB. After that he left for the Soviet Union to be part of a new vision and the Worpswede dream was finally over. The white room where he and Martha, Paula and Otto, Clara and Rilke sang and made music has been turned into a refectory smelling of pork fat and boiled cabbage.

After Paula died Otto and Heinrich went to her studio. I think my father was quite humbled by what he found. Her visceral paintings filled the room with her presence. Forgetting and remembering are a balancing act. We try to hold on to the past, but there's always something missing; a texture, a colour or smell.

I can't give you anything but lo-ve bay-bee...

... your mouth on my ear, your palm pressed into the small of my back as you hold me in your arms and dance with me round your room. But I can't feel your breath on my cheek or smell your skin any more. I'm left only with the memory of a memory. There's no narrative coherence. Life pursues us like our own shadow. We simply search for what we've lost in order to try to relive it better.

By the time I return to the guesthouse I've made the decision to go back to Berlin. There's nothing for me here any more. I have to find out what's happening in the city, see for myself.

I can't shut myself away and deny what's going on in the wider world. And I'm worried about Hölderlin. I hope he hasn't run away. Also, unlike so many thousands of others, I have the possibility of a future and need to attend to the responsibility that imposes.

My mother would never have run away; Paula would never have given up.

I pack my bag and walk to the bus stop. As the bus pulls in I climb up the steps, followed by an old man carrying a basket of eggs. I sit at the back, my face pressed against the icy glass and watch the flat open country slip by; the windmill in the distance, and the little white church where Clara and Paula disturbed the whole village with their bell ringing.

Flakes of snow swirl outside the window. We pass a man in clogs carrying a bundle of furze and two village boys throwing snowballs. I close my eyes and try to imagine your face. Imagine your response to the news that you're about to become a father. I hope that you'd be pleased. I hope that one day you'll know our daughter. But I'm afraid of this war. There are rumours that there have been round-ups of all known political opponents, Communists as well as Jews. It feels as though we are heading towards an abyss and who knows how deep it will be.

But my body is offering its own resistance. However heavy my heart, however dark things might become, it's insisting on a future.

I hope it will be a girl. I hope she has auburn hair.